D1082186

For the greatest the greatest older brother a guy could have Love, Janie

Cypria

a vampire romance for young hearts

JAMES H. EDGAR

a red oak book

THE RED OAK PRESS
220 Winne Road
Delmar, New York 12054

Cypria (Grade 6 and up): Seventeen-year-old Alex Clarke is a nerdy boy from Pennsylvania Dutch country who finds himself the obsession of a sweet Mexican vampire girl. She's faces death if she's not ready to kill the one human she's allowed.

Cypria is the first book in the Minersville Vampire series.

ISBN: 0-692-16756-0
ISBN-13: 978-0-692-16756-4

DEDICATION

To the love of my life Elizabeth Allen Edgar,
though alas she does not like vampire stories

CONTENTS

PROLOGUE

I spotted a likely prospect at the other end of the alley, but I needed to act carefully. Already there were strange rumors among the homeless. The talk could still be dismissed as paranoia, but I wanted it to stop before I was forced to do something I'd regret.

The man was sitting against a wall alone, but I held back and looked to make sure no one could see me. It was a good thing I did. He called out to someone on the street beyond and got up. A boy in a prep school uniform joined him, and the two walked off together. I hadn't seen them well, mostly just dark figures silhouetted by light filtering into the alley, but it was an odd combination: the homeless black man and the privileged white boy. I wondered what strange business brought the boy into this neighborhood late at night to meet this man.

Nothing as strange as mine surely. I hated having to be here, and now I needed to find someone else.

As I started to withdraw, I heard a noise and froze. Was there someone else in the alley? I stared intently into the dark but couldn't make anyone out. Nevertheless, as I slipped away, I couldn't shake the feeling someone was watching me.

1. FAILURE

The headmaster asked me if I'd been sneaking out of the dorm at night, and I assured him I hadn't.

"Are you sure about that?" he asked.

Oh shit, I thought. There was something about the way he said it that made me think he must know.

We were in his office. He was sitting with me in front of his desk on a second chair. He got up and retrieved his laptop computer from where he'd been using it at his desk. This modern piece of technology contrasted strongly with an office that otherwise looked like it could have been from a hundred years ago.

He showed me a video from the security camera at the front door. There I was, slipping back inside the school. It was time and date stamped with just before midnight yesterday. I was busted.

The headmaster nodded at my expression. "Where have you been going at night?"

The way he phrased that suggested he might have other security camera footage. So much for pretending it was my first offense! I figured I'd better tell the truth. "I've just been going to get a burger and fries."

The headmaster sat back with a look of disbelief on his face. "The nearest fast food is fifteen blocks away, and it's in an economically stressed neighborhood."

"Yeah, that's the one," I admitted. It was always a long walk there and back.

He shook his head. "Why would you sneak out at night, risk getting in trouble with the school and endanger yourself? For a burger and fries? It's not like we're not feeding you well."

I shrugged. I didn't have a good answer. It's true there was plenty of food in the cafeteria; but I didn't fit in, I was miserable, and I felt a little better when I ate junk food.

"You know you're straining relations with the community, don't you? By showing a prep school uniform and a white face late at night. Do you have any idea how dangerous that is?"

That sounded racist to me, so I may've been a bit surly when I said, "Abe's cool."

His eyes narrowed. "Abe who?"

Abe was a guy I'd met when I was eating my first illicit burger. He was an old black guy wearing three coats who smelled like body odor and those deodorant cakes they use in rest room toilets. He'd asked me if I would buy him a burger, so I had. I didn't have a lot of money, but this guy looked like he had less. I'd seen him a couple of times since, and we chatted while we ate together. I told the headmaster about him.

"So Abe's a homeless guy. That's not safe. Many of the homeless are mentally ill or addicted to drugs." He sounded concerned for me but also dismissive of Abe.

I didn't know what Abe's problem was. I didn't want to think he was dangerous. "He just sleeps out of doors is all."

The headmaster didn't seem satisfied. "You're telling me the truth? This is really what you've been doing? You've been going out to eat burgers with a homeless man? You're not—I don't know—buying drugs or seeing a girl?"

"No, sir." I was definitely sullen this time. I didn't know which suggestion was more off base: the pipe or the pipe dream.

He sat back in his chair and thought for a while. Finally, he hit upon the real problem. "Alex, are you happy here?" That was the beginning of the end.

By Friday afternoon, I was on the train home. I wouldn't be returning to St. Augustine's.

It was unfortunate that the train ride from Philadelphia to Mt. Joy lasts as long as it does, which is almost an hour and a half, because that gave me far too much time to think. There was no escaping that my small town escape plan hadn't worked or that I was going back home a failure. After tenth grade, I'd decided I could enroll in a private school in Philadelphia and skip junior year. In all advanced classes at Minersville and old for my grade, I'd thought the plan made sense. It would get me out of Minersville two years early.

I'd been bored by small town life. Minersville only has a population of about five thousand. It's even smaller than neighboring Pottsville, the county seat, which is also pretty small. I'd been a star on the academic stage of our area high school, well prepared by my mother, an elementary school teacher in the district. My early success had given me the inflated self-image necessary to think I could switch to an elite boarding school and simultaneously skip a year. I'm not sure how I convinced my parents, who didn't want me to go; my grandmother, who paid for it; or the admissions director, who'd been properly skeptical. It was all embarrassingly arrogant in retrospect.

Academically, I was in over my head. Even in my strongest subject, English, I couldn't keep up. I'd always done well because I'm a reader: science fiction, fantasy, comic books, Greek myths, the Bible, you name it. But suddenly it wasn't about understanding the story any more; it was about understanding the critical theory and applying it. In math, I was in even worse shape. Since I'd been taking pre-calculus as a sophomore at Minersville, they put me in calculus at St. Augustine. Calculus is about rates of change, and the rate of change of my knowledge of math was not fast enough to keep up with my better-prepared, privileged peers.

My fellow students might have helped me except I'd inadvertently become a social outcast by failing to bridge the cultural differences and confirming my own isolation. In the common room after dinner, I mentioned once how my parents were big on the idea of "you eat what you shoot," but I didn't really like venison that much. Apparently, my fellow St. Augustine students were not hunters because into the shocked silence, this girl shrieked, "Oh my God! You killed Bambi?" I realize now that it was more of a fake, dramatic shriek—maybe to be funny—but at the time I was angry that I was being made fun of for saying something totally reasonable. So, I compounded my mistake by observing ironically (and not too kindly) that the animal that died to provide her handbag probably appreciated her defense of animal rights. Then, after another shocked silence, there was a buzz of angry voices, a muttered "Jerk!" and she exited.

One of her friends stared at me. "Just so you know, some Prada bags are pleather." I didn't know what either Prada or pleather was, but the girl's bag definitely looked like it was made out of the skin of some animal.

Even when I was right, I was still wrong. In this situation, my attitude had been wrong. I had embarrassed this girl, pissed off her friends and made sure none of them would talk to me again. That left me embarrassed, pissed off and with no friends. Clearly, I was the loser here.

When I found myself over my head academically, I went to the student-to-student afternoon help sessions. Unfortunately, the student in charge of the sessions was Prada-handbag girl.

Eventually, I gave up. I stopped trying to do well, and I stopped trying to make friends. I probably should've just called my parents and begged them to take me back home. Instead, I started sneaking out in October to have burgers with Abe.

I'm not sure I'd understood the connection between giving up and sneaking out until the headmaster asked me if I was happy. That's when I realized I wasn't and I needed to admit it. My whole plan had been a failure. The headmaster called my parents.

I thought they would tell me to try to stick it out longer, to try to last the year, that everything worth doing is hard work. Instead, they said, it was fine, and I could come home right away and enroll at Minersville for the second marking period. My dad said he preferred having me live at home. Apparently, losers' parents have depressingly low expectations.

No one said anything about the money, and I didn't ask about the refund policy because I was afraid the answer would just bring me more guilt. What if my grandmother had to pay for a whole semester even though I'd left halfway through?

They just told me to get on the train to Mt. Joy and come home. Fortunately, I didn't have a lot of stuff to take with me. I'd donated my expensive school uniforms. Half my suitcase was my collection of beloved fantasy novels and some illustrated retellings of Greek myths. I'd brought them not even knowing they'd be my refuge when I had no friends.

Let me repeat that: *when I had no friends.*

Who says that? Apparently me. It was true: I had no friends. At that moment, I realized how much of who I was I'd left behind when I left home. Then the train pulled up to the platform.

My thoughts began to improve immediately. My mother was there. She was still dressed for school, with her ID on a lanyard. She's the one from whom I got brown hair, brown eyes and a slender build. My father contributed the waves in my hair and a goofy face. It was good to see Mom. I hadn't seen her in two months, and I'd missed her. She gave me a hug and helped me load my bags into the SUV. Once we were on our way to Minersville, she didn't ask me about school or anything upsetting. She just told me that I should plan to unpack and make my bed before dinner—my father liked to eat early—and asked if there was any particular meal I'd like, so she could stop and pick up ingredients if necessary.

When we pulled onto my street, we drove past the Millers' house. It was a grand old Victorian house, with gables and everything. It has always been on the edge of falling apart, but now it was in great shape. It'd been repaired and repainted, and there were two new cars in the driveway. "The Millers' house looks great," I said.

"It's not the Millers' house any more," Mom informed me. "They moved across town, rather suddenly. A new family has moved into the house, the Garcías. They're Mexicans—though I believe the children were born in Texas. Sue Miller told me the house hadn't even been for sale, but Victor García knocked on the door and made a generous offer, well above market value. Sue said he wanted a 'historic' house, and apparently Victor is a bit of a handyman and likes to restore old things. I hope he's not a flipper. Anyway, they've got two children, a son at college and a daughter about your age." I just listened as Mom talked. I wondered if I'd see the girl at school.

As we pulled up to my house, I saw the school bus. My house was on the corner where the bus stops, which was convenient, as I knew I would soon be riding it again. I saw a girl I didn't know get off. I got a fleeting impression that she was well dressed—overdressed for school really—in a pretty long-sleeved shirt, navy blue skirt and dark tights. I saw a glimpse of what looked like an absolutely beautiful face, framed by long dark hair. Hmm, I thought, if she's that pretty, she won't be wasting time on me. Despite my grumpy thought, I could not help but feel a further lightening of my mood. Sometimes seeing a pretty girl was all it took to make me feel better.

When my brother Simon got off the bus, I smiled feeling an unexpected moment of real joy. I'd missed him. That surprised me because my brother had spent the summer before seventh grade being either painfully awkward or outright obnoxious. We had spent a lot of our time fighting over stupid stuff in the months before I'd decided to go to St. Augustine. It didn't help that we lived in the same house and went to the same school. Well, I guessed I'd be back on the bus with him soon enough, but that prospect didn't bother me as much anymore.

"Alex!" Simon was screaming. He gave me a big hug, which I returned with feeling until he said, "Enough hugging now," and went inside. I followed him.

Our dog, Inskeep, wagging his tail furiously, instantly jumped up on me and started licking my face. Normally, I hate being jumped on and licked. I'm not really a dog person like Simon. But today I was so happy to be home, I just said, "Is there room at the inn, Inskeep?" He kept wagging his tail and licking, which I took for a "yes."

My dad was home already. He's a postal carrier and sometimes works an early shift to be home before the school bus. He was still in uniform and gave me a big bear hug while ruffling my hair. Then he took my suitcase. "What have you got in here, Alex? Rocks?"

"Mostly books."

"Well don't plan on reading them all tomorrow. I've spoken for your helping out at the McCord place."

"Dad!" Home five minutes and already I was put to work. I gave him a reproachful look.

He ignored me and launched into a long explanation. "Well, it's like this. Tomorrow's a workday at the church because the rector volunteered us to help out with leaf cleanup at the Baber Cemetery. Bob McCord is the only guy in the church with a tractor that can pull the cart we'll use on the leaf piles, but he's got late broccoli to harvest before the weather kills it."

Dad put the suitcase down and extended the handle to wheel it. I put my hands in my pockets. He continued, "Jane put her foot down and said she wasn't going to do it all by herself. Well, the kid had a point. That broccoli patch is a lot to ask one sixteen-year-old girl to do by herself. So I said to Bob, 'That's all right. Alex will be home to give us a hand with the leaves, so we don't really need you, Bob.' Which wasn't exactly true on account of that tractor. And I wasn't going to ask him to lend an expensive piece of equipment like that. Anyways, as soon as I said your name, Jane perks up and says, 'Alex can help me then. That can be his service to the church.' I said, 'I suppose he could,' so Bob agreed to come with his tractor."

Thanks, Jane, I thought sourly. "How many leaves can there be? It's only just November, for goodness sake. Surely lots of leaves are still on the trees."

"The thing is," said Dad, "nothing got done in October." I'm screwed, I thought. Still, why did they have to use Mr. McCord's tractor?

"Surely someone else in the whole Pottsville area has a tractor you could use? Maybe someone who lives closer to the cemetery than Jane's dad? Won't he have to put it on his flatbed?"

"Those are all Presbyterian tractors." My dad actually said that with a straight face.

"Are you kidding me? You're saying a 'Presbyterian tractor' cannot pull our cart? Do the tractors object to episcopal oversight?" I spoiled the effect of my sarcasm by cracking myself up.

Dad wasn't impressed. "No, smarty-pants, I'm saying they'd charge us by the hour. Those Presbyterians are good businesspeople." He turned to take the suitcase up to my room.

I followed. "Dad, I wanted a day to myself. To settle in."

He didn't seem at all sorry about condemning me to a day of picking broccoli. "Settle in today. Tomorrow, you're helping at the McCords." He put down the bag and left me at the door to my room. "Sheets are in the linen closet, like always. Oh, and your mother got you reenrolled in school for Monday."

Okay, fine, I got the message. My parents weren't going to let me mope.

When I looked at my phone, I saw I had an email from the headmaster at St. Augustine. I was instantly anxious again. Why would he be writing me? I just wanted to put the whole experience behind me.

I read the message: "It is with sincere regret that I write to tell you of the passing of Abraham Brown. I heard about his death at our community outreach board meeting from a friend who runs a local food bank. I believe this was your Abe and he meant something to you. No man is an island, and we are all diminished by his passing."

There was a link to a news story. It was pretty gruesome: "Police find a third homeless man with slit wrists over a storm drain grate." I was too shocked to cry. I just sat on my bed, numb.

When I got off the bus, I smoothed my skirt. I was glad to put another tedious day of high school behind me. It felt like I'd been going to high school forever. Fortunately, I was one day closer to graduation. At least I was free for the rest of the day.

I looked up and saw one of the neighbors, Sarah Clarke, getting out of her SUV with a boy who looked high school age. That must be her son Alex. I guessed he must be back from boarding school in Philadelphia. I wondered idly if he was home for some weird extended Thanksgiving break. My brother wouldn't be back from college for two more weeks. I'd ask Mom what was up with Alex. She'd know.

Then I saw him: a tall Mennonite man standing on the sidewalk just ahead. He wore a black jacket and hat and had the air of a preacher. He was well over six feet, thin, and bearded. He stared at my face so intently that it was definitely rude. He didn't move; even his facial expression was frozen. As I walked past, I briefly glanced into his eyes.

Okay, I had a serious problem here.

As I turned to go into my house, I felt my phone buzz. I had a coded text message. My hands shook as I opened the secure app that would let me talk encrypted and untraceably. They couldn't possibly know already, could they?

"Hello?"

"Is this Maria Morales?" He sounded pleasant but that didn't make him any less terrifying. At a word he could have me and my entire family killed.

"I go by Helen García now."

"I'm calling from Philadelphia. We're having a problem with someone who's been indiscreet. I was wondering if you could look into one of your neighbors, Alex Clarke. See if he knows more than he should."

Despite his phrasing, this was a command. At least it wasn't what I'd been afraid of. "Okay. Should I call you back if he does?"

"No, take care of it yourself. Make it look like an accident."

Since I really didn't want to do this, I pretended I didn't know what he meant. "What do you mean?"

"Oh, you know, he had a hunting accident or went hiking and fell off a cliff. You're in Minersville, right? Fell down a mineshaft, maybe. Use your imagination."

2. BROCCOLI

The best thing about Saturday morning at my house is the pancakes. My dad always cooks bacon and pancakes, with real maple syrup, which is like super expensive. My dad says it's a luxury worth the price, and it almost makes it worth getting up at the ungodly hour of 8 a.m. I awoke to the dog licking my face. "Aw, gross. Stop that," I said. Simon was at my door, looking bleary-eyed. Simon must've opened my door for the dog.

"Get up, Alex!" Simon ordered. "If I have to get up, you have to get up. You'd better hurry up, or I'll eat your pancakes." I groaned and rolled over, but then I got out of bed. The smell was pretty enticing.

I ate my way through the best breakfast I'd had in two months while listening to my parents argue about what to bring to the church's workday. That reminded me that they'd obligated me to pick broccoli all day with Jane McCord. Not a pleasant prospect. They were planning to leave soon, so I went and got dressed in work clothes.

We were delayed when the doorbell rang. My parents were in the garage loading up my dad's truck with rakes and leaf blowers, so I answered the door.

Standing there was an absolutely gorgeous girl. She was about my height of five feet eight inches, which is perfectly fine for a girl though not so impressive for me. Consequently, I found myself level with a pair of brown eyes in what had to be the most beautiful face I had ever seen. There were no striking features, except maybe for a perfect complexion of light brown skin, framed by lustrous, straight dark hair that went down her back. Nothing else stood out because every feature on this girl's face was so absolutely what it should be that I didn't notice any of them individually but received only the impression of collective perfection. I was fixated by her eyes. I belatedly realized that this was the girl who got off the school bus before Simon yesterday.

"Hi," I said. I felt a little shy.

She had been distracted waiting for me to answer the door. When she turned to look at me, her expression changed dramatically. Her face slowly morphed from stunned surprise to furious denial.

"You're dead," she said.

There was an awkward silence. I kept my face blank to hide my confusion. "Excuse me?" I said.

"You're Alex. I meant to say you're Alex." She suddenly looked embarrassed.

"Yeah, I know," I said.

She laughed nervously. "Sorry, slip of the tongue." This was so weird. I wondered why she was here.

"I'm your neighbor, Helen García. My mom baked this banana bread to welcome you home." She gave me an odd smile.

I looked down and saw that she was indeed holding a loaf wrapped in aluminum foil. I took the bread when she offered. "Thanks."

She took a deep breath and gave me a more natural smile. "Are you going back to school in Philadelphia or are you home to stay?"

"Home to stay." I tried to make that sound like I was looking forward to it, like being home wasn't a failure.

"So, will I see you at the bus stop on Monday?" I didn't understand the hopefulness in her voice.

"I think so." It's not like I had any other way to get to school.

"Nice to meet you, Alex." She gave me one last quick smile. Then she left.

Despite her strangeness, this girl was way out of my league. I didn't get why she'd bothered. Then, as I looked at the banana bread, I figured it out. Her mom must be one of those head-of-the-social-committee types who did nice things for everyone. She must have made it her business to find out who I was and then made her daughter come and welcome me out of policy. Helen was a socialite-in-training.

The banana bread smelled really good. Even full of pancakes, I cut myself a slice and stuffed it in my mouth before I put the rest in the cupboard and went to join my parents.

Mom gave me the keys to her SUV, so I could get to Jane's house. It's a bit of a drive, and I took my time because I wasn't eager to begin work as a field hand. When I got there, Jane seemed happy—no, that's too strong a word—*relieved* to see me.

"Hi, Alex!" she said. Then, "Let me grab you a pair of gloves and show you the broccoli patch."

Great, I thought sarcastically, I'm all about the vegetables.

I was a little alarmed when I saw the size of the patch we were going to harvest. Jane seemed to divine my lack of enthusiasm. "Look, Alex, we would have been doing leaf cleanup all day—until at least five o'clock. I figured if I invited you over here to help, we'd get done by two and then go hunting. Mr. Martin said it was all right if I hunted his woods today." Henry Martin was an old Mennonite farmer who lived on the other side of the woods that bordered the McCord farm. Mennonites are like the Amish, who live completely without modern technology, but Mennonites follow a less strict set of rules. I hadn't realized he owned the woods. "Dad said I could, so long as we got all the broccoli picked."

"Jane, I didn't bring my gun or camo."

"That's all right. I'll take my rifle, and you can use my shotgun. Dad's got an old orange vest you can wear though there shouldn't be anyone in those woods but us."

"Okay, sounds like a plan." I was warming up to this idea.

Of course, I hadn't really understood what was involved. Jane had me cutting florets as fast as I could, without cutting my hands with the knife or missing the side sprouts or taking the ones that had gone to flower.

"I hate broccoli," I said, "and that was before I knew how much work it is."

"Hey, that's high-quality, organic produce you got in that basket. That's going to help put me through school."

"Good. Someone else can pay you lots of money to eat it. I don't like the way it tastes."

"You got to cook it right. I like it pan-fried in a little oil with bacon bits. We can have some tonight along with whatever we shoot."

"What if we don't bag anything?"

"Then, it's broccoli for dinner." Jane's sense of humor was always deadpan, but when she got me to laugh, she'd join me with a smile.

"Broccoli for dinner, I'll starve." I made it into a dramatic whine.

"You and I both know you're going to stop on the way home to pick up a burger and fries 'cause you can't stay away from junk food." She knew me too well. I'd already built the time into my schedule.

"I have boy metabolism, and you're driving me like a slave. I'm going to need more food than broccoli."

"That's why the oil and bacon bits, and why you should leave the shooting to me unless you get a really clear shot." Jane hunted frequently, and I did it only when someone else made the plan.

My back really hurt before Jane allowed us a short break for lunch. Then we were back at it. She was really sick of cajoling me by the time we finished at exactly two o'clock. She's good at time management.

Jane gave me the shotgun and the orange vest before we headed to the woods. "We can shoot rabbits or turkeys today. We can't shoot deer yet, which is a shame 'cause they're all over the place like an infestation. I don't care if your license is for this year or not, but we aren't shooting anything out of season that I can't explain to my dad. That clear?"

"Yes."

"Good."

It was fun stalking through the woods even though it became clear that none of the game we were hunting was likely to be making itself obvious in the mid-afternoon.

That's when I caught a glimpse of some wild turkeys. They were on the edge of the woods, on grass by a drainage ditch next to a field. It isn't unusual to see turkeys around Minersville though my parents always act like they're some endangered species.

I didn't think I could get any closer without startling the birds. I looked for Jane, who was some distance from me, checking the low brush growing by the wood's edge. I signaled to her with my arms, but she wasn't paying attention, and I didn't want to make any noise. I didn't know what to do. I didn't want to miss the moment.

I checked my shot to make sure the land sloped upwards, and then I looked for Mr. Martin's house. It was far to the left and more than the required distance away. I sighted a bird and squeezed the trigger.

Of course I missed. The shot was too far for my unpracticed aim, and I didn't really know what the effective range of my shotgun was or even what size shot Jane had used to load it. It occurred to me belatedly that a successful hunter might have asked some more questions beforehand.

The sound of the report scared all the birds into the air, and Jane came running over just in time to see them fly away. "I thought you were going to let me take the shot," Jane said.

"You weren't paying attention. I didn't know what else to do."

"That's all right. I didn't expect to find anything out at this time of day." I looked at her quizzically. She shrugged. "I didn't want to spend the rest of my Saturday working. Look, here's old man Martin coming. He's probably come to see about the noise."

Indeed, my shot had caused Jane's elderly neighbor to investigate. When he reached us, I saw he was a white-bearded man who looked to be in his seventies or eighties.

"Hello, Jane, I see it's you, come to hunt, as you said you would. You're welcome to, especially as your father's so handy with a butcher's knife and you're so good about sharing. Who's this young man?"

After Jane introduced me and told him where I lived, he said, "Ah, I know the street. When I was a young man, I heard a story about a house nearby yours, a proper ghost story." He described the house he meant, and I recognized the Garcías' house. I told him as much, and he regaled us with the story he'd heard:

"Back in 1925, it was, right before the illness. There was a young schoolteacher named Mary, who lived there before she disappeared under mysterious circumstances. The night she went missing, she killed a man from my church." Mr. Miller paused dramatically. "His wife said Mary did it, but no one believed her at first. The man's body had been so torn apart that it was impossible to imagine a human being could have done it. It looked like a bear had gotten him." Mr. Miller's face lit up with relish as he related these sensational details.

"That was fortunate for his wife, or she'd have been suspected herself. She had a black eye that night, and it seemed likely her husband had given it to her. Everyone was aware that the man was given to ungodly behavior, such as drinking to excess, and he had a history of beating his wife. So she might have killed him herself, you see, except it didn't seem possible.

"They only started to believe Mary was the killer when they discovered she'd disappeared."

Mr. Miller interrupted himself. "This first part is all true, mind you. I've seen an old newspaper article about the killing and disappearance." He looked at us sharply. "But this next part didn't make the paper."

His voice started building in intensity as he went on. "There was no trace of Mary at the house. What's more, there was no sign she'd ever lived there. There were no records of her existence anywhere in town. That's when folks remembered she always looked young and never grew old." Mr. Miller's tone had become really spooky as he continued: "Mary was a ghost, a murdered woman, now an avenging spirit who killed men for mistreating womenfolk." Then he laughed.

"Now, that's what I call a proper ghost story." Jane and I agreed it was a good story. I told him that I'd met one of the new residents.

Mr. Miller seemed to feel obliged to add, "This story isn't religion, mind. This is superstitious nonsense."

"I understand, Mr. Miller," I said, "Everyone tells ghost stories. Charlotte Brontë was a good Anglican, and she wrote ghost stories."

"It's as you say," he agreed. "I thought young folks still liked a good ghost story. I don't know these Anglican writers, but ghost stories are what you might call universal."

We left him to whatever he does on Saturday afternoons when guests of neighbors aren't disturbing the peace. On the way back to her house, Jane quizzed me about Helen. "So, you've seen this new girl," she began. Jane had seen her at school, she said, but hardly knew anything about her. She acted unimpressed by my description of her face and seemed to feel that I should've discovered more details about her in our brief conversation.

"Look, I get all flustered when I'm talking to a pretty girl," I explained.

"Standing right here, you jerk!" She gave me a shove.

"I'm sorry. I didn't mean you're not..." At least, I stopped myself from the idiocy of finishing with "a girl."

"Alex Clarke, you can be an idiot sometimes." She ordered me to put the guns away while she cooked us a dinner of bacon and broccoli fried in oil.

I made a face of mock-horror. "Don't make my punishment more than I can bear!"

"Clown." She sounded disgusted, but she was smiling. I laughed.

As it turns out, the broccoli was really delicious the way she made it. My mom only ever steamed broccoli, and this tasted like it belonged in a completely different food group. I mean, it wasn't much of a dinner that Jane had made, just fried broccoli with bacon bits and cans of diet root beer, and I *did* still stop at a drive-through fast food place to get a burger on the way home. But I didn't get fries.

As I ate my burger, I tried to calm myself down. I'd gotten all creeped out driving back from Jane's because I'd thought the car behind was following me. It had matched my route, turn for turn, for miles—as though it were headed directly for my house. It'd been following too closely, too; not tailgating exactly but impatient for sure. When I turned into the drive-through, it had continued on, and my paranoid fantasy shattered. I decided Mr. Miller's ghost story must've affected me more than I'd realized. The burger cured me.

When I got home, I saw the car parked in Helen's driveway.

Alex's face came as a shock. The familiar features triggered a surge of memories, and I was overwhelmed by emotion for a moment. Alex looked exactly like the young man who'd taken my innocence. I hadn't expected that.

Of course, it couldn't be him because he was dead. In my surprise, I accidently blurted out my thought. Alex didn't bat an eye. I covered the slip as best I could and made pleasant small talk with him. As good an actress as I've become, I'm not sure how I managed without betraying the turmoil of my feelings.

I had to keep reminding myself Alex wasn't the one he looked like. It was another time and place. I shouldn't feel revulsion or shame. It wasn't him.

I looked closely into Alex's light brown eyes to see if he was alert to any hint of my strange reaction. I usually avoided eye contact when meeting guys because often what I saw there was revolting, but I got none of that from Alex. His gaze was sincere admiration. He naively saw me as wholesome and good, theoretically worth having but beyond his merit.

I felt the opposite.

I knew the truth. I'd justly hated myself ever since the one Alex resembled had made me over in his likeness. Alex didn't deserve to have someone like me interested in him. He could do so much better.

Still, I couldn't shake off the perfect vision of myself I'd seen reflected in his eyes. I desperately wanted to be that again. I wondered whether I could become innocent and trusting enough to go on a journey with this boy to find the person I truly wanted to be.

I wondered at the irony that the mirror image of the one who made me hate myself, who routinely starred in my second worst nightmare, should become the catalyst in my decision to try to transform into someone I could love.

Only after I'd left did I remember I was supposed to be finding out whether he knew anything he shouldn't. I resolved to take care of that next week at school.

The more immediate problem was the situation with the preacher. I'd have to borrow Mom's car.

3. GRANDMA

I had thought Sunday afternoon would be free, so I could settle back in at home, but my family's conspiracy to keep me from moping apparently extended to my grandma as well. My mother's mother, Mary Jane Fulton, lived in town and had a passion for genealogy, which we occasionally shared. I loved her ancestor stories that brought history alive for me. Grandma Fulton had fully embraced the technological advancements in genealogy, creating a massive family tree on the Internet and occasionally spending an afternoon in an old graveyard photographing headstones with her cell phone so she could upload them to a website that featured graveyards. Gravestones are often the only record of a person's birth and death dates in the 1800s. I was Grandma's partner in genealogy (and the only person under 50 who could tell everyone at a family reunion how they were all related), so she claimed me for a graveyard trip.

When she picked me up, she asked, "Do I have to pay you by the hour for this?"

"No, this is fun. You can still pay me for gardening though."

She laughed and agreed. We went north of town to a Mennonite graveyard we'd never visited before. Apparently, there was a request by a researcher for photographs of the headstones of several dozen people from three interrelated families. I was a little disappointed. "So, I'm not related to any of these people?"

"No, Alex, you aren't. I've photographed anyone related to us already. I'm doing this because I like helping people. Thanks to volunteers, I just got a photograph of your three times great grandfather's stone in Centre County without actually having to go there. I got facts off that stone I couldn't get from the genealogical society's published book."

Before I could ask her for the details, she asked about our new neighbors. I told her I'd met Helen. When I mentioned how beautiful she was, Grandma said, "You mean the Mexican one, the brown-skinned one?"

I didn't want to talk about that, so I just said, "She brought me this delicious banana bread." I left out the "You're dead" part because Grandma would get ahold of that and never let it go.

Grandma sniffed. "Be careful with her. She might be after an American boy to get herself a green card."

I wished Grandma wouldn't say things like that. It was offensive on so many levels. If the girl was born in Texas, she was a citizen already. I kept quiet because saying anything would just wind Grandma up. Also, did a beautiful girl need an ulterior motive to be interested in me? Sadly, the answer to that was yes.

Grandma took my silence for acceptance of her advice. She asked, "Have you met the rest of the family?"

"No," I admitted.

"I heard that the college boy has himself a Negro girlfriend." I realized this was going to be one of those conversations where Grandma kept saying really embarrassing old-person things. At least we were alone.

"Please don't say 'Negro,' grandma. No one says that anymore." Maybe she could learn.

"It's certainly not the word my mother sometimes used." I really didn't want Grandma to say what word she meant.

"Can we keep that bit of family history to ourselves, please?" I begged.

"All right. What I am supposed to say instead of Negro?"

"Black or African American," I suggested.

"She certainly is black. I heard from your father that she's as black as the ace of spades. I wonder if they'll get married and have, what-do-you-call-them, mulatto babies."

"Oh Jesus, Grandma, please don't say 'mulatto.' You mean 'biracial,' I'm sure, like President Obama." I loved my grandma, but she could be really mortifying.

"Don't take the Lord's name in vain. The world sure is changing. A black president! Don't think I'm prejudiced, Alex. These are good changes, I'm sure. It's good we have our first black president, even if he is a Democrat. I'd have preferred that black general, myself. It's a better world you are growing up in than the one I was born to. Marry whatever girl you like, even if she's as black as the ace of spades."

"Okay." It was time to admit defeat. I couldn't fix Grandma. At least she didn't seem totally against the idea of my marrying a dark skinned girl. That might be progress for her.

Grandma looked at me closely, suddenly worried. "It will be a girl, right? I know gay marriage is legal and all now."

"I think it's just called marriage. And, yes, Grandma, if I marry, it will be to a girl." Maybe I was being prejudiced too, but I knew I was only attracted to girls.

"Well, that's all right then. I'd try to be open minded, but I am hoping for babies to carry on the family." I hoped she didn't expect them any time soon.

Grandma showed me the map of the cemetery from a spiral bound book purchased from our local genealogical society. She had printed out the list of all the gravestones we were supposed to photograph.

I looked around and saw that there was another person in the graveyard. She was some distance away and wearing a scarf around her head, but something about the way she moved reminded me of Helen. Of course, I couldn't think of any reason why she would be here in this graveyard. I must just have her stuck in my head. Given how beautiful she was, that was an exercise in futility. I was just about as likely to succeed with her as I had been at St. Augustine.

After we'd photographed a few stones, Grandma asked me, "How do you like being back at home?"

"It's a relief." That was true, but I thought Grandma deserved the truth. "I'm actually really worried about school tomorrow. I told everyone about my plans, and now I feel like a fool, coming back a failure."

She nodded and walked with me to the next plot. She told me a story while we photographed.

"I remember a boy named Maurice that I knew in high school. He was a skinny sort of weakling, and people made fun of him. Senior year he told everyone that he was going to join the Marines and serve his country in Vietnam. Well, of course, the Marines wouldn't take him. Somehow, he managed to enlist in the regular army, but they kicked him out after basic training because he couldn't pass the physical."

I felt sorry for Maurice. That must have been humiliating.

"When he came back home, he went to work in his father's hardware store, and he joined a veteran's support group, which was mostly army wives. People made nasty remarks, said he was just trying to 'put the make' on some army wife while her husband was away."

That's mean, I thought, but... "Was he?" I asked.

"No! It was just a mean-spirited thing people said." Grandma looked at me sharply. "A couple years later, your grandpa came back from the war. Things were different for veterans then. Some people called them 'baby killers' because they'd heard about atrocities on TV. Emergency responders could get attacked in the projects just for wearing a uniform. Your Grandpa Bob got rid of all his uniforms. He had a difficult time readjusting, getting a job and paying our bills." I knew that Grandpa Fulton had gone to Vietnam, but I hadn't known they'd struggled financially when he got back. I realized that Grandma Fulton had inherited her money later.

"When a tree branch punched a big old hole in our roof, Maurice's father didn't want to give us credit. Maurice stuck up for us. He told his father that he hadn't risked his life for his country the way Bob had, and the least they could do was provide some plywood and shingles. Maurice's father came around, and Maurice even helped Bob with the repair."

Grandma continued, "After what Maurice did for Bob and me, no one could ever say a bad word about him around either of us. Bob would tell people he was a stand-up guy. One time, this fellow tried to make a joke of how Maurice got kicked out of the army. Bob told him that he'd waited to be drafted but since Maurice had signed up, he figured Maurice was the bigger patriot."

Grandma Fulton looked at me to see if I'd gotten the point. "Sometimes we all look foolish. Sometimes it feels like everyone's turned on you. But if you help others, one at a time, you'll win friends for yourself."

"Thanks, Grandma." I wondered if I could do that—win friends, one at a time.

The day was becoming overcast. Surprisingly, that made it easier to take legible photographs of the headstones because we weren't dealing with harsh sun shadows. It was getting cold though.

As we went through the graveyard, I noticed a surprisingly large number of stones with the same year of death. I commented, "About half these stones give 1925 as the death date. That must've been a bad year for this church."

Grandma looked at me and nodded. "Oh yes, and not just for this church. My father told me that an epidemic swept through the area. It took the lives of the mayor, the whole police department and the entire staff of the local newspaper."

"Wow, what'd they do?"

"Well, the borough president got appointed interim mayor. For a while, the county sheriff and his deputies had to take over policing Minersville. The newspaper folded."

I tried to imagine it. "What disease caused all that?"

She shook her head as she snapped another picture. "I don't know. My father said it was very mysterious. Of course, in those days lots of people died in epidemics: smallpox, influenza, typhus, you name it."

I was suddenly grateful I'd been born in the twenty first century. "Thank God for vaccines," I said.

"Amen to that. Every time I hear those liberals going on about opting-out of vaccinations for their children, I want to smack some sense into them."

I agreed with her about the vaccines, I didn't appreciate her smug assumption of conservative superiority. "Grandma, there's nothing wrong with being liberal," I insisted.

Grandma smiled at me. "I forgot you get your politics from your mother. How goes the war on war?" That deflated me a little.

"Not well, based on how often Mom screams at the radio," I admitted. "She went to a protest in Philadelphia last month."

Grandma shook her head. "It's a good thing that girl has tenure. In my day, the principal would fire her for criticizing the government." I thought that tenure might be a good thing, then. She looked at me. "I'm proud of my girl. I'm sick of war. It's always the wrong people who suffer." She said it with a bitterness I didn't understand.

I'd yet to experience enough violence to know why she felt that way. I still thought there were good wars and bad wars. "But not all wars are bad," I contradicted. "Without the unions winning the coal wars, the mines would still be unsafe." I was probably being disrespectful, but Grandma was tolerant.

"I don't know 'winning' is the right word. Seems to me that my grandfather Hopkins told me the army won the battle of Blair Mountain." She smiled with the memory. "He was proud of the fact he could hide a shot gun down the pants of his 'overhalls,' as he called them."

"Well, the mines got safer afterwards, didn't they?" I crossed three names off the list since Grandma had finished photographing that family's plot.

"Yes, I suppose they did. Certainly, Grandpa Hopkins outlived his father, John, who died of black lung."

"The Welshman who settled in Minersville?" I thought I remembered her telling me about John.

"Yes, he did, but he already had the black lung from the mines in Wales. He only lasted a while here before he bought the farm in Ohio. His family struggled after he died."

As we walked down the rows of stones, I noticed someone had left fresh cut flowers on one of the graves recently. The stone was that of a young woman, wife of somebody or other. Her dates were 1896 to 1925, but I noticed she'd died some three months before most of the people who'd had the mysterious illness. I wondered if she'd be one of the first to die.

Grandma paused a moment, with her hand on a gravestone, resting. She seemed to be breathing heavily.

"That's enough for today, Alex."

"We haven't finished photographing all the stones on the list." I didn't want to have to come back another day.

"We'll get the rest later. I'm not feeling well right now. Let's go home. Do you think you could manage to upload these photos to the website for me? I don't think I'm up to it tonight." I agreed that I would, worried that she seemed so tired. We packed up, and she took me home.

It was nearly five o'clock. I saw Helen driving up to the front of her house in the car that looked like the one that had followed me home yesterday. If it had been Helen, she wasn't following me home so much as going to her own home, of course, though I had no idea what would take her out Jane's way. I wondered where she'd gone today. It was hard to tell at this distance, but she looked upset. I wondered idly what was up with her. I guessed being beautiful didn't mean a life free of problems.

I went to raid the kitchen, but my mother, who was already making dinner, thwarted me. She asked how things went today with

Grandma. I gave her a blow-by-blow account, and she smiled throughout until I got to the end. Then Mom started crying.

"Mom, is Grandma all right?" I was getting worried.

"No, sweetie, she's really sick. She has cancer. She's been getting treatment from specialists in Philadelphia, but she's not getting any better. We're not sure how long she has to live." My dad came in at that point. I think his original mission might have been the same as mine because he had started out in the direction of the refrigerator, but once he saw Mom crying, he went to give her a hug.

"The bombings?" he mouthed at me over her shoulder. I realized the radio was on in the background, and there was a horrific story about a Middle East dictator who had ordered airstrikes against civilians.

I shook my head, and mouthed, "Grandma."

He nodded, and I left.

The day had brought one miserable revelation after another. I thought I'd made her life better once he was dead and couldn't hurt her anymore, but I hadn't helped her at all. I'd just gotten her killed. Somehow, she'd remembered what she shouldn't have and gotten ahold of things she shouldn't have. She'd drawn too much attention, and they killed her. Well, I'd done my crying for her this afternoon. She'd left so much evidence that now I needed to worry about myself. Now I had to admit to my parents the mess I'd made before they found out for themselves.

"So what did you find out?" Mom asked from the kitchen counter by the sink. Dad looked intently from a small wooden table in the kitchen. His opened bottle of beer was untouched. I swallowed, wishing I could put this

off. What would they think of me? I'd always had their trust, and I was about to lose that. I started off with the easiest part.

"His name is Elias Brubacher, and he's the minister of the Mennonite Church a few miles to north of town. He'd come to town to specifically to this address to see if it was true that a girl who looks like me lives in this house."

"Why would he do that?" Dad stroked his chin.

I struggled to stay calm. I didn't want him to know. How would he look at me, knowing how foolish I'd been? But I had to own up to at least this part of the truth.

"He has seen a compromising picture of me."

Dad was stunned. "What do you mean? A photograph? How could he have seen such a thing? You wouldn't let someone take compromising pictures of you, would you?"

I was silent for a moment, and that was my answer. My parents looked disgusted, so I tried to explain. "I gave it to someone I loved and trusted." My voice was very small. My parents took a moment to consider what I'd admitted.

Dad was angry. "When was this?" I was terrified of Dad when he got angry.

"A long time ago. I wouldn't do it now. I was naive. Everyone was doing it, and it seemed harmless." Please understand, I thought.

My father was still angry. "So the secret's out now, huh? What were you thinking?"

My mother was incredulous. "How would a Mennonite preacher come to see such a thing? Why would he associate it with this house?" I really didn't want to answer that, but I had to.

"It's an enlarged print. On the back is written this address and who I am and what I did. It was left for him to find. It was meant as warning

about me, to keep the men of his church safe. He came to see if any of it was true. He didn't expect it to be." But, of course, it was.

"And now here we are," Dad said pointedly. "We came to this house to make a new life for you, and here's your old life coming back to haunt us. You should've admitted what you'd done before now, so we'd have known this was possible."

"How could you be so irresponsible?" My mother was angry, too. I was shaking.

"I didn't think it would be a problem. I don't always tell you what I do when I'm alone. We all have private lives. I'm sorry. I know I made a mistake. I thought it was in the past and wouldn't matter now." Please forgive me, I thought. I knew it wouldn't be that easy.

My mother looked pained. "Of course it affects us."

"Does he know it's you? In the photograph?" my father wanted to know.

"Yes." I couldn't deny it.

Neither of my parents liked that answer. There was a pause while they considered.

"At least it's not on the Internet," my father concluded. "Then there would be little we could do to prevent it from being out there for people to see, little we could do without the police's help—and we don't want them involved."

No, I thought, if the police got involved, they might find out how stupid I'd been. They might decide I'd broken the law. Of course, I hadn't realized that I was breaking the law at the time though it was obvious in retrospect. I could end up running for the rest of my life if the police found out about the picture.

Dad looked at me. "Well, you'll just have to get it back."

4. FRIENDS

I was so nervous about school on Monday, I got up an hour early instead of waking up at the last minute. I took a shower and put on some smart, pressed newer clothes. Then, when I checked myself in the mirror, I realized I looked like I was trying too hard. It might look to people like I still thought I was too good for the school. I put on an old pair of pants and a faded shirt. Then, I noticed a tear and realized I looked too much like a slob, so I put on a better shirt.

I never used to worry about what people thought of my appearance. In the old days, I'd just rolled out of bed with ten minutes to spare, pulled on whatever was handy and wolfed down a bowl of cereal or grabbed a banana if the bus seemed imminent. Seriously, I thought, what happened to me at St. Augustine? I suddenly had more sympathy for girls getting ready in the morning. They faced much more pressure to look good than I did, and I was having trouble with just pants and a shirt. I didn't even have to worry about makeup, jewelry or hairstyle.

I almost missed the bus I was so late getting out the door. Simon was at the bus stop with a girl in a pink hoodie sweatshirt, with the hood up against the early November crispness. She turned, and I saw it was Helen. She gave me a big smile and a wave before getting on the bus. I ran to get on just behind them. Helen had paused in the aisle next to an empty seat and turned towards me. For a second, I thought she was going to offer to share a seat, and my heart raced. Then, some girls shouted her name and claimed her for themselves. Of course they did, I thought sourly. A girl like that wouldn't have to sit next to a loser like me.

I sat down by myself, put my legs up on the seat in front of me and rested my head. That's what I'd always done before to grab a few minutes extra sleep, but now it felt lonely. Simon would not have appreciated me sitting with his friends because he complained I bossed them around.

Later, at school, I carefully watched to see how my old friends treated me. After I'd gone to the office and gotten my schedule and locker assignment, I was sent to class. I'd worried and worried about how my friends would react seeing me back at Minersville: Would they tease me? Would they give me the cold shoulder?

The reality was much worse than my worst fears. My old friends really didn't really care that I was back. They were busy going on about their school business, and they made time to say "hi" and exchanged a few words, but they had all made plans without me included. No one was mean to me. They'd just gone on with their lives.

With a shock, I realized that I hadn't really had many friends. I'd had lots of friendly acquaintances. I hadn't even realized how superficial these relationships had been until now. If two months absence (plus summer vacation) could make people this indifferent, I could only conclude maybe they weren't real friends.

The one exception to this general indifference was the enthusiastic reception I got from Jimmy and Jon. These two had been inseparable since kindergarten where each had found a perfect audience for his brand of crude humor. Now they palled around during and after school performing a sort of Dumb-and-Dumber comedy routine, which I found mildly entertaining, though I was never quite sure how much of it was an act and how much was them being themselves. Often they crossed the line into being really obnoxious, but they never intended any harm, so it was usually easy to forgive them.

When Jimmy saw me in the halls, he yelled, "Aleeeeeeeex!" That was apparently a signal because he and Jon came at me and body slammed me between their two chests.

"Ow," I said. Body slams really hurt.

"We're glad you're back, man," said Jon.

At lunch, Jimmy was waving me over to the table where he was sitting with Jon. The other tables were either full or completely empty, so I was grateful for the invite.

"So, how was school in Philadelphia?" Jon wanted to know.

"I couldn't handle it," I confessed.

"Philly sucks," said Jimmy. "That's why I'm going to Penn State where I'm going to root for the Pirates."

"If you get in," said Jon. "I heard Penn State has a minimum I.Q. cut off."

"I'm out then. You just crushed my dream." Jimmy mocked sadness.

Jon looked aside at me. "He only wants to go because he heard they had a major in drinking beer."

"They don't?" Jimmy demanded.

At that moment, I saw Helen sit down with a mixed group of fairly popular athletes. I watched her for a moment, but I couldn't tell if she was especially friendly with anyone.

"Hey, guys, what do you know about this new girl, Helen?"

Jimmy was full of opinions. "She's a complete babe, of course, and totally bang-able." Jimmy took another bite of pizza.

"Can we please not talk about her like that? Her mom made me banana bread. I feel like it's rude." My attempt to tactfully shut down this line of conversation before it got more inappropriate didn't work.

Jon looked at me with his finger on the slide of his nose. "Good strategy. Be respectful and polite. That might actually get you somewhere."

Jimmy jumped in, "With her mom!" The two high fived.

I put my head in my hands and briefly considered whether sitting alone would've been preferable. No, I decided, that would've marked me as standoffish or alienated. Having friends was better, and these two were mine. I should be grateful.

It turned out Jimmy and Jon did have information on Helen. I found out from them that I had zero chance with her (no big surprise there) because close to half the junior and senior boys had asked her out by October and she had turned down graciously all but one. That lucky boy was Manny Spartoli, who took her to the Halloween dance. Jon added that it wasn't clear he was her boyfriend because afterwards she had called him a pig and said she wasn't going to any more dances. The only non-gossip item that either of them knew was that she went to Philadelphia every Saturday for classes in Spanish language and Mexican culture. Jimmy said that was bullshit because immigrants should assimilate. Jon said he thought it was her parents' idea, not hers, and that he was jealous because they let her go by herself and have dinner in the city, so she always came back late. I thought of my late-night dinners with Abe, and the reminder caused me to choke up a bit. By then, lunch period was over, and I went back to class.

Academically, school was a mostly a breeze. The classes at Minersville all seemed comfortable and easy after the rigor of St. Augustine, all of them except math. Guidance had put me in the next course in the sequence, naturally, and my brain still had the same rate-of-change problem. I went to the teacher after class and asked about switching to another level. It was the same teacher I'd had the year before, Mrs. Lohnas. She said, "Alex, you've missed two months of curriculum, so you can't expect to understand everything right away. I know you're a capable student. Let's wait until the end of the next unit before we talk about changing classes. Anyway, there isn't any other class you can take without repeating." That wasn't reassuring.

On Tuesday, I felt like I had fallen quickly into a pattern: sit by myself on the bus, with Jimmy and Jon at lunch and with my math teacher during extra help sessions. The latter worried me. Mrs. Lohnas had to help a large number of students, and I basically needed her to reteach close to two months of material. She gave me pointers to help me on whatever was the immediate problem on the particular homework, but I was still totally dependent on her.

Wednesday brought a surprise. Helen asked if she could sit next to me on the bus. Since I hadn't seen her at the bus stop, this time she must've been the one running to get on at the last moment. She wasn't wearing her hoodie today, and I almost didn't recognize her because of the way she had cut her hair. It was a radical change. On Saturday, it had gone all the way down her back; today, it was a pixie cut. She still looked like a magazine cover girl, but maybe it was a different magazine.

I hoped my "sure" didn't sound too eager. I was a little ashamed of the fact that I barely knew her and was only enthusiastic because she was so beautiful. She didn't seem to notice. Maybe she just expects guys to be shallow that way, I thought, in which case I was sure not to disappoint.

"So, girls really do spend Saturday doing their hair. I thought they were just saying that to avoid going out with me," I said.

She looked surprised and then seemed to divine that I was trying to be funny. "Maybe it's both," she said.

"Probably." I gave a fake sigh.

She cocked her head to the side. "Maybe you're asking the wrong girls."

"Definitely," I agreed.

She laughed. "Yes, I got my hair cut." She made a disgusted noise. "I hate it. My parents more or less made me do it. It was time for a change, they said. Mom cut it herself. She said it gave me a 'more contemporary look.' What do you think, does it?"

"Oh yes, very kid's-channel-turned-adult-pop-star. Your mom did it? She's a talented hairstylist then."

"I'll tell her you said so. That way Mom might not think I'm resentful or ungrateful. I miss my long hair because it's always been that way and managing it is second nature to me now. This new cut—well, I haven't figured it out yet, and it's taking me a lot of extra time in the morning."

"I'm pretty sure what you just said about long vs. short hair is the exact opposite of what every other girl has said ever."

She laughed. That was good. At least I was an amusing clown. I'd liked her long hair too, but I knew I didn't get a vote, so I didn't say anything. Also, my experience with my mother was that she would eventually persuade herself that she liked her hair, but she'd remember I hadn't. I wondered if that's why she'd worn her hood up on Monday.

So I changed the subject. "I hear you go to Philadelphia most Saturdays for classes in Spanish language and Mexican culture." What I really wanted to ask her is whether she was the one I'd seen driving back from Jane's on Saturday or walking through the graveyard on Sunday, but I was almost sure the answer would be "no," and the question itself would be far too revealing of how much I'd been obsessing about her.

"Just Mexican culture," Helen corrected. "Since Spanish was my first language, I'm fluent already. The classes are more about twentieth century history and literature."

I was surprised to hear that Spanish was her first language because she didn't have an accent. That got me wondering why she didn't have a Texas accent either. "I'd never have guessed English was your second language. I think it's better than mine."

Helen smiled. "Thanks. My family is trying to assimilate. We usually speak English, even at home, now. That's why I use the English version of my name. But we also want to keep our culture. That's why my parents have me take the class."

"Good for you." I was impressed. Helen was like two people, with two languages and two cultures. I felt a little self-conscious about the fact I only had one of each.

She winked at me, and my breath sped up. "Plus, it gives me an excuse to go the city once a week with my parents' approval." Then she changed the subject. "How's your first week back going?"

"It's nice to be home."

She smiled wistfully. "Yeah, I guess it is, if home hasn't changed too much and if you haven't changed too much."

"It's only been a couple months. Nothing's changed." As soon as I said that, I realized it was a lie.

Helen smiled at me, and that got my heart racing, so I almost missed what she said next. "Maybe you can show me around a little? You've lived here your whole life, I think. I heard that from one of your mother's former students."

"You want *me* to show you around?" That slipped out before I had a chance to censor it. I was just shocked. Guys had been asking her out since she'd moved here. Most of them had lived here their whole lives too. Why was she suddenly interested in me? I was nothing special, and she was. Still, I wasn't going to toss a winning lottery ticket just because it made no sense that I'd won.

"I'd love to!" I assured her. Then reality came back. "Um, I think I'm more or less grounded by math homework until I catch up."

"Maybe I can help tutor you? I'm good at math." Helen had an earnest expression.

"That would be awesome. I can use all the help I can get." I was grateful even if I didn't understand the offer. My calculus class was the most advanced class in the school, and I would've noticed if she were in it. It didn't seem likely that she would've already taken calculus as a sophomore in Texas. Still, it was friendly of her to offer.

Getting to school ended the conversation.

I didn't see Helen again on the bus or anywhere else until she walked into my math class on Friday. Mrs. Lohnas just nodded at her to take one of the open seats in the back row. That was next to me because I'd also been added late to the seating chart. She sat and explained, "I asked to take the placement test and switch classes."

"Why didn't you take the placement test when you first came?"

"My family has had to move around a lot, so I've started at a new school a few times. That's a lot of first impressions. People can resent it if you seem too good at everything."

I didn't miss the implication she was good at everything. I didn't doubt her, but I did wonder why she'd had a change of heart. This couldn't be a result of our Wednesday school bus conversation, could it? Then I mentally kicked myself for being self-centered. I thought sarcastically, "A girl tells you that she wants to study math at her own level, and you think it's about you."

What I said was: "If you're trying to avoid envy, why don't you tone down the whole beauty thing?"

She smiled. "Beauty thing? Flatterer. Anyway, I let my mom cut my hair." She pointed at her head, but I just shook mine. "You'd better start paying attention to Mrs. Lohnas because I think she's started class." Oops, she had.

When the bell rang, I groaned. "I have absolutely no idea what's going on in this class."

Helen heard me and said, "Why don't you meet me in the library after school, and we can work on homework together?"

"Thanks," I said, so grateful for any lifeline that I didn't even think about the fact that Helen was paying special attention to me. Later, I did wonder. It still didn't make sense that a girl like Helen would spend so much effort on someone she barely knew.

At lunch, I told Jimmy and Jon that I'd be meeting Helen for help after school. Jon said, "When did you two become friends? Weren't you just asking us at the beginning of the week who she was?" He sounded puzzled, but I realized I didn't have a good answer for him.

"She just offered," I said.

Jimmy wagged his head at me. "No way, man. No way she just offered. A total babe like that? *You?*" He raised his eyebrows. "Nah, I bet you asked her. You saw how hot she was. You did the research with us. And then you scored with some puppy-dog help-me eyes." He made his eyes real big and folded his hands in prayer. Then, he laughed and put up his hands. "Not that I don't admire your technique, bro."

We were all laughing at this point, but I wanted to protest that's not how it happened. It wasn't my game. It was Helen's. Except that didn't make sense. And I had to admit I *had* acted pitifully in front of her before she'd offered. Maybe Jimmy had it mostly right.

Our exchange must have been overheard because Manny Spartoli confronted me in the halls after last bell.

"Hey! Clarke, I hear my girlfriend is giving you remedial help in math."

His tone really irked me, and I wanted to lash out, but I remembered Prada handbag girl. There was no use in pissing off someone and potentially alienating all his friends, so I sighed away any aggression and let myself deflate. "Yeah, I really need the help. I'm total crap in math this year."

Manny seemed satisfied by my pitifulness. All he said was, "She's nice like that, likes to lend a helping hand. Hope you appreciate it, or you and I will have a problem, understand?"

"Yes, I appreciate it. Message received." I got his message: hands off my girlfriend.

When I met Helen after school in the library, I didn't meet her eyes, but just got out my math book and sat down at one of the tables. "Alex, is anything wrong?"

I looked at her and lied. "No."

Her eyes narrowed. "What happened?" She didn't look like she was going to let this drop. I figured I'd better fess up.

"Manny Spartoli and I have an understanding."

Helen muttered something angrily under her breath. It sounded a bit like "*hijo de puta*." She said, "Listen, Manny is not my boyfriend. He invited me to the Halloween dance where a group of us were going. He seemed to think that my agreeing to dance with him gave him license to put his hands where they didn't belong. I convinced him to move them by stamping on his foot. He's lucky I didn't break his toes. Afterwards, I told him not to ask me to any more dances. If Manny is still under the delusion that I'm his girlfriend, I'll straighten him out. In fact, I don't know why I'm telling you this. I'll talk to Manny."

I was starting to worry that Helen was a little crazy. There could be repercussions. "Ah, I really don't need any trouble with Manny."

She patted my hand. "Don't worry. I'm not about creating unnecessary drama. It will be all right." My hand tingled where she touched it.

"You really stamped on his foot?" I was having trouble picturing it.

"With three inch stilettos." She smiled wickedly. "He won't be wearing those shoes again. Let's get to this math."

Helen was a really good tutor. In fact, she was better at explaining math than the teacher. When I didn't understand her first explanation, she would try again by explaining it a different way. In a little while, I stopped thinking about her as a beautiful girl (who was not Manny's girlfriend) and began to be impressed by her skill as math instructor. She seemed practiced and professional. A couple of times when I was being really stupid, she showed a flash of disgust, but she covered that up almost instantly with more help. When we were done, I told her, "You have a gift. You should consider becoming a math teacher." She looked sheepish.

She drove me home in her mother's car. Apparently, her mother let her drive sometimes when her job had her working at home. That explained why I didn't see Helen on the bus every day. I thanked her profusely. I was just as grateful for the time she was bestowing on my loser self as Manny Spartoli would have liked. She might not have been Manny's girlfriend, but she wasn't mine either.

Mom asked me how I'd gotten home from school. When I told her Helen drove me, she seemed surprised. "Have you gotten to know her, then?" Mom asked. I told everything and realized how little "everything" was. Before today, I'd only talked to Helen twice, for a few minutes total. Mom gave me a strange look, and I wondered at it myself.

My plans to spend time with Alex kept having to be put on hold in order to track down everyone who knew anything about the photograph.

It was frustrating. Full of inspiration from the vision of myself I'd seen in Alex's eyes, I wanted to make progress. I wanted to seek my lost innocence with him. He wasn't completely necessary to the plan, but I confess I did love the way he looked at me. He was so prepared to find perfection and so grateful for any attention that I couldn't help but be flattered.

I'd always allowed myself to have innocent friends. Otherwise, life wouldn't have been bearable. However, I usually began such friendships within a comfortable pattern with set limits. Very safe, very responsible, very careful. With Alex, I was trying something different. I was leaving myself open.

There was another reason I wasn't making much progress.

Spending time with Alex at school inevitably brought the old, painful memory to mind. I hoped that frequent exposure to him would eventually inoculate me. If my plan to change myself were to succeed, I would need to see only the boy and not the monster. Alex had many promising qualities:

his heart had thrived at the center of a loving circle of family and friends, and he had cultivated his intelligence and humor with wide range of reading material from comic books to literature. For now though, his face looked like the monster, and I could not escape the horrible memory:

The boy Alex resembled managed to lure me to his room by a combination of flattery, drink and hints that I would enjoy his attentions. I was naive and mistook what he wanted for what I wanted. What he wanted was so far outside my experience, I couldn't have conceived of it.

Once we were alone, he attacked me viciously, smothering my screams with his hand. What he forced me to do—I felt defiled and degraded by it. What I'd done seemed unforgivable to me, and I felt so much shame, I didn't want to be seen by anyone or even to look at myself in a mirror. I still feel a barely-controlled rage when I remember.

When he'd done, I lost consciousness. I discovered later that he dumped me unceremoniously at the door of my parents' home. I was spared the ordeal of having to describe what had happened because my parents immediately understood my situation. They were kind, and I loved them for it.

My parents explained what had happened to me. They did not blame me but put the responsibility for it squarely on my attacker. They condemned him for using force and for inflicting himself on one so young and unknowing. They informed the police even though there was nothing they could do because he was long gone.

Later, I was astonished and squeamish when I learned from my mother that both she and my father had regularly done with each other the act that I thought defiled and degraded me. She said it was different when the circumstances were right.

That was a bitter time in my life. I lost all of my ability to trust and feared intimacy of any kind with any man, including my father, who patiently accepted that I couldn't be approached by him or touched even in the most casual way. My parents cut me off from all former acquaintances rather than let me harm them by association. Eventually, I made a new life for myself, but one that included a legacy of poor choices and worse luck at times.

Perhaps, I thought, this move to Minersville will give me a chance to remake myself. Perhaps Alex's face can replace the monster's in my mind. But, I added to myself, only if I can spend more time with him.

With a start, I remembered the other reason I was supposed to be spending time with Alex. I'd never reported back to the guy in Philadelphia. That, at least, I could take care of right away.

I made the secure call, and the same voice answered. I truthfully told him I'd had several face-to-face conversations and checked out Alex's connections and found no evidence he knew anything he shouldn't.

"I didn't really expect you to. He was a very casual secondary contact of one of the victims. Well, that about wraps this up. Thank you for your help and your thoroughness."

"Does that mean you've dealt with the problem?"

"Oh yes, we got the guy responsible for the rumors. He was a real idiot, killing too often in the same location and staging all his victims the same way." That was a huge relief because I'd been afraid I'd somehow I'd been at fault.

I laughed nervously, with relief. "So you weren't after me, then?"

"Have you been operating in this area? No, we didn't get a whiff of you. Good job on the low profile."

"May I ask why you had me check into Alex, instead of a more regular investigator? Not that I mind." I did, but it was pointless and dangerous to say so.

"Oh, that...well, the regular people from your area are all out of Williamsport. They can be a bit old fashioned in their attitude. You know, they act like a photograph is a big deal, and tend to overkill when it comes to containment." My heart started racing. This was not good news. If they found out about the photograph, they might come after me.

He went on, "It's like they've never heard of computers. Don't they get facial recognition cuts both ways? Lots of people have the same faces; you can always deny it was you or, if you can't, switch your identity. And with police and doctors using computers to look for patterns in premature death, eliminating people without good reason is just stupid." When he ended the call, I had an even greater sense of urgency.

I absolutely had to fix the problem of Elias Brubacher's photograph.

5. HIKING

I didn't see Helen over the weekend. Once school started again on Monday, I didn't see much of her during the week either. She wasn't riding the bus and put off tutoring me after school on Monday. She was distracted on Tuesday when she did tutor me though she was certainly helpful with the math. Only once on Tuesday did she say anything personal, which was, "Oh, I just remembered I've still got to speak to Manny." I kind of hoped she would be distracted enough to forget that one because I figured talking to Manny would just stir the pot. She must've done so, though, because of what happened on Wednesday.

Manny Spartoli came running down the hall. "Clarke, I need to talk to you!"

I sighed to myself. I really didn't need this right now. "Manny, I really don't want a problem with you. I'm not trying to cause any trouble here. Whatever's going on with you guys is between the two of you. I'm not going to do anything to disrespect either one of you." I felt craven saying it. Helen had made it perfectly clear that Manny had no rights, but here I was treating Manny's possessiveness as legitimate. Perhaps I was being a spineless coward, but what I mainly felt at that moment was exhausted. I desperately wanted to be accepted back at Minersville, and I didn't want Manny for an enemy.

Surprisingly, that was not going to be a problem. When Manny caught up to me, he seemed a little embarrassed, if anything.

"Look, Alex, we don't have a problem. Helen came to see me, and she explained how things are. She told me I owed you an apology. I guess I got everything wrong. She's not my girlfriend."

I just nodded.

"She only went to the dance with me because she thought we were going as a group, but I made a mistake." Manny paused like he was done. Then, almost as if he was forcing himself, he said, "And, ah, it was a total bad on my part that I grabbed her ass. That was completely unacceptable behavior, and I'm just lucky she didn't rat me out to my mom." Manny looked around like he was afraid someone might have overheard what he'd done and be about to tell his mother. He was actually sweating. "That *was* lucky 'cause Mom would've had my balls. Anyway, I totally deserved to have my foot stomped on." He winced at the memory. "So Helen wants me to tell you that whatever she does is up to her and none of my damn business—and that I'm sorry and that we're good, you and me. What do you say? We good?" He stuck his hand out for me to shake.

I was stunned. I took his hand in dumb reflex and shook it before I managed to get out a "Yeah, Manny, we're good." He looked relieved and beat a hasty retreat.

This was beyond weird. This was *bizarre*. This was not how I would've expected the story to go. It made no sense. How did Manny go from being a Neanderthal who thought any girl would like being groped in public at a dance to someone who apologized to a complete loser for warning him off his girlfriend? How did Helen accomplish this?

I knew Helen was odd. After all, she had shown interest in average guy like me, which proved she was at least eccentric. Still, she was so beautiful that she could bestow her attention anywhere she wanted. Her power meant she didn't have to conform to anyone's expectations. She could defy the universe and choose whomever she deigned.

But none of that explained what had just happened here. Manny had made a complete and total about face, and he didn't even seem angry about it. That fell outside my understanding of the usual parameters of human behavior. Struggling to understand, I remembered Helen's mother and the banana bread. Ah, I thought with inspiration, maybe her mother the socialite master had brought her apprentice to a level of social skill beyond my conception. She was a horse whisperer for people and had soothed Manny into doing her will. I wished *I* knew how to do that. Maybe her mother could give me lessons, I thought.

I didn't believe it, though, not really. As an explanation, it felt thin. What I really believed was something had gone on between Helen and Manny that I didn't understand.

I couldn't ask her about it because she wasn't in math that day. When Mrs. Lohnas was taking attendance, she asked if anyone knew where Helen was, and a girl said she thought she might be cutting class. I was shocked both that Helen would cut class—she didn't seem like the type—and that this girl would snitch. Mrs. Lohnas looked surprised too, and asked, "Why do you say that?" The girl said she'd seen Helen get into her car and drive off after first period.

Since Helen hadn't specifically cancelled Wednesday, I showed up at the end of the day to see if she was there. She wasn't, so I went to find Mrs. Lohnas. She didn't have time to help me at that moment, but I explained I was looking for Helen. Mrs. Lohnas told me she was sick. I said, "So she wasn't cutting?"

Mrs. Lohnas looked annoyed. "Don't go spreading that rumor. That girl was *mistaken*. I had it from the nurse herself that Helen's mother signed her out sick today." The way she said "mistaken" made it sound like she thought the girl had lied.

In some ways, that was weirder than if Helen had cut. Why would a girl spitefully lie about Helen like that?

She wasn't on the bus or in math on Thursday either. I couldn't call or text her because she'd never given me her number—and anyway, we didn't really have any defined relationship other than tutoring. My understanding of math was definitely suffering from the missed tutoring, so I planned on going to the regular extra help sessions again. Idly, I daydreamed about just walking over to her house after school, but I imagined my mom's reaction to my imposing myself on Helen's sickbed and tried to be patient.

At lunch, I sat with Jimmy and Jon as usual. The one time I'd tried sitting with some of my other old friends, they'd said a pleasant welcome, asked me a couple questions about how I liked being back and then returned to their previous discussion and lives. My dad said to be patient and I'd gradually be reabsorbed. That was probably good advice. However, I found I preferred to sit with Jimmy and Jon.

Jon said, "The weather's gonna be clear and in the seventies on Saturday. We probably won't get another day like this until spring." That's unusually warm for mid-November in Minersville. Jon added, "I was thinking we three ought to hike some of the trails outside of town, like we did in our Boy Scout days." Boy Scouts was how I'd met Jimmy and Jon.

Jimmy said, "Global warming is the best!" He pumped his fist.

I disapproved. "Jimmy, you know how wrong it is to be psyched about an impending world-wide disaster, don't you?" I don't know why I tried to educate Jimmy. It wouldn't do any good, and it might just start a pointless argument.

Jon seemed to think that too because he tried to redirect the conversation back to the hike. "It should be pretty with all of the leaves turned colors and some still on the trees."

Jimmy said, "My dad's going to want me to rake."

"That mean you can't go?" I wanted to know.

"No, that means I'm *definitely* going, so I don't have to rake. I'll ask Mom today about the hike, and then when Dad wants me to rake Saturday, I can be all like 'Mom already said I can go.'"

Jon looked admiringly at him. "That's pretty deep strategy, Jimmy. So, are we all going?"

"I'll be there. We don't have leaves to rake." We had bushes but no trees.

"Then I'll see you guys at eleven at the trailhead. We can hike the trail to the ridge. I'll get my mom to make sandwiches and stuff."

Lunch was over, and I had something to look forward to that weekend.

Helen was back on the bus Friday, and she sat down next to me, looking gloomy. "Hi, Helen, feeling better?"

"Not really," she said, "I just don't want to miss too much school."

"There's that honors student mentality," I said brightly. "I bet your parents are really proud."

"They used to be." Helen sounded glum.

"Oh come on! They can't be down on you because you missed a day and a half for being sick." I hoped they weren't putting too much pressure on her.

She ignored that. "What'd I miss?"

I thought about telling her about the girl who'd claimed she'd cut class. I decided I didn't want to bring her down any more. Instead, I said, "Well, my friend Jon Dingle has a Saturday hike planned up to a ridge that overlooks town. The weather is supposed to be beautiful, and we're going to have a picnic. Jimmy Fisher and I are going." Lost in those beautiful brown eyes of hers, I impulsively added, "Do you want to come? We'd love to have you." That last part was true— though I realized I might have to speak to Jimmy about not drooling over Helen. In fact, those two had the potential to be seriously embarrassing around any girl, but I was willing to take the risk if Helen wanted to go.

She said, "No, I don't think I'll be able to. I just need to get through today. Thanks for the offer though. I really would've liked to go on a hike with you. It would've been nice to do something fun together as friends, instead of just tutoring."

Her smile was so sincere that I couldn't believe she was just putting me off politely. Then I remembered how she'd somehow horse whispered Manny and realized that maybe she was doing the same thing to me: rejecting my offer while simultaneously leaving me feeling like I was special to her. She'd used the word "friends," and I treasured that for a moment—at least until I had parsed her grammar enough to worry that "would've been nice to do something as friends" meant that we weren't because it only "would've been." I reflected with chagrin that this girl literally had me hanging on her every word.

"All right. See you in math," I said as the bus pulled into the school.

However, I didn't see her in math as she had gone home early again.

I didn't mention the invite to Jimmy and Jon over lunch because I was sure they would razz me about getting "shot down" by a "total babe" who was "out of my league." Since I already knew what they were going to say, I didn't need them to say it, right? Of course, I probably *had* been overreaching, but if Helen smiled at me like that every time she rejected me, I'd probably keep trying forever.

Saturday morning started with pancakes and developed into a late fall day more worthy of July. Jon sure had picked the right day for his plan. My parents seemed to approve of my spending the day in the outdoors with friends. That might change when they saw my mid-term math grade in three weeks, but for now, I was good to go. I only spared one regretful glance at Helen's house on the way to the trailhead.

It wasn't much of a trail. In fact, I'm not one hundred percent sure that Jon's proposed track didn't take us trespassing over private land. On the other hand, if I didn't ask, I could always truthfully claim later that I hadn't known. It took us close to an hour to wind around in the woods behind the cliff, slowly climbing until the trail took us towards the edge. While in the woods, we couldn't see much but trees. At the edge of the ridge, it was different.

The overlook commanded a breath-taking view. We were all affected by the vista of wooded mountains—okay, hills maybe—all in the glory of fall foliage, surrounding the town. We were on the top of a sheer drop. There were trees behind us but nothing in front but a view of clear, blue sky and the town below. The houses of the town carved a space out of the colorful trees in what looked to me like the shape of a hand. I could see the five fingers.

For Jimmy and Jon, "breath-taking" was a cliché. It simply meant they forgot about the fact that they were breathing while they enjoyed the view and exchanged banter and roughhoused. For me, "breath-taking" was literal because I have a complete phobia about heights. I panicked whenever faced with a situation where my feet were more than my height above ground level. Airplanes weren't a problem, and I was fine with looking out the windows of tall buildings, but ladders, stairwells, balconies all freaked me out. I'd freeze, muscles clenched, taking rapid shallow breaths. My neck would break out in hives.

I stepped back a bit onto the forest trail where I could still enjoy the view but safely. I wished Jimmy and Jon would back off the edge. Just watching them fooling around in proximity to that fall was causing me to feel alarm.

Unfortunately, I got my wish because they came after me.

Jimmy caught sight of me backing up and somehow sensed my fear. It's not like he's super sensitive. I was probably whiter than my usual pale self, and my hands and legs were probably shaking a bit. "Alex, don't be a wuss," he said. "You can't hike all the way here and not take a proper look." I didn't move.

Jon looked at Jimmy. "Jimmy, I think we need to help Alex man up, so he can enjoy the view." This wasn't funny to me. Usually their goofing around wasn't a problem, but if they tried to drag me toward that ledge, I was going to hate it. Why did my friends find amusement in torturing me?

I turned to run, but they moved faster. They grabbed me, and I couldn't fight back effectively because my muscles were already fatigued and trembling from the fear of the heights. I tried to plant my feet. "Guys, quit it! I don't want to go to the edge."

"You'll thank us later, man." I don't know which idiot said that. Oddly enough, I would feel like thanking them later, but not for the view—for what happened afterwards.

They pulled me closer and closer. I didn't know how close because I was keeping my face turned. Jimmy said, "Here, just take one good look," and used his hands to force my head around. I should have closed my eyes, but I looked. Out would have been fine, but I looked out and down. I saw a vertical drop of about a hundred feet where the landscape had completely fallen away, no vegetation, just vertical ridges of dirt and rock going straight down.

That's when I completely lost it. I thrashed uncontrollably. Since Jimmy was holding my head, it was only Jon holding me in place and I broke free of his grip. I lurched out on one foot, right arm forward like you do when you fall—over the edge of the precipice. It was like I was moving in slow motion. I felt it when my center of mass passed the point of no return and I realized there was nothing I could do to prevent myself from falling to my death. I figured my next thought was about to be the last I ever had.

Shit, I thought.

When I got home Friday afternoon, I got my parents together, so I could share the good news with them.

"I got the photo!"

"You did? You really did?" my mom asked.

"I got it and destroyed it. No one will ever see it again." I smiled.

"Are you sure he hadn't made a copy?" Dad asked.

That was an unpleasant thought. But, no, I didn't see how it would be possible. "There was absolutely no technology in that house, certainly no camera or scanner. Elias Brubacher does not seem like the kind of man to stroll into a copy center and ask for a copy of a photo like that."

"'Doesn't seem like?'" Dad repeated. "You don't know for sure then."

I was frustrated by his skepticism and didn't appreciate being second-guessed. "I didn't get the chance to interrogate him!"

Dad relented. "I think we're in the clear. I don't mean to spoil your good news. I agree that it seems unlikely he would've made a copy, he being a preacher. He could've explained having the original—he found it—but he would have had to justify making copies."

Mom was happy. "What a relief! You've saved us all a world of trouble. How'd you find it?"

"I heard he'd be out Friday afternoon, so I went to his house and searched it. I didn't even have to break in. He doesn't lock his doors."

Dad looked puzzled. "Why did it take you until today then? We've been worried all week, and you wouldn't tell us anything except that you were 'handling it.'"

"Maybe you should tell us everything, Helen," said Mom.

I knew I should. I'd solved the main problem, but I'd also uncovered some disturbing facts they should probably know. I briefly considered editing my story. They wouldn't know. Then I looked at their faces and saw how much they loved me. They deserved the truth.

"I started at the church because that's where he found the photo in the first place. Someone had left it in the church records with a note. Anyway, I went at night, but I couldn't get inside."

That surprised Mom. "I don't understand. You couldn't get in?"

Dad added, "A girl with your abilities shouldn't have had any trouble."

I said, "I know. It's disturbing. The locks had strange markings on them I didn't recognize. I don't think you could have gotten in either."

My parents digested that for a minute. "Along with the marks, there was a symbol, like a letter M with a vertical line through it."

Dad looked at me sharply. "Were these old locks with old markings or new ones with new markings?"

I wasn't sure. "The marks looked old, but it's hard to tell because the locks had all been polished to a bright finish recently."

My dad put his hand to his face and mused. "That's a bit of a puzzle." He looked at Mom, who shrugged.

I was impatient to get to my good news. "I am hoping it doesn't matter. I visited each of the church elders this week under various pretexts. None of them recognized me from the photograph. I learned from one of the elders that the minister would be visiting him all Friday afternoon, so I took advantage to go to his house today and search. I found the photo in a drawer of his desk with the note I told you about. I got out of his house and burned them both."

Dad smiled broadly. "This is good, very good. If the elders didn't recognize you from the photo, then Brubacher never showed it to them or they didn't get a good enough look. Even better, with the original destroyed, Brubacher would have to be a fool to say anything. Without proof, he'd look like he had a sick obsession with an innocent schoolgirl."

Mom looked really happy, too.

I asked, "Can I let my hair grow out, now?"

Mom looked at Dad. He said, "I don't see why not. By the time it grows back, the photo will be a distant memory—if they remember it at all."

Mom said, "Remember that it will take a year to grow six inches."

"I know, I know," I said. "It's such a pain."

We celebrated that night with a special dinner of roast chicken and a bottle of sparkling cider. They might've given me champagne in Texas, which permits parents to give their own children alcohol on private premises, but this was Pennsylvania, where that was not allowed. My parents studiously avoided any unnecessary, minor law breaking. Dad said it prevented calling attention to the absolutely necessary, major law breaking. During dinner, we all relaxed. I'd been lucky.

I suddenly thought of Alex's hiking trip, and wanted nothing more than to go with him on a jaunt in the woods. I needed him to look at me the way he did. I watched my parents feasting comfortably and imagined myself telling them I was going hiking with Alex. I really didn't want to have Alex's name introduced in the context of that photograph. I wasn't sure they would have approved of my spending time with a boy before, but they certainly wouldn't now. I had really strained their trust in me.

I wanted to see Alex badly. I decided to track him down tomorrow on the hike and surprise him. I was pushing my luck.

6. RESCUE

A hand grabbed my left forearm from behind and pulled me hard, back to safety. It hurt like hell. I barely noticed the pain from the fingers crushing my forearm because my shoulder felt like something had broken inside it. At least, it felt that way for a brief moment of searing pain before the whole pain thing short-circuited my brain and I went numb. A moment later, I collapsed and was lowered to the ground, my head cradled gently by someone's hand, to keep it off the rocks.

I looked up into Helen's face. I couldn't process it. Helen wasn't here. How could I be seeing her? Briefly I was mesmerized by the angelic beauty of her face, which lost nothing to the worry etched there. "Are you okay, Alex?" she asked. My arm hurt so badly I couldn't answer. "You're in shock," she said. "Don't worry. You'll be fine. I'll take care of you."

"Where did you come from?" asked Jimmy.

Helen's face went from concerned to wrathful with a suddenness that was frightening. I'd never seen someone so full of rage in real life. In school, I'd seen a video of an angry Malcolm X where his every word and gesture radiated anger, and later I'd seen an actor do the same speech for a movie. The actor was nominated for an

Oscar—but he fell far short of the reality. I'd concluded it's not possible to fake the emotions of a lifetime of pain and outrage. Where did this girl get that level of rage?

Helen turned on Jimmy. "You!" She sounded furious. "You nearly murdered your friend with your carelessness! What is wrong with you? How could you be so irresponsible?" Her hands were balled into fists at her side and were shaking.

"Is he all right?" Jimmy wanted to know.

"No thanks to you." She fixed him with her stare. "That's what I'm trying to find out. Just stand there a second until I see if I need you to summon help." She turned back to me, muttering to herself.

Her expression softened to reassuring. "Can you speak to me, Alex?"

I could speak again. "My shoulder really hurts. I'm afraid it might be broken."

"Let me check."

I didn't want her touching it because it hurt so much. "I think maybe we should wait for a doctor."

Her lips thinned. "We're going to have to move you. Help's not likely to come up here. I need to know what kind of injury you have before we decide how to do that." That explanation sounded reasonable. Her calm demeanor helped. "Alex, look at me." I did. "I will be gentle, and you won't feel any pain. Understand?"

I nodded tightly, so as not to move the shoulder. She replaced her right hand, which had been holding the back of my head, with her left. She used her right hand to carefully feel my shoulder. I noticed I was on my back on the ground, her kneeling beside me. "The good news is that you haven't broken your shoulder. The bad news is it *is* dislocated." She delivered her conclusion with a wry expression.

Jon asked, "How'd you move so fast? You weren't even with us."

Helen pursed her lips. She had that look I remembered getting so often at St. Augustine, the look that says, "Well this boy is going to be a problem."

Jon asked, "How did you even do that? Pull him back so hard you dislocated his arm?" That was a surprisingly good question. I hadn't wondered at her strength because I was used to strong girls. Jane could lift nearly as much as I could—and she could do it all day long whereas I got tired quickly. However, I hadn't thought about what Helen had done logically or quantitatively. I had assumed gravity and my own weight had dislocated my arm, as it might have done if I'd fallen on the ground, but it was actually Helen's arresting and reversing my momentum. To accelerate my 150 pounds as quickly as she had would have taken an astonishing amount of strength.

Helen's lips were pressed together in disapproval. "You should be thanking me for saving his life and keeping you out of a world of trouble. You think girls can't be strong? You know this is the twenty first century, right?"

"Sorry," said Jon.

"Thanks," added Jimmy.

"What are we gonna do?" Jon wanted to know.

Helen looked at them and then at me. "These really are your friends, right? They were just roughhousing? They didn't intend to hurt you?"

"Yes," I admitted.

She turned back to Jon and Jimmy and took a deep breath. "Hi," she said with a smile that seemed sincere if rueful. "I think we got off to a bad start. Let's try again, shall we? My name is Helen." She paused, staring at them.

Jon said, "I'm Jon, and this is Jimmy." Jimmy gave a half-hearted wave.

"In terms of what we are going to do, may I suggest that it would for the best if none of us ever told anyone about what just happened? At the very least, I'll bet your parents wouldn't let you go hiking on your own again if they heard you'd nearly gotten your friend killed." Jimmy's eyes were huge, and Jon was nodding agreement. Helen smiled tightly.

Jimmy said, "I won't say nothing."

Jon said, "Doesn't he need medical help?"

Helen took another deep breath. "I think I was wrong about the shoulder. I'm no doctor. I've probably just watched too many medical shows." She gave a forced laugh. "I'm sure he's totally fine and can walk out of here on his own and doesn't even need to see a doctor—which is good because a doctor would certainly call his parents and that'd get us all into trouble." Helen looked at them significantly.

Jon said, "You really think he's okay?"

Helen gave him a reassuring look. "He's totally fine," she said. Jon looked relieved.

Helen added, "So, are we agreed to say nothing about the near fall?" Jon and Jimmy both nodded.

"Good. I'm sure his arm hurts a lot, and he'll want to act like a tough guy as long as you're around. You probably feel like you're responsible and want to help right now. But if you care about his feelings, you won't inflict yourselves on him. You'll leave him to me." I looked at Helen in surprise. She wanted them to leave?

"You want us to leave?" Jimmy was surprised too.

"Please," she said.

"We really can't do that," said Jon. "It's our fault he got hurt. He's our friend. We can't leave him." Good for you, Jon.

Helen turned to me. "Alex, would you please tell your friends they're totally forgiven, you're just fine and it's all right to leave you with me?"

I wasn't sure about any of that, but reflexive masculine pride kicked in, and I found myself saying, "Yeah, guys, I'm good. Don't worry. You can leave me."

Helen turned back to them, "He really is fine. I think he was just afraid from the scare of it all."

"No harm, no foul," I said. I literally do not know what that phrase means. I just said it because I'd heard people say it.

I could see Helen and I were getting through with our combined reassurance, but the guys still hesitated.

"Please?" Helen begged. "Would you please leave me alone with my boyfriend?"

"Boyfriend?" Jon echoed. He and Jimmy looked shocked.

Boyfriend? I was stunned.

"Yeah, right," Jimmy said sarcastically. "We'd know if he had a girlfriend."

I'd know, I thought. At least, I think I would.

Helen gave them a pleading look. I couldn't tell if it was an act. "It's a recent thing," she explained. "I'd kind of like to spend the afternoon alone with him."

Jimmy looked at Jon, who shrugged his shoulders.

"Okay, we'll go," said Jimmy.

"Yeah, three's a crowd. We get it," said Jon. By this point, they were smiling a bit.

"Thank you." Helen said the words like they were end punctuation and gave them a well-get-on-with-it look. They left us some of the sandwiches and cans of Coke that we had brought for lunch and then took off.

Once they were gone, I asked, "So I'm your boyfriend now?" I was all mixed up. I totally wanted to be, but it was a little crazy that she'd just announced it without telling anyone first. Like me.

We hadn't moved from our positions on the ground. I didn't know if she was comfortable kneeling.

"I really needed them to leave, and they weren't going to unless they thought I had a claim on you that superseded theirs."

What kind of explanation was that? "So I'm not your boyfriend, and you just said it because it would make them leave? Is that what you're saying?" That seemed a little less crazy. Still, she must know it would get around.

"I said it to make them leave, yes," she said. "As to whether you're my boyfriend, that's up to you. If you want to be, I think the position's open."

"What do you mean, you *think* the position's open? Do you mean that you have a boyfriend right now who's ignoring you?" She was going to use me to make Manny jealous, I thought. That made sense. I wasn't boyfriend material for a girl like her, but I would do as an expedient. The fact that I was seriously considering taking this role in her little play just so I could act opposite her—well, that was humiliating.

"No, I've never had a boyfriend." The admission came quietly. "I've never wanted for one. I just meant that I would consider opening the position to you if you were to put in an application."

Whoa, I thought. Boyfriend. Her boyfriend. I really liked that idea. Maybe I wasn't such a loser after all. Or maybe I was a loser, but I'd have a really hot girlfriend. Like every nerd movie every made. Cool.

"You know that the idiots you just sent away will already be telling everyone in town that we're a couple." I wasn't inclined to be charitable to my best friends after nearly falling off a cliff.

She didn't agree. "I think I made it quite clear to them that it's in their self-interest not to broadcast the details of this incident."

"Maybe that's true about nearly shoving me off a mountain, but the boyfriend bit—there is no way they're keeping that to themselves." I couldn't believe she was that clueless. She had to know how much interest she generated.

"Oh," she said. "I didn't...Oh," she said again. "Then I guess I better say something to my parents before they hear it from somewhere else. What should I tell them? You never answered me. Is that because you're dating that Jane girl, Jane McCord?"

I wondered why Helen would think that. I couldn't remember if I'd ever spoken of Jane to her. "No, she's just a buddy. We were the only two children in the same grade in our Sunday school, so we were thrown together a lot. She's a friend, but she doesn't have a lot of patience for me. She calls me a jerk a lot."

"So she's not your girlfriend?" Helen looked at me intently.

"No." I shook my head. "I never had a girlfriend."

"What do you think about me? Would I be acceptable? We haven't known each other very long, but do you want to be my boyfriend?"

Hell, yeah! Why would she say "acceptable"? Awesome was more like it.

I tried to play it cool. "Yeah."

"Then I'm your girlfriend," she said. "I'll try to be a good one."

I couldn't believe my luck. I mean I really couldn't believe it. For me, a catch like her couldn't be without a catch, and I wondered if she was crazy.

That's when I made the mistake of trying to shift position. My shoulder was suddenly screaming in pain.

Helen instantly focused. "Oh, I'm so sorry, Alex. Here I am making plans for the future, and I should have been paying attention to the present. The thing is that your shoulder really *is* dislocated. We need to do something about that."

Wait! What? No!

Before I could react—before I could even see her move—she had her hands on my collarbone and humerus and yanked hard. I shouted in pain. I looked at her accusingly. "That really hurt!"

"Yes, but it's fixed now." She put her face a few inches from mine. I thought for a second she was going to kiss me. I held my breath and hoped. Instead, she said, "It doesn't hurt now, does it, Alex?"

It didn't at all. That was weird. Shouldn't it be sore?

"Now why don't we have that picnic?" she suggested.

"Can we move a little further from the ledge?" It was still making me nervous.

"Sure." She smiled. My day got a whole lot better.

I was hungry, so we didn't do a lot of talking while we had lunch. Later, I was caught up just looking at her. I was fearful of saying anything that might cause her to change her mind about the whole boyfriend / girlfriend relationship. I worried if I opened my big, fat mouth, I'd say something offensive, and she'd come to her senses and tell me the deal was off. So we looked out at the view—from a safe distance from the ledge—in what I hoped was companionable rather than awkward silence.

This gave me time to think about Helen's strangeness. Not the unaccountable strangeness of her wanting me as a boyfriend. No, I was remembering the mystery of her inexplicable physical strength. Also, how did she know how to fix my shoulder? That one, I asked her over lunch. She said she'd received "Red Cross training." Her answer didn't really make sense to me. The tiny amount of first aid training I'd received as a Boy Scout was pretty clear that anything not immediately life-threatening should be left for an actual medical doctor to treat. The most surprising thing was the confident way she had taken charge of all of us. She just assessed the situation and told us what to do, and somehow we all did it. She reminded me of a teacher, like my mom. I really didn't want to go there (since she was my girlfriend now), so I promptly repressed that thought.

When it was time to go back down the trail, she didn't exactly hold my hand, but she kept taking ahold of my good arm, like she needed it for support. Actually, I think she was supporting me, keeping me from stumbling or straining my re-located shoulder.

Injured or not, I walked her to her door. I wanted to be courteous, and guys always walk girls to the door in the movies. I didn't really think my new girlfriend would kiss me goodbye. I'd never been kissed, and we hadn't known each other long. Distracted by the thought of the kiss I didn't expect, I missed the approach of a dark-suited, hatted Mennonite man.

Helen recognized him. "Reverend Brubacher, welcome," she said, sounding surprised.

The Reverend Brubacher was imposingly tall and stern faced. "I know what you are, girl. I know what you did." He delivered his accusation like a judgment from God. He lifted his finger and pointed at her. "I don't know how you made everyone forget, but I haven't forgotten." He was angry, and it was a little scary.

Helen looked at him and me with anxiety. She said to Brubacher, "Whatever you think, you should discuss this inside the house, with me and my parents. Go inside and wait for me."

He did.

I looked at Helen in shock. I was trembling a little bit, but she seemed perfectly calm. She was maybe a little embarrassed. "Alex, I'm sorry you had to be a witness to that. Don't worry about him. He's crazy. We'll get this sorted out."

I didn't think I should leave her alone to face this man. "Do you want me to come inside? For extra protection?"

She covered her face to hide a smile. "No, I'll be fine. Go home. I'll see you tomorrow at school." She disappeared into her house.

Obviously, there was a whole lot I didn't know about this girl. Was she for real?

My reception at home also came across as unreal—surreal even. Despite the fact that I had predicted what Jimmy and Jon would do, I was unprepared when my mother said, "So, I hear from Mrs. Fisher that you have a girlfriend now. The neighbor girl, Helen."

"Uh, yeah."

"I would have preferred hearing this from you."

"Sorry, Mom. Helen and I just decided this today. Jimmy's got a big mouth is all."

"Mrs. Fisher also tells me that Jimmy and Jon left the two of you on the trail alone for the afternoon."

Uh oh. I had caught on too late to the fact that I was in trouble.

Mom continued, "We trust you, Alex, and we don't mind your going off hiking with Jimmy and Jon, but we expect you three to stay together on the trail."

"Mom, I promise you that Helen and I behaved ourselves. There was absolutely no hanky-panky of any kind." I'm not sure whether I was coming across as earnest or flippant though it was all perfectly true.

My mother didn't seem sure of how take my assurance. "I'm certainly glad to hear that you behaved yourselves. You father and I expect nothing less. But, be that as it may, if you are going somewhere with Helen in the future, we expect to know where you are going to be and who's going to be there with you. Beforehand. Am I being clear?"

"Yes, Mom."

"Now, I've already spoken to Helen's mom..." Of course, she had, I thought. Her often-voiced philosophy was: "People get all upset, they hear rumors, and they feel resentful—when what they ought to do is pick up the damn phone!" Of course, she had called Helen's mom and talked it out. I hoped Helen didn't face too much trouble when she got home. "...and I assured her that this was not *typical* behavior from you and that she could expect better in the future. Do not make me a liar."

"I don't understand how what I did was so disrespectful. You let me hunt with Jane in the woods last Saturday."

Mom nodded thoughtfully. "I see how that could be confusing. Of course, I didn't exactly know the two of you would be doing that when we agreed to the broccoli picking. I don't mind you hunting alone with Jane. She's a sensible girl, and we know her father well. He trusts her alone in the woods, and he trusts her alone with you. But you and Jane have always been just friends. Jane doesn't call you her boyfriend. That makes a big difference."

My father had entered the room in the middle of the conversation. He seemed to have understood what we were talking about immediately—maybe Mom had talked to him earlier—because he said, "If Helen comes to visit—and we'd like to meet her—don't try to take her upstairs or in your bedroom. I know you've been used to hanging out with Jimmy and Jon up there, but the rules with girls are different." Mom nodded agreement. Dad added, "Those are the rules in this house, and they are not going to change until you're married."

"For heaven's sake, Dad, she's my first girlfriend, and we've only been going out for like five hours! You're getting ahead of yourself there." Mom gave Dad a look, like maybe she agreed with me—though I suspected she was in agreement with him on the substance of the prohibition.

"Don't you get ahead of yourself, son. That's what I'm saying. I know she's pretty, but take the time to get to know her. Slower is safer when it comes to matters of the heart." Mom now looked like she was in complete accord.

"I'll try, Dad."

"I knew your mom for twenty five years before I married her."

"Oh come on, Dad, that's just because you two were in the same kindergarten class." We all laughed at that one. It was an old story, and laughter carried us into dinner.

On the whole, it had been an unreal day.

Homework brought me back to reality.

I left Alex at the door and went inside. I was furious with Brubacher. Why couldn't the man act sensibly? He was waiting for me in the living room with my parents. Before he could speak, I glared at him and said, "You have no proof. No one will believe you."

He said stiffly, "I've seen the proof with my own eyes. I will testify to the truth."

I was not going to let him do that. Besides embarrassing me in front of Alex, he'd be endangering my entire family. Given what I'd heard about the attitudes of the investigators out of Williamsport, I was terrified of the idea of them getting involved. Even without proof, this story alone might be enough to get us killed.

I stared into his eyes. "You'll say nothing about this. You'll go home and forget this."

He didn't blink. Standing tall he said, "God will remember, and he will judge you, evil creature that you are."

He wasn't wrong about that, I thought.

Dad looked at him menacingly. "You say one word about that photograph, you will die. If hear you've so much as breathed my daughter's name, I will kill you with my bare hands."

Brubacher looked a little daunted at that. He glanced at me then, and I saw worry but also stubbornness.

The trouble was he wasn't nearly as afraid of me as he needed to be. What if he didn't do what I told him? That was not acceptable. I had to let him see a little bit of the monster, or I might have to show him all of it. I stared him down and said in a cold, tight voice, "If you keep talking about me, I will destroy you. You will lose everything. Believe it." I looked right into his eyes and made sure he did.

The man flinched and took a step back. "St. Michael protect me," he said.

Mom and Dad exchanged a significant glance. I wasn't sure what it was about.

Mom turned to Brubacher and said, "Go home now. Say nothing about what you know about Helen, and no harm will come to you."

He left.

We all breathed a sigh of relief.

We talked it over. My parents had known something like this could happen, but they seemed to feel I'd done everything I could at this point. Mom especially was optimistic that it was really over. Dad was surprised Brubacher had found the courage to confront us, but he seriously doubted he'd do anything more at this point. Mom approved of the way I'd carried myself.

So it came out of the blue when Dad said, "Should we move again? Just to be on the safe side?"

No, I thought, I don't want to leave Alex now, just when I'm getting started.

Mom didn't look surprised at all. She said, "You think he might've told the wrong people already."

"If there's any chance at all they'll coming looking for us, it'd be better not to be here."

"No, Dad," I said, "surely there's not so much danger as that? Who would he tell? You just got the whole house restored."

He and Mom exchanged another significant glance.

Dad exhaled through his nose. "I would like to enjoy the fruits of my labor a little bit longer."

Mom said, "We can keep alert. Maybe get a security camera and alarm system." That seemed to end the conversation.

After dinner, Mom came to talk to me in my room. I thought she wanted to talk more about Brubacher, but she wanted to talk about Alex. Unfortunately, she was surprisingly well informed. I'd meant to ease my parents gently into the whole Alex situation.

Alex was right about the lack of discretion of his friends. That was a fact to keep in mind. Mom and Dad already knew Alex and I were now dating by the time I got home. Alex's mother had called mine up on the phone to discuss the situation. Mom had given all our new neighbors our phone number and invited them to call us if they ever had any problems or concerns about anything going on at our house, not that she expected any, she'd said. It's a good policy, Mom had told me, because it encourages people to call us before little problems become big ones.

Alex's mother seems to have the same philosophy. She told Mom she'd just heard from the mother of Jimmy Fisher that we'd met up on the trail, I had called Alex "my boyfriend" and we'd spent the afternoon alone in the woods. She'd added that she "couldn't say for sure" that we hadn't planned this. She apologized for her son's disrespectful behavior and promised to speak to him about it. She also reassured my mother that Alex had always behaved as a decent and honorable young man (though I believe the phrase she used was "good boy"), and she'd hoped that my parents wouldn't judge him too quickly based on one mistake. Somehow she managed to hint that her son's lack of romantic experience and my "exceptional good looks" might have caused him to err without actually saying as much.

So, there it was. Alex was a decent, honorable, impressionable innocent, whose biggest mistake in life thus far was choosing to be alone with me. I couldn't have agreed more.

After describing the entire conversation, Mom said, "Your desire to stay in Minersville wouldn't be because of this boy Alex, would it?"

I didn't say anything.

Mom looked at me sympathetically. "Cuidado, hija. There may be more than one danger here. Promise me you'll be careful."

I nodded my head. I was a little hurt that she'd asked for my promise. In my family, trust usually goes unspoken. We all try to respect each other's privacy and to trust each other implicitly. I supposed it was fair since I'd recently violated my family's trust in a major way.

"Can I date Alex?" I hated having to ask permission, but if my parents were dead set against it, the whole plan was a no-go from the start.

"Of course. You don't have to ask. Your dad and I trust your choices." Mom left me alone.

Maybe my screw-up hadn't been as bad as I'd feared. It didn't seem to have changed our family dynamic fundamentally. Apparently, whether I chose to spend time with Alex and what we did together was up to me. My parents wouldn't ask, and they didn't necessarily expect me to tell. I think this was their way of trying to show me they still had faith in me.

I wished I trusted myself as much.

7. GIRLFRIEND

The next day I didn't see or hear from Helen at all. At first, I didn't realize that I wasn't going to see her because I spent the morning at church. I took out my phone to text her after lunch, but I remembered that I still didn't have her cell phone number. I realized that I wasn't just new to be being her boyfriend, I was still new to being her friend. I would've walked over to her house—I mean she lived right there—but I worried that it'd be rude to arrive uninvited. I didn't know whether being Helen's boyfriend gave me drop-in privileges. Ultimately, I had to go to my mom to get Helen's home phone number. I knew my mom had it after yesterday, and she gave it to me easily enough. Maybe I only imagined that the look she gave me meant "go slow." When I called, I didn't get Helen, I got her father.

"*Diga*," he said.

"Ah, hello, this is Alex Clarke. Is Helen there?"

"I know who you are. This is Victor García. Helen is not home right now, but I expect she will see you at school tomorrow."

"Ah, thanks, Mr. García." He hung up. I was glad I hadn't walked over since Helen wasn't there, and I didn't get the impression Mr. García would approve of drop-in privileges.

The next day, Helen explained while we were waiting for the bus that her class in Philadelphia had been moved to Sunday afternoon because of a teacher scheduling conflict. That was why she had been free Saturday (and why I was alive today).

I asked Helen what was up with that Mennonite guy. I'd been burning to ask her all the day before. Helen looked irritated, and I hoped it wasn't with me. "Reverend Brubacher is crazy. He's been spreading lies about me—which no one believes. Yesterday, Dad threatened him with lawyers. I hope that's the end of it." She hugged herself and sighed.

"What's he been saying?" I was intensely curious about anything involving Helen, but for once she didn't answer.

She shook her head and said, "I don't want to talk about him any more."

So I asked Helen about what she was learning in her culture class. I knew nothing about Mexican history and culture, so we spent the whole bus ride and much of the time between classes with her telling me about it. I listened eagerly partly because I liked learning what she could teach me and partly for the joy of having this charismatic girl talking animatedly to me.

We sat together at lunch at the end of a large group of friends, who were together and didn't include us. It was almost like being alone together. Jimmy and Jon made themselves scarce, which was wise, considering Helen probably hadn't completely forgiven them yet. I saw the occasional surprised looks, and some people kept glancing at us furtively.

Helen proposed that we stay after school for her to give me extra help and for me to walk her home. I liked the generosity of her implication that I was doing something for her by escorting her home, rather than other way around. Helen pointed out that the weather had stayed really warm, that it was supposed to get to seventy degrees by the mid-afternoon and that a major cool down was expected tomorrow, so this would be our last chance to walk home in nice weather. I texted Mom and got permission so long as I was home by four thirty.

(I had asked Mom once how come she was allowed to have her phone on during class, and I wasn't. She had said because she was a teacher and I was a student, and don't tell her principal.)

I raced through my math homework with Helen and walked slowly on the way home. We crossed the parking lot and cut through the narrow woods to the grassy fields beyond. The fields are sheltered from view of the road by more woods. Since the sky was clear and the sun shining, I was in no hurry to get home. I checked my phone and realized we had plenty of time. Helen saw me looking and said, "Did you want to stop here for a while?" I did. "Let's sit, and you can tell me more about yourself."

Helen lay down and closed her eyes while she listened. She asked about Mom and Dad and Simon, she asked about Trinity Church, and she asked about Jane and Jimmy and Jon. She asked just enough questions to keep me going and show she was listening until I got self-conscious and fell silent. She was quiet then too, and I simply watched her.

She looked beautiful on the grass, an exquisite combination of sexy and sweet. The curves of her face and body made interesting shadows in the afternoon sunlight, and the light brown of her skin and blue of her shirt contrasted strongly with the fading green of the fall grass. I thought of my phone's camera. "Helen, may I take your picture?"

"No!" That was certainly emphatic, I thought. I felt a little disappointed. I really was unsure of how much latitude I had with Helen.

Her eyes snapped open, and she sat up. "You haven't been taking any pictures of me already, have you?" she demanded.

"No." I might have sounded sullen.

"Give me your phone." I did, a little reluctantly.

"Now tell me your password." I did that too, a little more reluctantly.

She scrolled through all my pictures. There were my friends, my mom and dad, a few of me, lots of my brother Simon, a bunch from the first week at St. Augustine but none of her. I didn't know whether to be relieved that she hadn't busted me with an unauthorized candid or sad that someone I now thought of as a major part of my life was so little represented on my camera roll.

"Can I have my phone back?" She gave it back.

"I don't want you taking my picture."

"Obviously," I deadpanned. Then, "Why not? I know my mom doesn't like to have her picture taken, but that's because she always hates the way she looks in them. You're so perfect I can't believe that's your problem."

"That's sweet."

"That's not an answer."

"Would you believe that I have a need to maintain total control of my image?"

"Hm," I thought. "If it's about control, what if you take the picture? You could take selfies of us until you're satisfied, and you then could post it online—maybe with a relationship update?" I was only half serious. My mother would possibly have a cow.

"Absolutely not. No social media. No postings of any kind." She seemed really upset. "You aren't planning to do something like that, are you?" She looked me in the eyes intently.

"No, I wasn't." She seemed satisfied.

"Good. Don't forget. I don't want you taking my picture."

"I still don't get why." I thought we were close.

"Would you believe that I'd been bullied online?"

Yes, I'd totally believe that. Of course, she would've been bullied online. Helen was so beautiful (not to mention smart, well-off, bilingual) that common junior high envy and resentment would more or less guarantee she was cyber-bullied. I suddenly felt like a huge cretin for pushing her on this.

"Helen, I'm so sorry. I didn't know. I've never been a victim myself, so I have no idea how you feel about pictures, but I promise I won't ask you again."

Helen was quiet for a moment. "Why did you want picture of me? Did you want to post something about us? Is that what's expected? I'm afraid I'm being a bad girlfriend here." She seemed uncertain of herself.

"No, all my friends already know we're going out. I just wanted a picture of you for myself. You looked so beautiful lying there on the grass." That was the truth. "I love looking at you. I might have put it up in my room."

"Oh," she said. She brightened considerably. "Look at me all you like." She lay back on the grass as she had been before and closed her eyes again. "You don't need a picture when you've got me."

"Won't you be uncomfortable with me staring at you?" I tried to imagine myself doing that. It seemed rude to stare.

"If I were uncomfortable with you staring at me, I'd probably be uncomfortable with you staring at my picture in your room. No,

Alex, I don't mind you looking at me. In fact, I rather like it." She said it like she meant it.

We were out of time if I was to meet Mom's deadline, so I had to enjoy the privilege of looking as we walked home.

The next two weeks were a happy time for me. We spent every moment we could together at school. Since the weather had turned cold, we were taking the bus and sitting together. We ate lunch together, and we still had math class and extra help sessions.

We didn't spend much time with each other outside of school. We both had homework that kept us busy in the evenings, and I wasn't ready to invite her to my house and meet my family because I was afraid Simon might be embarrassing—or my parents. She didn't invite me, and I wondered if that was because she didn't think her parents would approve. Her father hadn't given me a warm and fuzzy feeling on the phone. On weekends, she had her Saturday class in Philadelphia, and I had Sunday church.

There had been no social media announcement, but the news that we were a couple seemed to have spread instantaneously in our small town. Jimmy and Jon joined us at lunch after that first day. Jimmy proved better behaved than I had expected him to be. He just kept staring at her with a big, goofy grin. Periodically, he would glance at me and shake his head, as if to say, "What does she see in you?"

Jon was mostly his normal self, which meant he kept introducing geeky conversations about various fantasy and superhero movies and TV shows. Normally, I loved these conversations, but I kept furtively looking at Helen to make sure she wasn't ready to bolt back to her previous crowd to avoid being the audience for one more passionate debate of Dumbledore vs. Gandalf, Superman vs. Spider-man or zombies vs. unicorns. Still, I couldn't help but vigorously defend my deeply held convictions, which were respectively: Gandalf, depends on which version of Spider-man and unicorns (because their horns have healing powers). The quality of our debates was limited by the fact that Jon didn't read anything he didn't have to, even graphic novels, so his evidence was always from the movies and TV shows. Helen sat patiently through these arguments, having little to offer except for the Dumbledore vs. Gandalf debate. It turns out she'd read all of Tolkien and the *Harry Potter* series once. She even offered to watch season five of Doctor Who with me if I could get it recorded on our DVR.

I began to hope she might inexplicably feel some attraction to me, some tiny echo of what I felt to her. That gave me the courage to finally ask for her cell phone number.

I need not have worried that my geekiness would rub off on Helen because what happened was that her popularity began to rub off on me. Maybe I should have known that someone with 24 charisma points and a hefty dose of comeliness would be able to weather an association with the kind of boy who thought of her in terms of Dungeons and Dragons character traits. I was completely floored when the cheer captain invited me to her birthday party in December. Since she had invited Helen too, I assume she invited me as a courtesy to Helen. The editor of the school newspaper also suddenly remembered I was on staff and found me at lunch to ask if I would contribute an article for the next edition. I cracked up when Helen suggested that I write one on the cheer team. "Go fighting miners!" I chanted.

It wasn't just Helen who was changing my life. Being Helen's boyfriend was changing my life.

Mrs. Lohnas was the only teacher to take official note of our change in relationship status. She was thrilled that Helen was providing me so much help in math, and I think she might have been a little relieved that she didn't see me at her overcrowded help sessions any more. She confided in me that Helen had scored the highest grade on the pre-test she had ever seen and advised me to stick with her. Mrs. Lohnas seemed to imply that my success in math would depend on my success in love, and I wasn't sure that I disagreed with her about that.

When Jimmy discovered I was getting help from Helen in math, he asked if I thought she would help him too. He was having trouble in algebra. I was glad of a chance to do something for him since Jane, Jon and he had turned out to be my only real friends. When I asked Helen, she seemed surprised. "You wouldn't mind not having me all to yourself?" she asked. I told her I was doing better in math, and I had no objections to her helping others—as long as she wasn't *dating* them. She laughed at the idea of going out with Jimmy.

After Jimmy joined our help sessions, he started doing a lot better, and he told everyone it was thanks to Helen. After that, Helen got a lot more requests for help and our sessions became almost as busy as Mrs. Lohnas's. She didn't mind the competition at all and even started referring some kids waiting for her help to us.

Strangely, I ended up helping people most times. When Helen was busy, I was often able to help someone else with the algebra or geometry that I'd already mastered. Explaining it to others was a good refresher for me as well. I realized I had inadvertently taken the advice my grandma had given me about doing nice things for others, one at a time. I noticed more people saying "hi" to me in the halls, and Helen and I often sat in much larger groups at lunch.

I noticed the girls I tutored all asked me at some point if Helen was my girlfriend. They'd obviously heard it, but they asked like they wanted to hear it from me. Mostly, I think it made them more comfortable that I was already taken. They were reassured that I wasn't helping them as an excuse to hit on them. Once or twice though, it sounded like maybe they were hoping I was available. The old me—the one with the inflated ego—might have gotten into some real trouble at that point, but the new me knew enough to be grateful for what I had. Helen once asked me what I thought of the girls I tutored, and I could look her in the eye and tell her truthfully that I really liked helping people, but it didn't much matter to me whether they were boys or girls.

She said, "But you think the girls are prettier, right?"

"Prettier than Jimmy," I agreed. Helen laughed. Okay, I was ducking the question because the answer was embarrassing and weird.

I had been looking at Helen's beautiful brown face so much that other girls started to look pale to me. These other girls had the same skin color I did, for heaven's sake! I didn't want them to go tanning and give themselves cancer. I realized my personal notion of beauty had shifted because of the way I felt about Helen. In other words, girls that looked like Helen were beautiful to me. And no one looked more like Helen than she did.

I hoped I wasn't being racist, like my grandma sometimes was. I wasn't suddenly into Mexican girls. I was into Helen. Whatever she was, that was good to me.

Manny Spartoli once came to an extra help session. Afterwards, he said to me quietly, "Clarke, I hear you are Helen's boyfriend. A word of advice? Don't try anything with her." He raised his eyebrows suggestively. "She'll eff you up."

I hadn't tried anything, not because I didn't want to but because I was afraid to. I was well aware that my loser status was only being eclipsed by Helen's aura of awesomeness. There was no doubt that I wanted her. My body was letting me know that, and my imagination was frankly out of control. However, I kept a tight rein on those feelings when I was around Helen because I didn't want to risk offending her. I didn't want this relationship to end.

The only people who seemed to harbor any reservations about Helen being my girlfriend were the people I'd known longest and who loved me the best. Dad still told me to take it slow. Mom wanted me to remember to spend time with my other friends. I could put both my parents off by pointing out how Helen was helping me with math, and they liked that. Simon, on the other hand, refused to believe in a girlfriend who didn't come over to our house. He made a joke of pretending that she "was just not that into me." It wasn't like he didn't see me sitting with her on the bus every day! I think this was Simon's way of pushing me to invite her to our house, but it got under my skin because I really was secretly worried about the same thing myself.

Jane McCord brought Helen up on Sunday when we were working in the church nursery together. We only had a couple children that day, and they were occupied. Jane said, "Your mom mentioned that you're now going out with Helen García."

"That's true."

"I guess you overcame your inhibition when it comes to talking with pretty girls."

I remembered the shove she'd given me. She wouldn't catch me the same way twice. I said, "Thanks for letting me practice on you. Now, I have a chance to be successful in love." I bowed with an ironic flourish.

Jane laughed a bit, and added dryly, "You're welcome, I guess, though I thought at the time I was just talking to you, not training you. Is it love, then?"

It was easy to talk to Jane. She understood me—sometimes too well—so I confessed. "For me, I think it is. I can't speak for her. I don't really know what she's sees in me, to tell the truth."

Jane's eyes narrowed. "Don't let her walk all over you."

Of course I would, I thought.

Jane continued, "She should feel the same way about you as you do about her. You're a decent guy, and she should appreciate you."

"Thanks. Usually you call me a jerk."

"Only when you're being one—which I admit is often." She made a face. "So, when I am going to get to meet this girl?"

"Ah, I don't know." I thought about it. "We don't share any classes, and you have second lunch period. Maybe I could invite her to come to services at Trinity?" I kind of wanted her to see the church since it was such a big part of my life.

"Is she Episcopalian?" Jane asked.

I wasn't sure. "Her parents are Mexican, so I'd guess that means they are Catholic."

Jane looked disgusted with me. "You don't know? You didn't ask?"

"Er, no," I admitted embarrassed.

"You might want to find that out before you start arguing over in which faith to raise your children." Children. That was a scary thought.

I'd always assumed I'd raise my kids the way I'd been raised. "Episcopalian, of course." I couldn't imagine anything else.

"Jerk!" Jane was playful, but she obviously disapproved. "You need to get to know this girl, you know, if you're serious about her."

She had a point. "Now, you sound like my dad." That's when one of the toddlers started crying, ending our conversation.

After Thanksgiving dinner, Julio and Nabila were doing the dishes, so I was sitting with Mom and Dad at the table. My father asked, "Will you be going to Philadelphia this week?"

"Of course," I said.

Mom looked up at me. "We wondered if you were because you've been spending so much time with Alex. We were afraid you'd want to spend the day with him. We're not making you go to Philadelphia, you know. We just think it's better for you than spending too much time with Alex."

"Safer," said my dad. "There could be consequences for him and for you."

"We're not doing anything like that! Please trust me," I said to my parents. "I won't let you down like I did before."

"It's not just what you did before that worries us," said my mom. "It's what you're doing now. You seem to care about Alex far too much. You need to think about your life and your future." She sounded really worried.

"We know you usually make good choices, but it can be hard when your body needs something else," said my dad. "If you're going to involve yourself with him, you need to be prepared to do what's necessary." I didn't want to hear this. I wasn't ready.

"Dad, please stop talking. I'm going to Philadelphia with Julio on Friday. I won't see Alex until Saturday."

8. FAMILY

School was closed on Thanksgiving and the day after, but my parents were clear that this was "family time." I was not allowed to invite Helen over or accept any invitations to her house on Thursday or Friday. Her parents felt the same way, Helen told me. Her brother Julio would be back from college in Philadelphia, and they would be taking him back to college late Friday night. It would be all right if I wanted to see Helen on Saturday, my parents said, so I invited her over. Helen agreed since her culture class was on holiday for Thanksgiving weekend. Simon was ecstatic. He said that if she actually showed up, he'd admit she was, in fact, my girlfriend.

Helen did not disappoint. She came over around ten o'clock and introduced herself to my parents. She was ingratiating, and my parents were not too embarrassing. After welcoming her in a friendly way, they went back to their own Saturday morning projects and left us alone, which was exactly what I wanted. I even wondered if they had spoken to Simon because he went upstairs to play in his room when I would've expected him to hang around us all morning.

Helen said, "What do you want to do? Homework?" Only Helen could make that seem like the best plan ever. We spread our books out across the living room floor and worked until lunchtime. By that point, I had done all my homework except to read the chapters for English, which I preferred to do on my own.

Saturday lunch was usually make-your-own sandwiches, and this week it was as well, but Mom made a big production of getting all the food out on the counters to create an assembly line. I assume she was doing this so Helen would not be underwhelmed by our lack of hospitality, and I thought it was nice of Mom to make an effort. Afterwards, Dad made chocolate chip cookies, which he usually did every two or three weeks. He never varied from the recipe on the package of Tollhouse chips because he claimed that they were the best cookies in the whole world, so why try to improve upon perfection? Simon, Helen and I all enjoyed some of the dough, though Mom did fuss a bit, asking if Helen's parents would be okay with her eating the batter even though it contained raw eggs. I was embarrassed for Helen, but she just smiled like she thought it was funny.

After lunch, we went back to the living room and were going to listen to music when I remembered the conversation I'd had with Jane.

"Helen, do you go to church?"

"No, I was raised Catholic, but I'm not really anything now."

"Why?"

"I am afraid my answer will shock a nice church-going boy like you."

Maybe that should have warned me off, but I had been stung by Jane's implication that I didn't know Helen very well, so I naively plunged ahead. "Are you an atheist then? It's okay with me if you are. I know plenty of good people who are atheists."

She smiled sardonically. "Some of your best friends are atheists, you mean?"

"No, not really," I said. Then I realized she was teasing me. I blushed.

"I wouldn't expect atheism to shock you. I *believe* in God. I just *hate* him. That's why I'm not a Catholic any more." She said it without particular anger and with perfect sincerity.

Just as she predicted, I was shocked. I had never heard anyone say that before. "Why?" I didn't understand how someone could hate God. God was love.

"Evil," she said shortly.

I gave her a puzzled look. "I don't understand."

Helen took a breath and explained. "It's the ancient conundrum: if God is all-powerful, all-knowing and all-good, why does he allow evil to exist in the world? I have a problem with theodicy, with God's justice. My problem is that it doesn't seem to exist. Evil reigns unchecked."

The phrase "God's justice" rang a bell for me. When we read the book *Night* about the Holocaust in tenth grade, I remember Eli Wiesel wrote that his faith died in the camps. He said he did not deny God's existence but doubted his absolute justice. I told her what Wiesel had written.

"Yes," said Helen emphatically, "that is *exactly* how I feel."

"Oh." I was in denial that Helen's feelings about God would be a problem for us, but deep down I realized I was probably going to be really upset later. I didn't want to think about how I could have a relationship with someone who hated God. I certainly wouldn't be taking her to church with me.

Helen gave me a puzzled look. "Alex, why did you want to know about my faith?"

Time to fess up. "I'd wondered if you might want to come with me to Trinity." I smiled apologetically.

"Oh!" Now it seemed that I had shocked Helen. "I never thought!" She seemed to be taking a moment to consider. She said, "Well...maybe. Let me think about it." I was surprised she was giving it so much thought when she'd already told me how she felt about God. Was that because of me? If so, I was flattered.

Helen looked pretty agitated. Did I just imagine that she was breathing rapidly? It almost looked like she was panicking. She said, "So, how about a tour of the house?"

"Um, I'm not allowed to take you upstairs." I wished my parents weren't such freaks about it.

"Show me what you can, then," Helen suggested.

That wasn't much. She'd seen the living room, kitchen, and dining room, so I showed her the breezeway to the garage and the basement. My father had finished most of the basement to be a playroom for Simon and me when we were little. When I was in eighth grade, I'd begged my parents to buy a TV for it. They just moved the one from the living room downstairs, so now the living room was mainly a sitting and music room for my mom. Once there was a TV downstairs, we got a sofa there as well. Now Simon and I mostly came downstairs to watch TV or play video games. My parents didn't watch much TV though Mom listened to a lot of public radio news.

As soon as Helen got to the basement, she went from very tense to more relaxed. She sat on the sofa, and I sat on a beanbag chair. I wanted to sit next to Helen, but I figured if Mom or Dad came down and found us both on the sofa, we might soon find ourselves restricted from the basement as well as the upstairs.

Simon opened the door and bounced down the stairs. "Mom said I could play video games. Hey, Helen, do you want to play too?"

She said she did. Simon sat in front of her and kind of leaned on her. He played and narrated what he was doing, occasionally telling Helen what her character should do. She had very little gaming experience. Helen was patient with Simon's pedantry and bossiness, and I thought she had never looked more adorable than when she was sitting there with him on the sofa.

She looked up at me and said, "I would like to go to Trinity with you some Sunday. Not tomorrow. But I would like to try going to your church." My heart swelled. She would try, and that was all the reassurance I needed.

Before she left, we made plans to see each other Sunday afternoon. Since Grandma Fulton was coming over for a special family dinner, I figured Helen could meet her before she left. Fortunately Mom and Dad agreed to this plan, impressed by all the homework done that morning.

Grandma called Saturday evening to say she had gotten more gravestone photo requests, and would I help her after church? It was a local Minersville graveyard this time where we'd gone many times before. She said, "I probably should just do every stone in that graveyard, but I'm not up to that. At least I can get these current requests done. What do you say? Can you help, Alex?" I'd taken Grandma's call on the kitchen phone, and Mom was standing right there hearing every word because Grandma had her phone volume set so high.

Mom gave me a pleading look.

"Grandma, I have Helen coming over tomorrow afternoon," I said.

"Ask her if she wants to help," Grandma said.

I said I'd call her house to check and call back. As it turned out, Helen was willing, which seemed to score major points with my grandmother and made Mom happy too. It was all arranged that I'd go to the graveyard from church with my grandmother and Helen would meet us there.

That's what happened. When we got to the graveyard, it was really cold. There hadn't been snow yet, and the weather was clear, so we could still take good pictures, but the temperature wasn't much above freezing, especially with the wind. Grandma didn't last too long.

"Maybe you two could finish up these requests and do the postings. You have my username and password, right?"

"Yes, Grandma, I do. We've got this." Since Helen had come in her mom's car, Grandma could go home to get warm. We had to search for the names on Grandma's list by checking every stone because we didn't have a map of this graveyard.

Walking down the rows of stones, I noticed Helen had disappeared. I turned around and saw the she had stopped, transfixed, by a particular monument. I walked back and found her with tears running down her face. "What's wrong?" I asked, but she ignored me. I read the stone. It was a monument to nine people who had died in one night in the Atwell boarding house due to carbon monoxide poisoning from a faulty furnace. It happened in fall of 1925.

"All those innocent people," Helen said in quiet misery.

"I know. It's scary." I imagined how awful a discovery that must've been for whoever found all those bodies the next day. "That was a bad year for Minersville."

"What do you mean?" Helen asked sharply.

I told her what I'd learned from my grandmother in the Mennonite cemetery.

Helen let out a quiet wail of pain and closed her eyes. Her posture grew rigid, her hands balled into fists at her side. "Damn you, Williamsport," she muttered. "All those people. All those innocent people." Tears rolled down her cheeks.

I was a little alarmed. "What's Williamsport got to do with it?"

Helen didn't answer directly. Eventually she just said, "All those deaths made me sad."

"Me too," I said. "I think it's time to get warm."

Helen was still acting oddly when we got into her car and turned on the heater. I bathed my hands in the air from the car's vents waiting for the engine to warm it enough to do any good. Out of the blue, Helen asked, "If someone you cared about had done something awful, would you want to know?"

"What do you mean?"

"Like if your mother had driven drunk and killed someone before you were born?"

"What are you talking about?" I was upset and a little angry. "Why would you say something like that about my mother? She wouldn't drive drunk. She barely even drinks. Jesus, why would you say such a thing? What's wrong with you?"

"I'm sorry. I don't mean your mother. I just meant for instance." Helen looked upset too. She started wringing her hands. "Would you want to know?"

"No!" Then I reconsidered. The truth was important to me. When I was doing genealogy, I needed the facts to be accurate, or the stories meant nothing to me. It had to be true. If I loved someone, didn't I need to know the truth?

I said to Helen, "I guess I'd want to know. If someone I loved had done something awful, I'd want to know. I'd want to know why, and I'd try to understand. Why'd you ask me that?"

Helen just said, "Thank you." Then she asked, "Are you hungry for a late lunch?"

I was always hungry. "You are aware that I'm a seventeen-year-old boy?"

"I'll take that as a 'yes.'" She laughed.

Helen drove us back into Minersville and parked on the street in front of the neon sign for Myrtle May's Cafe, which occupied the whole first floor of the building. It was a one-room family restaurant, with booths along the side, tables in the middle and Bible quotes painted on the walls in flowing script. Honestly, I didn't understand why Helen chose this place until she said, "I've heard they have good burgers and fries. Did you know the homecoming queen works here?" That explained it. Helen had no doubt heard about the place from the queen herself.

It was nearly closing time, but they were kind and agreed to serve us if we didn't mind them cleaning up while we finished. Since the burgers had bacon and the fries were exactly how I like them, I was just about in heaven. When we were done, we were the only customers left in the place.

"I want to dance," Helen said.

"Helen, this isn't the kind of restaurant where people dance, and I'm sure they're about to kick us out." I was wrong. I'd reckoned without the reality-altering factor of Helen's charisma. She simply strolled into the kitchen like she owned the place, and returned with a plug-in radio boom box, saying that the kitchen staff were very friendly. Bemused, I told her I wasn't sure that dancing was my thing, but she should knock herself out.

She plugged in the radio and found a station playing a pop song that was fast and loud and really sad—if you paid attention to the lyrics. I wasn't because I was paying attention to Helen. She'd pushed some tables aside to create a space where she could dance. She closed her eyes and went at it with spastic energy like a goofy little kid dancing with one hundred percent commitment and zero embarrassment. As the song sped up, she became more frenetic, like a punk rocker—head pumping, short hair flying. Because she was neither kid nor punk but all beautiful young woman, I found the whole performance intensely sexy. In a moment of pure lust, I struggled with the urge to take out my phone and make a video.

I was ashamed of myself. She'd been completely clear that I was free to watch her all I liked but I was forbidden to take a picture. How was I different from those who'd abused her online if I took her picture when she'd made it crystal clear that she didn't want that? What would I do with such a video anyway? The idea was as unworthy of me as I was unworthy of her.

Then the song ended and a new song started playing. The new song was slower, lyrical and full of longing. Her dance morphed as well, and the mood changed. I'm no expert, but it seemed like she was executing a series of classical ballet positions in an improvised choreography that matched the song perfectly. I was the sole witness to what I began to suspect was a mature and sophisticated piece of performance art that was far beyond my ability to understand or fully appreciate. I wondered what the school's dance teacher would make of Helen's talent. I was in awe.

Helen opened her eyes, and beckoned me to join her on the dance floor. That would be a travesty, I thought, but then when a third song came on the radio, it was a completely silly one. Helen became goofy again, and I thought, "I can do this." I joined her in uninhibited childish expression until we were both exhausted and the staff finally kicked us out.

When she pulled up to her house, I walked her to her door. She looked at me intently, and then quickly leaned in and kissed me on the lips. It was my first kiss, and all I remember is that her lips were soft. Before I could say anything, she had gone into her house.

It felt like the best day of my life.

Dinner brought me down a little. We were having our usual Sunday dinner, and everyone wanted to talk about Helen.

Dad said, "It's nice we got to meet her. You two have been going out for what? Like two weeks?"

Had it really only been two weeks, I wondered. I did the calendar math and realized Dad was right. "Yeah, I guess." I didn't want to be reminded how short a time I'd known her. I was in love, but if I told my parents that, they'd say I barely knew her. I thought of all the mysteries that surrounded her, and I couldn't say they were wrong. It didn't change how I felt.

Mom said, "I really like her. I think Simon did too." Mom had no doubt been swayed by the manners, the homework and helping Grandma. Simon was probably impressed that she played video games with him.

Simon blushed. "Yeah, she's totally awesome. Like an eleven." That pissed me off. He was going to rate her with a number, like out of ten? I totally agreed with him on the rating, of course, but I didn't want to hear *him* say it, the little seventh grade horndog. I glanced at my parents and realized I'd have to talk privately to Simon about my girlfriend and limits.

Simon added sarcastically, "What's she see in Alex?"

"Shut up!" I told him, fed up.

Mom told him not to be rude.

I consoled myself with the memory of Helen's lips.

I hoped Alex hadn't paid too much attention to my falling apart at the graveyard. I'd been far too upset to conceal my feelings. It was bad enough that they'd killed the woman I'd thought I'd saved. It was my mistake leaving her knowing too much; her tears had fooled me. They didn't have to kill everyone she knew as well. Just the ones who heard the story and believed it. Not the ones who didn't believe it. Not the ones who could've heard it but didn't. They didn't have to kill everyone I'd lived with. Poor Mr. and Mrs. Atwell, no one remembered them, not even my parents, who slept in their bedroom.

I hoped Alex had paid much more attention to me later. I hoped I'd distracted him by the food and dancing and kiss. Why hadn't I looked when he was watching? I tried to tell myself it was long-ingrained habit, but I knew the real answer was cowardice.

Because looking in the eyes of teen boys was tedious, I generally didn't. I knew what I'd see. Nothing shocked me, and nothing disgusted me any more when it came to their vivid fantasies. Honestly, I would have been bored to actual tears if I hadn't learned early on to ignore them. They thought I was shy—and apparently that added to my allure—but as long as I was blocking it all out, I didn't really care.

I told myself that habit was why I hadn't looked to see what Alex thought as he watched me dance. Later, I realized to my surprise that I wouldn't have minded seeing lust in him. I was almost astonished to discover that I wanted him to feel those desires for me. I was starting to feel that way about him myself.

So why hadn't I looked, I wondered? Why didn't I want to know for sure?

Then I admitted I was afraid. I was afraid to see his desire under false pretenses. I didn't want him to desire me as he thought I was—but as I really was. I would be hurt otherwise.

When I came in the door, Dad saw me. "Did you spend the whole day with Alex?" he asked.

I nodded my head, still smiling from the kiss. I wanted to hug myself.

Dad looked concerned. "I don't understand," he said. "You went to Philadelphia yesterday. You got what you needed there."

He didn't understand what I really needed from Alex. I'm not sure I did either. I no longer had a plan. I smiled at Dad. "It just makes me happy to be with Alex."

He looked even more concerned. "You can't love him."

Why can't I? I thought, still in my happy bubble, refusing to acknowledge what Dad was saying.

Dad could tell I wasn't taking him seriously and became more urgent. "Look, we've already installed a security camera and a burglar alarm in case St. Michael comes calling—"

"I don't think—"

"That's just it. You're not thinking. If you can't control your feelings, we could have a lot worse people than the Order after us. What if we get a visit from Williamsport? A camera and an alarm won't help against them." He stopped to emphasize his point.

I didn't want to hear this.

"You're allowed to make him yours. You can do anything you want with him. Just remember that you can't love him. You have to be able to end it at any time." I stared at the wall, ignoring him. He went to find Mom to worry her with my strange behavior.

How could I forget the first rule of my life?

But I already had.

9. ACCIDENT

Helen fulfilled her offer to come to church with me on the first Sunday in December. Mom checked with Helen's parents to make sure it was all right with them. Victor García confirmed that they were not usually churchgoing folk but that he had no objections to Helen going with us if that's what she wanted to do.

My family always went about an hour before the service began because my mom sang in the choir, which had a last-minute practice and warm-up. That's how I had originally gotten roped into helping with the nursery: I was able to be there before parents showed up. I took Helen to the nursery with me to wait for the children.

We got several takers and were busy keeping a trio of toddlers entertained when Jane showed up. An expression of irritation at finding the pair of us already taking care of things was quickly replaced by a forced smile. "You must be Helen García. I've seen you at school even though we don't have any classes together. I'm Jane McCord."

"Hi, Jane." Helen said it warmly, and she gave a genuine smile. "I'm glad to meet you. I gather you've known Alex a long time."

Jane nodded. "Alex and I've been doing nursery together for years. I was really glad when he came back from Philadelphia because it was dead dull in here with him gone."

"I'm very glad he came back, too. Otherwise, I wouldn't have met him." Helen smiled again, and this time Jane smiled more easily.

Thank goodness they were getting along, I thought. For a second, I'd worried Jane was about to get territorial. We all played with the kids for a while until Jane started a game. Helen and I sat back and watched. Helen wore a smile that seemed increasingly sad, which I didn't understand. She commented, "You do a wonderful job of taking care of these young ones, Jane."

Jane said, "I like looking out for them. They're my friends. I watch out for all my friends." She nodded significantly at me. "That one there needs a lot of watching."

Helen laughed. "Alex needs a guardian angel—especially if he's going to hang out with Jimmy and Jon." Jane laughed too.

About halfway through the service time, Jane suggested that she had the place covered and why didn't we join my family for the Eucharist? Helen looked a little apprehensive but agreed. She asked if we could slip in quietly at the back, so she wouldn't draw undue attention.

When we entered, Helen took a look at the great Gothic arch of ornate stone and stained glass that formed the backdrop of the high altar with its brass candlesticks and tall cross. She looked at me anxiously. "I don't know if I belong here," she whispered. "Can we sit in the back? Don't make me go up and sit with your dad."

I said it was all right, so we got in a back pew. Helen dropped to her knees and prayed. Very quietly she said, *"Por favor, Dios, si me escucha, déjeme ser buena. Déjeme tener a Alex y olvide mi otra oración."* I didn't understand her.

"Were you just praying for me?"

"Yes," she said, "and for myself as well."

When it came time for communion, Helen refused to go up and receive. "Is that because you're Catholic?" I asked.

"It's because I haven't made a confession." I didn't remind her about the general confession we had all said moments before because I figured Helen must've meant something more specific.

Helen acted a little weird on the way home from church, but she was normal enough after that. In the two weeks that followed, we went to school together, did homework together and even went Christmas shopping together once.

Then, something a whole lot weirder happened.

Helen was visiting on the Saturday afternoon before Christmas. Her class was off these next two weeks for Christmas break. We had been watching TV in the basement by ourselves, which wasn't unusual any more. In the past month, my parents had gotten a whole lot more chill about supervising us, and I'd noticed that Simon had not come down to play video games as much either. I began to suspect that Mom had initially been encouraging him to come down as a way of chaperoning us.

I went upstairs to make some popcorn, but when I came back down, I forgot to duck my head. I must have been paying too much attention to not spilling the bowl. Our basement stairs had a spot in the ceiling where an angle stuck out because it was part of the first floor, and even someone who is only five foot eight inches had to lean back or duck to avoid it.

I hit the top of my forehead going full bore down the stairs and nearly knocked myself out. I instinctively clapped my free hand over my head to try to stop the pain, but the pressure didn't help. I got a little worried when I noticed that the place on the ceiling where I hit now had a popped drywall nail with some blood on it. One hand clamped on my head, the other holding the bowl, I winced with one eye shut.

Helen had heard the commotion, and said, "Alex, are you all right?" When I didn't immediately respond, she jumped up to quickly relieve me of the bowl. Then, she helped me down the stairs and had me lie on the sofa. I now had both hands clamped on my head. "Here, let me look at that." I didn't want to take my hands off my head. I took the top hand off and then took a quick glance at the other one. My palm was covered with blood. Well shit, I thought, I may end up in the emergency room for Saturday night. I clamped my hand back down on my head to keep up the pressure. Also, I didn't want to bleed all over the sofa.

"Let me look," Helen insisted. She climbed on top of me straddling my hips and took me by the wrists. I barely noticed that she was doing something that would have been pretty exciting under other circumstances. As it was, I was embarrassed that I'd hurt myself, my head hurt like hell, and she was invading my space. "Please get off," I said.

"I need to see how bad it is." I remembered how Helen had taken charge at the ledge and her doctor-in-charge manner was back (except for the whole straddling the patient bit, which had to be unprofessional). I also remembered how much it hurt when she snapped my dislocated arm back into the socket. "No, please," I said.

She stared me down. "Alex, let me look." That time it was a mom voice, and I responded by letting her move my hands aside. "Okay, it is a long but shallow cut. Superficial, I'd say. Since it's by the hairline where it won't show, you don't need stitches. There's a lot of blood. That's normal for a head wound." Her clinical manner reassured me even though I had no idea how she could be so absolutely sure of herself.

That's when it got weird. Her expression went from concerned to enthusiastic. "I have an idea for cleaning you up," she said. She leaned down over me. With her throat above my eyes, I felt her lips touch my cut in a puckered kiss. What was she thinking? My head already hurt and even the light touch of her lips stung.

"Ow, Helen!" I protested. I tried to move, but she still had my wrists trapped in her hands. I'd forgotten how strong she had been at the ledge. This was just as incredible a feat of strength: her arms didn't give at all when I pushed against them. It was like I was straddled by a bronze statue and my hands were trapped in its unmovable fingers. I briefly considered the fact that I was a pathetic weakling compared to every girl I knew and that maybe I needed to start some weight training to keep up.

Helen stopped the kiss, and I felt the gentle rasping of her tongue licking. "Stop, that really hurts!" What in God's name was she doing? Then I realized that she was washing me like a cat. She was licking the blood off my head. That was totally gross. "Stop it! That's disgusting." I made a more serious effort to shake her off, and that's when I realized that I had absolutely no control in this situation. I was at her mercy.

"Please, Helen, stop!" I sounded desperate to myself.

She stopped. She sat up, with bloody lips and a puzzled expression.

"What the hell were you doing?" I demanded.

"I kissed your boo boo to make it better, and I was cleaning you up," she said with hurt innocence.

I was so upset I started to rant uncontrollably. "Are you kidding me? Kissing a 'boo boo to make it all better' is for moms and preschoolers. I am not three years old, and you are not my mom. Gross! Speaking of which, you were licking up my blood. That's beyond disgusting. Plus, it hurt like hell. I thought you were going to help bandage me. I did not expect—what you did! I'm completely freaking out here." I wasn't exaggerating about that. I looked from my own shaking bloody hands, which Helen had released, to her face.

She looked as though I'd slapped her. Tears welled up in her eyes. She jumped off of me and sat down on the far side of the sofa, knees pulled up in front of her and hands on her face. "I'm sorry. I'm sorry. I'm so sorry." Her chest heaved with sobs as she began to rock back and forth.

I still really hurt. I was still freaking out over how gross the whole thing was. Who knew how many germs she had in her mouth? That last thought was a bit unfair since I wouldn't have hesitated a second to let her kiss me under less painful circumstances. I looked at her crying and felt manipulated. Like, my boyfriend's mad, so I'll turn on the waterworks. I wasn't the crazy one here, was I? I tried not to think about the fear I'd felt when I realized she had me trapped and helpless. That wouldn't have bothered me if she'd responded to my pleas to stop right away, but as it was, I felt a distrust for Helen that I'd never felt before. I didn't want to think about it.

Helen was still sobbing. She was saying, "I'm so sorry, Alex. Please don't think I'm disgusting. Please don't hate me."

The revulsion I felt at being covered in blood and licked morphed into a different kind of shame. "Look, Helen, maybe I overreacted. I shouldn't have yelled at you. I was surprised is all."

She quieted but she didn't take her hands from her face. I hesitated to touch her because my hands were bloody, but then I thought blood obviously doesn't bother her. I took her wrists in my hands, just as she had done moments ago to me. She allowed me to pry them off her face, just as I had done. I looked at her face, which was beautiful to me despite her tears and my blood. "You are not disgusting to me. I don't hate you." I almost added how I did feel, but I didn't think this was a good moment for that.

Helen gave a tiny nod. She leaned towards my face, eyes locked with mine, and I thought for a minute that she might try to kiss me with my own blood on her lips—gross!—but she backed off and shook her head as if to clear it.

"I think I should go to a bathroom and clean up now," I said.

"Am I forgiven enough that you'll let me help with the disinfectant and bandage?" She sounded really anxious.

"Sure. Am I forgiven enough that you'll wash away those tears and not let my family see that you've been crying? I don't want to tell them what happened." I didn't want to imagine what my parents would assume if Helen came up from the basement with tears on her face. I was sure they'd blame me.

She sniffled and gave a wan smile. "Good idea."

After we had both cleaned up, we watched some TV. My stomach was way too unsettled for popcorn at that point, but Helen ate the whole bowl almost manically. She went home for dinner at her house.

When Mom saw the bandage on my head, she said, "Alex, what happened?"

I told her about hitting my head and how Helen had disinfected and bandaged it—leaving out everything that had occurred in between. Mom made me peel the bandage back so she could confirm the presumed shallow, non-disfiguring nature of the cut. She tsk, tsked and said, "Joe, you really should do something about that nail in the ceiling."

Dad went to check it out. After dinner, he spent about a half hour down in the basement making various hammering noises. When he was done, he called out, "Hey, Sarah, Alex, come see what I did."

When we got to the top of the basement stairs, we could see that he had folded over a piece of thin blue padding multiple times and nailed it to the edge of the angle of the ceiling. "Joe, is that the mat I gave you so we could do yoga together?"

He ran his hand over his hair as he let out a slow, "Yeah."

She looked at him and raised an eyebrow. "I thought you were just nailing down the nail."

"Yoga is more your thing, Sarah. We never did that much of it together."

"I don't know that I want a yoga mat to greet everyone going to the basement."

"But this way, if Alex hits his head again, he won't get hurt." Dad demonstrated by deliberately bumping his head on the pad. "See, no worries?"

Mom laughed. Then, she looked at my head. "All right, the padding can stay. Helen may not be here to bandage him up next time."

I wished that was all Helen had done. The whole day had been emotionally taxing. I went to bed that night feeling nauseous and woke up to a nightmare about being crushed underground.

"Mama, I'm so ashamed. It is not just that I took advantage of his ignorance. What I hate is that when he tried to push me off, I held him down with all my strength. I forced him."

My mother looked at me in dawning comprehension. She nodded her head.

"Now I see why you're so upset. You did very wrong tonight, and you must not do it again. Your father and I wondered if you'd keep going to Philadelphia for your needs. We'd hoped you'd keep this boy ignorant for his safety and ours. We aren't fools, so we could see that you might choose to make him yours. I can see now that you will—that you already have. That's allowed. But this, what you did this afternoon, this is unacceptable." She looked at me sternly.

"Mi hija, I forbid you to taste this boy's blood without his full, free consent."

I was shocked. My mom never forbade me anything. She always let me make my own choices. Using force was not against the rules, and the police would not have come for me. As long as I kept him from revealing the secret to anyone else, this was permitted to me. Even Dad had said it: Alex was mine to do with as I would. I had to be willing to end it, of course, but only if necessary—and it wouldn't be—but until then, Alex belonged to me. He was mine. I didn't know why my mother was so emphatic about consent. She saw my confusion and explained.

"I've known you a long time, and I remember the beginning when you came to us. If you force this boy, I will not know you as my daughter any more. If you become the monster to him, you will not know yourself."

10. REVELATION

The next two weeks went by without anything terribly unusual happening. Helen and I spent just as much time together as we had before, but we were not as free or easy with each other. We were more polite than we'd been, more considerate and respectful of personal space. We still held hands sometimes, but there was a little more awkward hesitation about reaching out, by Helen especially.

Neither of us ever alluded to what had happened in the basement even though I had a big bandage on my forehead for several days before I ripped it off and combed my hair over the healing cut. I was still freaked out by what she'd done, but I didn't let myself think about it because I wanted to pretend it didn't happen. We'd both made each other so upset that I sensed revisiting the topic might lead to our breaking up. Having Helen as a girlfriend was too important to me.

When I asked her what she wanted for Christmas, she said she wanted to have a private heart-to-heart conversation with me beforehand. "That sounds like you want to break up with me," I said. I was proud of how little emotion I let creep into my tone, but I could feel my chest tightening. I wondered if that's where the cliché about broken hearts originated.

"I don't, but you might want to." She sounded like she really thought so.

I didn't want to hear it. "That sounds bad, like you have another boyfriend."

"It is bad, but don't try to guess. You won't get it right. I can't tell you right now because we need time and privacy to talk. Why don't you come over to my house on Sunday afternoon?"

"All right," I said. I hoped I didn't sound as glum as I felt.

That Sunday morning, I was working the nursery with Jane at Trinity. There were no children that morning, perhaps because their parents figured they were about to come back to church on Thursday night for Christmas Eve services so they could skip the last Sunday of Advent. Whatever the reason, Jane and I were alone.

"Alex, did you tell anyone that ghost story Mr. Miller told us?"

"I told Helen."

"I guess that was predictable. How'd she take it—that her house was supposed to be haunted and all?"

I tried to recall. It'd been back around Thanksgiving. "She seemed startled, but then she laughed and said people will believe all sorts of nonsense, and she was fine as long as they were talking about her house and not her." Jane suddenly looked very uncomfortable. "Then, she joked that I'd better be careful around her if there was a ghost in her house that avenged disrespected women." It made me a little sad now to recall how easygoing Helen and I had been with each other back then. I dreaded our planned conversation this afternoon.

"Did you tell anyone else?" Jane was being weird.

"No, why are you asking about this?"

"Mr. Miller asked me not to tell anyone that ghost story. He doesn't want you repeating it either. He says he thought it was harmless, but now he doesn't. He's really sorry he told us."

"Well, it's too late for me to un-tell the story to Helen, but I can ask her not to repeat it. Why did Mr. Miller change his mind? It did seem harmless."

"I'm not supposed to tell anyone that part." Jane seemed embarrassed.

"Jane!" I protested.

Jane gave me a pleading look. "Mr. Miller was really upset. He's my neighbor, and he's always been nice to me. He asked me not to tell."

"All right, fine." I wouldn't push her if it made her break a confidence.

"No, I think I do have to tell you. I owe it to you. There's a new story that's not so harmless—about Helen."

"What?" That made me angry. Jane held up her hands.

"Let me explain. Mr. Miller used to be a church elder. Now that he's older, he's gotten less active in the church and doesn't go to meetings as often, but he's still friends with the other elders. One of those came to him all agitated back in early November. The minister had found an old photograph in the church's archive from the 1920s. I guess they had a minister back then who went crazy and was eventually fired. Apparently, he'd written on the back of the photo that the woman in it was a vampire. He had also written the address of the Garcías' house, and the name Mary. There was a note to say that this vampire had killed a man belonging to the church and warned that if she ever came back, she could be recognized by the photograph."

"What's this got to do with Helen? Maybe that's where the ghost story Mr. Miller told us came from, but I don't see what an old story has to do with Helen's parents buying that house."

Jane looked at me with sympathy. "The current minister, Reverend Brubacher, told the elders he thinks Helen is the vampire from the photo. He said he'd seen her on the street, and she's definitely the one."

I was stunned. I remembered our scary encounter at Helen's front door. No wonder Helen had said he was crazy and her father had threatened lawyers.

"Mr. Miller doesn't want this story spread because he thinks too many bigoted people already say Mennonites are nuts, and this story plays right into that perception."

"I'll say. This is beyond absurd. A grown man, a respected minister, is going around and saying Helen is a vampire." I just couldn't wrap my brain around it.

"I know, right? No one believes in vampires. Also, even if you did—hello!—she walks around in the sun. She's not burning up or sparkling or anything." Jane said that with a twinkle in her eye but then became serious again. "The whole thing would be too silly for words, except that it is mean to spread rumors about a girl like that. Alex, I am truly sorry about this."

I could barely contain my outrage. "Did you know that Helen won't even let people take her picture because she was bullied on social media?" This stupid rumor was hurtful enough without the photograph. I was sure the picture would make it worse.

"No, I didn't know that," said Jane. "That's terrible!"

I was so mad, I was nearly ranting. "How could a minister spread a ridiculous story about Helen like that? What kind of man would do that?"

Jane nodded her head. "I told you. Mr. Miller thinks Reverend Brubacher is mentally ill. I'd guess the photograph set him off, and he created this paranoid fantasy about it. The only good news is that the story doesn't seem to be spreading. Mr. Miller said he talked to his friend about it later, and his friend said that he didn't know what he was talking about, so Mr. Miller figures the whole thing was being hushed up. That's a good thing, right?"

I wondered what I was supposed to do. The whole thing was crazy. "I've got to tell Helen, don't I?"

Jane bit her lip. Then, she said, "That's up to you. She's your girlfriend. You'll have to decide if you think telling her can do any good."

I was recovering from my initial surprise, but my stomach was starting to hurt. I felt really sick and excused myself from Jane and the nursery. I sat in the bathroom and my head started to spin. I ought to tell this story to Helen because she had a right to know. However, if I so much as breathed the word "vampire," she was sure to think I was bringing up the whole blood-licking episode again. I didn't know what to do.

I went over to Helen's house after lunch. Apparently, her parents don't have any kind of a no-boys-in-the-bedroom policy because she took me right to her room and closed the door. I hoped that it never occurred to my parents to compare rules with the Garcías, or I might not be allowed to come over to her house any more. Helen's room had pink and frilly curtains and bedspread, an old-fashioned wooden bed and matching vanity, but no desk or posters or toys or mementos. I wondered where she did her homework. She gestured for me to sit on the chair at the vanity and sat on the bed.

"Alex, what's wrong?" Helen asked.

I was reluctant to tell her, but I guessed I had to. "I heard a rumor from Jane at church that upset me. I don't think I want to talk about it."

"Tell me." She said it sympathetically.

"I don't want you to be upset too. It was about you," I admitted.

Helen looked me in the eye and said firmly, "Tell me what you heard."

"Someone has made up a story that you're a vampire named Mary who killed a man nine decades ago while living in this house." Why did I say all that? I hadn't meant to.

Helen suddenly laughed. "Well, this is unexpected. I bring you over here to listen to my big secret and apparently you've already heard it from Jane McCord!"

"Please, Helen, I don't know why I said that." I was really anxious.

"It's true enough," Helen insisted.

"Of course it isn't true. It can't be true!" What was she saying? Did she expect me to believe she was a vampire?

"It is. Jane was right. I'd really like to know how she heard it though. Tell me that."

I told her everything Jane had said. Afterwards, Helen asked, "So what do you think?"

"I think it's ridiculous."

"Do you? I licked the blood off your head." She said like it was a reasonable point.

Aw shit! I knew she would take it this way. "Please, Helen, I'm not trying to bring that up again. I know I overreacted. I'm sorry about that. I know it was just a momentary impulse on your part."

"It truly was impulsive," Helen said. She radiated earnestness. "Please forgive me. I shouldn't have forced you to let me drink your blood, and I'm ashamed of that. It won't happen like that again."

I wondered what she meant by "like that." Then, I realized she meant she *would* drink my blood again but not *like that*. She was still going on with the pretense she was a vampire.

"What are you talking about? You're not making any sense. Please, if you brought me here to break up with me, I get it. Just don't torture me." This was agony. It was bad enough if she was done with me, but she didn't have to make fun of me while she did it.

Helen looked at me in total frustration. "I'm not breaking up with you, stupid!"

I looked at Helen in confusion. I didn't know whether to feel relieved or hurt.

There was silence for a few moments. Then, Helen said, "I love that you're my boyfriend. I love who I am when I'm with you."

That didn't make sense either. "I can't believe that's what you wanted to tell me."

"It isn't. I wanted to tell you the truth about myself. The way you feel about me is based on a lie." She read my face intently.

"Which is?" I still had no idea what she meant. Sure, there were many things I'd found mysterious about her, but I was no closer to the answers than I'd ever been.

"You think I'm human, like you. I'm not. I'm a vampire." There we were again. She *was* going to torture me.

"Impossible." I was trying to be reasonable, but she wasn't giving me a chance.

"Here, give me your finger." I held out my hand to her, and she flipped it so that it was palm up and took ahold of my index finger. She opened her mouth wide and put my finger inside it. I thought this had some sexy possibilities. However, she didn't close her mouth or touch my finger with her tongue. She touched the pad of the finger to her left canine tooth. I felt a prick. She took the finger out of her mouth and showed me the pad, which now had a drop of blood on it. Then the tip of my finger went numb.

"My fangs are very sharp. I can make them secrete a short-term anesthetic, so the wounds don't hurt." I was really worried. This sounded like a whole new level of crazy. I understood the vampire bit. That was just her torturing me with the idea I'd brought up. This fang thing was very specific and totally her invention.

"You don't have fangs. Those are perfectly normal canine teeth." I was still trying to be reasonable.

"Tell that to your finger." I looked at the drop of blood.

"Do you have something I could use to clean this up?" I looked around for tissues.

Helen grinned. "Me? With your permission this time?"

I gave up. "Knock yourself out."

I held out the finger to her, and this time she did suck it. It was still totally not sexy because the whole tip was numb. But it was playful. Maybe she wasn't breaking up with me. Maybe she was just getting some payback. I could live with that if it meant I got to keep Helen. "Okay, you've got a sharp tooth. You're not a vampire."

She sat back down on her bed and sighed. "Usually, I'm trying to convince people that I'm normal. What will it take to convince you I'm not?"

I shook my head. I wasn't going to be convinced. The whole idea was completely preposterous. No one believed in vampires outside of stories. She didn't even seem like the stories: she wasn't pale, she didn't have an Eastern European accent and she didn't live in an old castle. I remembered Jane's point, so I said, "It's daylight, and you aren't sleeping in a grave. If you were a vampire, you'd burn."

Helen smiled. "Maybe I'm the sparkly kind." She laughed.

God, did everybody read those books? I got up and gently took her hand and put it in the shaft of afternoon sunlight that was coming through her curtains. The light showed nothing but her beautiful brown skin, just as it had that time when I'd asked to take her picture after school. I realized I was touching her while she was sitting on her bed, and my pulse quickened. I quickly released her hand and sat back down.

"You're not a vampire."

Helen shook her head back at me. "The stories about vampires are myths, and fact and metaphor get blurred in the world of myth."

Okay, I'd play along. Maybe Helen just wanted to explore a fantasy with me, like we were playing Dungeons and Dragons and she was inventing her character. "So what's the truth?"

"I'll tell you the truth, but there's a price to be paid." Helen looked grave. She must be really getting into the role. "I'm permitted to tell one human the truth about me, but you must promise to keep the secret—and I must guarantee that promise." I bit my lip to keep from laughing. Her acting was so intense it was over-the-top.

Still playing along, I asked, "What's the price?"

"I'll tell you anything you want to know, but you must promise to keep it secret. I'll make sure that you keep that promise." Helen paused.

"Okay, I agree," I said easily. Helen looked at me like she expected more reservation on my part.

"What do you want to know?" she asked.

"Why are you telling me all this? If you're a vampire, why not just kill me now and drink my blood?"

Helen smiled. "I don't want to kill you. I've lived a long time—and, yes, I did live in this house ninety years ago—but I've never felt about someone else, or about myself, the way I feel when I'm with you. I want you to know the truth about me, and I'm hoping you can still feel the same way. That's why I'm telling you all this."

I tried to figure that out. "You're saying you're a vampire, but you don't want to kill me and drink my blood because you want me for a boyfriend?"

"Basically, yes. What do you think about that?" Helen cocked her head.

It sounded insane. "I think you're a better girlfriend than you are a vampire."

Helen started laughing hysterically. I joined her for a bit, but then it was a little weird. She wiped tears from her eyes and said, "That's exactly what I wanted you to say." She got off the bed and came over to me on the chair. I tilted my head up, and she bowed down to kiss me.

I kissed her back and felt a great release of tension in my chest. If she rewarded me like this for playing her game, I'd play any time.

When she stopped, we both opened our eyes. She smiled, but the side of her mouth turned down. "I haven't convinced you of anything, have I? You're just playing along because you like kissing me."

"I like *you*," I corrected. "but yeah, basically, I don't believe in vampires."

"Why not?"

"I like stories about magic, but that doesn't make them real." I thought about it for a moment and then admitted, "I guess I don't believe in anything that can't be scientifically observed."

"What about God?" Helen asked.

Okay, she had me there. "I believe in God." I tried to explain the apparent contradiction. "The Bible's not just a story. It's not fiction, I mean." I couldn't really explain why I accepted the authority of the

Bible but not stories about vampires. It was a matter of faith. Helen had me confused.

Helen pressed her lips together and took a deep breath. "Alex, look at me. Look me in the eyes." I did, and I was lost in them. "I *am* a vampire," she said. "Believe it."

Suddenly, her eyes were the scariest things I'd ever seen. I remembered the old preacher's accusing finger as he said, "I know what you are girl. I know what you did." I felt my heart race as I moved to get up from the chair, slowly to see if she'd let me. She did. Warily, I backed towards the door, with my eyes on Helen. "You're really her. You're vampire Mary. It's not a story. You really killed that man."

She nodded.

For a moment, she seemed a stranger to me. She hadn't changed in almost a century and would never change. That wasn't human. She wasn't what I'd thought she was. She certainly wasn't a teen girl. That was merely her predator disguise. I remembered the strength and speed with which she'd dislocated my arm and saved my life. Was that so she could kill me now, here in the old house that had changed more than she had? It didn't matter that I knew her secret any more because I was too slow and weak to fight her. I remembered how she'd held me down while licking my head. Had she stopped only because my parents had been upstairs? My pulse pounded in my ears.

Then, she was Helen again. She'd been alone with me plenty of times. I didn't believe she wanted to kill me or that she'd only stopped because of my parents. She'd acted genuinely sorry about what happened in my basement, and she'd apologized again just now. I just couldn't sustain the feeling that I was in danger with her. She'd always been incredibly nice to me. She was nice to everyone. I had a hard time imagining her hurting anyone on purpose. (Manny's foot didn't count as he'd had it coming.)

I licked my dry lips. "Why did you kill him?" I asked. I knew it was a stupid question to ask a vampire. She had to drink blood, right? But she didn't act like she needed it all the time. She'd also implied she'd drink mine if I gave consent, like I had with the finger, and surely she didn't expect me to agree to my own murder. So I didn't understand why she'd killed him.

She took a deep breath. "Maybe..." she said, "here, let me show you something." She walked over to the vanity, opened a drawer—which contained papers, not beauty products—and produced an old brown typewritten document. She cautiously held it out to me.

"What is it?"

"It's the statement of the man's wife. Her minister figured out what I was and collected a lot of things. This statement, notes about vampires, notes about me—He even included a photograph of me from 1924. Brubacher found it all hidden in the church archives."

"That's why he confronted you?" I was thinking out loud. I made another connection. "That's why you didn't want me to take your picture."

"Yes," she said. "Anyway, I broke into his house and stole all that. I burned everything else, but I kept this. I wasn't supposed to, but I wanted it because I took some comfort from what it says at the end."

I was still figuring things out. "Is Brubacher why you got the security camera and alarm?" I remembered they'd installed that back in November. "You're afraid he'll come back?"

Helen shook her head. "No," she said. "He's been persuaded he was wrong about me. We got the cameras because—" She bit her lip. "It was something he said. My parents think he might have contacted a group of people who know about vampires." She took a deep breath. "Apparently, there's a secret group called the Order of St. Michael, which fights vampires. We're on the lookout in case Brubacher tipped them off. They might send people after us."

For a moment, I forgot to be afraid for myself because I was afraid for Helen. She looked at me, "You wanted to know the real story of vampire Mary." She nodded to the paper. "That's it. Read it. It'll probably horrify you though."

I looked down at the statement. A young farmer's wife described how Mary came to the house after seeing her with a black eye in town. When Mary confronted the husband, he broke a whiskey bottle over her head and slashed her all down her face. The wound had healed instantly. The last part was underlined in pencil with the words "not credible" written in the margin. I looked up at Helen's perfect face. "You don't have a scar," I said.

"The evil spirit that keeps me young eternally also heals minor injuries immediately."

"It doesn't sound like a minor injury here," I said. Helen didn't reply.

I read on. The husband called Helen a "meddling bitch" and "a damned darky." I was confused by the latter. "Doesn't this word mean black? Why'd he call you that?"

Helen gave me a sad smile. "I'm dark skinned. I'd made him angry. We're all the same to someone like that."

That made a twisted sort of sense, I supposed. My grandmother gave me the impression everyone in town had been more racist back then. That made me wonder how Helen could get work as a teacher, so I asked.

"Teachers back then were underpaid and overworked. I was highly qualified and dedicated. The school board was willing to overlook my being Mexican. Plus, I can turn on the charm." She smiled at me, and

I briefly forgot about everything else. Okay, I guess that made sense too. She stopped smiling. "Keep reading," she said.

I did. She'd killed the man by breaking his neck. She'd also dislocated his arm. I looked up at Helen. "What is it with you and arms?" I pretended exasperation and rubbed my shoulder as though it still hurt. Helen smiled a little at my pathetic attempt at humor. I read to the end. The wife praised God for sending Mary to deliver her from her abusive husband.

When I handed the paper back to Helen, she said, "How do you feel after reading that?" She looked worried. "I think she forgave me. Can you?" Her voice was trembling with anxiety.

"I don't see that you need forgiveness," I said. "So you killed a total asshole who was doing his best kill you—or cut your face off or something. It was self defense."

Helen shook her head. "It was naive. I provoked him by being there. I was young, and I just couldn't bear the pain I saw in her eyes. I wouldn't do it now, and he'd still be alive."

I didn't see how that would've been better. "And he'd still be beating his wife."

Helen smiled. "You're just as naive as I was, and I love you for that." Then she looked really sad. "I got her killed. I left her knowing too much, and other vampires killed her." I winced at that. We both paused a moment.

I wondered what I was supposed to do now.

"So," Helen said, "what are you going to do now?"

I shook my head in confusion. She clarified. "Can I still be your girlfriend?" She took a tentative step towards me with arms partly outstretched.

I shook my head again. "I don't see how. Not if you're a vampire."

Tears appeared in Helen's eyes. She let her arms fall to her sides and said nothing. I tried to explain.

"I can't keep kissing you and feeling the way I do if you kill people for their blood." Even if she kept me safe, I couldn't pretend I didn't know what she was doing to others. "I can't turn a blind eye to murder."

Helen looked suddenly hopeful. "But I don't kill for blood," she said.

"Really? In stories, vampires are all bloodthirsty murderers."

Helen sat back down on the bed. She patted the space beside her in invitation. I balked for a moment, and she raised an eyebrow as if to say, do you think you are safer from me across the room? I laughed at myself internally and sat down next to her. She leaned onto my chest, and I put my arms around her and let her talk.

"I don't need to kill to survive. I was made into what I am over a century ago by a vampire who drank my blood and forced me to drink his. That monster's evil spirit passed to me, and it has needs that must be fed. It must be fed blood regularly, and it must spend a certain amount of time underground. I can get by on a pint or so of blood a week and a few hours in the basement each day."

"But I've seen you eat regular food in the cafeteria," I objected.

"Yes, my body also has needs, just as yours does, to maintain its substance and strength. For that, I can eat regular food. Large quantities of blood could also serve that need, but that seems wasteful to me, profligate of human life. I don't take more than I need."

I thought about this. It didn't sound all that bad. It was like she had a medical condition and needed transfusions once in a while. But she'd left out an important detail. I asked, "Okay, so where do you get this blood?"

Helen didn't answer. I waited her out with a sinking feeling. The silence grew longer. "I'm ashamed to tell you," she said at last.

That's what I was afraid of. "Is that because you think I would reject you if I knew the truth?"

"Yes," the admission came.

"Then I think I need to know."

She hesitated and then began, "I go into Philadelphia once a week."

I interrupted, "For classes in Mexican culture, I know."

She sighed. "Alex, I was born in Mexico, not Texas, and I've spent nearly half my long life there."

I processed that. "You don't need classes in Mexican culture, then."

"No, I don't. I go because I need to hunt for blood. I find my victims among the poor and homeless, alcoholics and drug addicts. I enter crack houses and back alleys. When I find someone passed out and alone, I drink. I take only the pint I need. I put a bandage on the puncture, and I leave them money—twice what hospitals pay. I tell myself that they'd sell me their blood to feed their addictions if given the choice, but I can't give them the choice because I'm not allowed to explain. I'm only allowed one exception, like you." She said it sadly.

I was breathing heavily, in distress. I dropped my arms from Helen. I thought about Abe and how we'd spoken awkwardly over burgers on my unauthorized, late-night excursions from school. She was taking blood from people like him.

A terrible thought occurred: Abe had been found with slit wrists over a storm drain. Everyone assumed the blood had gone down the drain, but... "Helen, did you kill my friend Abe?" I felt cold.

"Who?"

"One of three homeless people found with slit wrists on drains in Philadelphia about the time I came back to Minersville. I used to sneak out to eat burgers with Abe."

Helen's puzzled blankness turned to comprehension. I could tell she knew exactly what I was talking about.

I felt even colder. "Don't you dare lie to me about this. This is important."

Helen face filled with sympathy. "I won't lie to you. I know the man you mean. I think I saw you with him once when I was scouting for blood."

"Did you kill him?" I said, suddenly hot and angry.

"No, Alex, I promise you I didn't. I don't kill when I take blood."

It sounded like the truth to me, but it also sounded like maybe she was still holding something back. My feelings for Helen struggled with outrage at what she did. "I'm having a hard time not being completely disgusted right now. I'm having a hard time not remembering that we find Christ in each and every person, no matter how low they may have sunk. You're telling me you are not a killer, but you take advantage of the most helpless and vulnerable people in society—every week." I was trying to stay calm, but I was starting to lose it.

Helen didn't say anything. She turned on her side and placed her cheek against my chest. "Now you know why I hate myself." She closed her eyes. "Please don't look at me. I don't think I could bear it if you looked at me the way I look at myself."

We were both quiet for a while. I thought about Abe some more. I remembered how quickly he'd devoured the burgers at first, like he was afraid someone would take them away. Later on, he ate more slowly and we talked a bit more. I realized Abe was always hungry, and I thought about the money Helen left. That could buy a lot of burgers.

She was so beautiful and so sad in her remorse, I found it difficult to maintain my outrage. "I've never been able to find the courage to kill myself," said Helen, "so I've stolen what I need to live and tried to justify it to myself."

I certainly didn't expect her to kill herself. I tried to put myself in her place, but I couldn't imagine it. At last I gave up trying to figure out what was right for her. There wasn't a simple answer here. "I'm not your judge. I can't be impartial with you. I don't know what I would have done if given your choices."

"Thank you for that," Helen said quietly.

"So you're a vampire, and you steal blood, but you don't kill— except in self-defense." I guessed I could live with that.

Helen was silent.

"Helen, you aren't a murderer, right?" I was getting upset again.

She was still silent. Angry, I shook her off, got off the bed and stood at the window, my back to her. "I told you I couldn't keep feeling the way I do about you if you're a murderer. You said you weren't. Now, I ask you again, and you say nothing." I was breathing heavily and my chest felt tight again.

Helen said, "I've killed to keep the secret. Any vampire who won't do as much isn't permitted to exist by the authorities of our kind."

I closed my eyes. "Explain."

"There are rules among vampires about keeping the secret. If a human learns the truth about us, any vampire must kill him immediately. If we don't, the authorities kill us and our entire vampire families. That's why I hunt the way I do. There is a minimum risk of detection, and if I'm seen, the witnesses aren't credible. I don't have to kill anyone."

That was sick. They made people kill? Or they killed their families? I couldn't imagine that kind of choice.

"How many people have you had to kill?"

"Too many, and yet not enough." I opened my eyes and looked at Helen, whose face expressed an infinite sadness.

"What does that mean?"

"It means I left that woman alive, the one who wrote the statement I showed you. It got her killed. It got everyone killed." Her chested heaved as she sobbed tearlessly. Once she had herself under control, she saw my puzzled expression and said gently, "There was no illness in 1925."

I felt stupid for not putting together the facts myself. I thought of all the stones in the Mennonite graveyard and the flowers Helen had laid on the grave. I remembered the name on the statement, and it was the same. Helen continued, "This was the Atwell boarding house. They killed everyone it because they'd lived in a house with me."

I remembered how she'd reacted at the monument. "Williamsport?"

"Yes, there are vampires there charged with keeping the secret. I was too lax, and they were too zealous. Damn them." Her anger this time was more resigned than it'd been in the graveyard.

"You didn't kill them, then. That's not your fault."

"No, but I need to be careful. I don't want anyone hurt."

I studied her lovely sad face. "Helen, I want to believe you. I am grasping at straws here trying to twist your lifestyle around in my head so that it's acceptable. I thought I'd won the lottery when you became my girlfriend. Now, I hope you're delusional. Otherwise, I'm living in a dark world where every moral choice is a terrible conundrum between the lesser of two evils."

Helen waited a moment and then spoke quietly. "If I were good, I wouldn't have dragged you into my world, but I'm not good. I'm selfish, and I want you to know me as I am. That's why I've told you what I have. I need to know if you still want me, even knowing the truth."

I'd thought I'd wanted her, but if she was a murderer, did I still? I felt a little sick. "I don't know how I feel."

"Please, would you turn around and look at me." I wrestled with myself for a moment and then I turned around and faced her. God, she was beautiful to me. She meant so much to me, I already didn't want to imagine my life without her.

"Tell me how you feel." Helen looked at me intently.

"I don't know how I feel." What did she want me to say?

She sighed with relief, and her face relaxed a bit. "You don't hate me."

"No, I guess not," I admitted.

"You still want me for a girlfriend."

"Yes, I guess so." That was true.

She put out her arms, so I went to her and curled up in them like a baby. I faced away from her because otherwise it would have been too much for me. She kissed my check once and said, "Let's take this slowly."

I went to the house of Jane McCord that evening. She answered her door. When she saw me, she said, "Alex told you." It wasn't a question.

"Yes," I agreed.

"I wasn't making trouble," she said. "I just wanted to help." She sounded defensive.

I hoped we could get along. "I'm not making trouble either. I just want to talk and maybe be friends with you. You're Alex's friend after all."

"Yes, I'm Alex's friend, and I'm worried you'll hurt him!" I liked Jane's honesty.

"Because you heard a story that I'm a vampire?" I made it sound like a ridiculous idea.

"No! Of course not! That's silly." Good, I thought. That's what I wanted to hear.

I looked her in the eye. "That's right. Forget all that nonsense." I was taking enough risks with Alex. I needed to minimize any others.

Strangely enough, she still thought I'd hurt him. I needed to know why. "Why do you think I'll hurt him?"

"I'm worried you'll break his heart." The poor girl clearly hadn't meant to admit that and looked embarrassed.

"Why do you care?" I demanded.

"He's a friend." I relaxed a bit. It was the truth, no more.

I could see that Jane cared deeply about Alex. She didn't love him, but she was open to the potential. There was a possibility here. I could leave Alex alone and perhaps he would discover that his feelings for her were more than friendship. Jane would not be long to discover that her feelings could match his. They would be good for each other. If I truly loved Alex, I would let Jane have him.

As I told Alex earlier in the day, I'm not that good a person.

"He's my boyfriend," I said, and I walked away.

11. EMBARRASSMENT

I was a little nervous about seeing Helen again. I'd been fine as long as I was with her, probably because my judgment was on hold in her presence. I'd started to think and worry afterwards. She came over Wednesday after school, which was the first day of Christmas vacation. I figured my parents probably wouldn't let me see her on Christmas Eve or on Christmas itself since they'd said Thanksgiving was for family. Helen had walked over to my house after going home to change. She'd worn a pretty dress and brought with her a boxed set of Doctor Who season five on Blu-ray disks.

"Is this your way of reassuring me that you're a normal girl? Because if so, you are way off."

"I thought you wanted to watch these with me." She looked confused.

"I do. You are totally awesome to bring them. I'm just saying that it's not normal: an average geek guy with a superhot girlfriend who also likes sci-fi. You clearly not part of the real world." I was joking, but I was also worried. Helen was trying too hard. I wondered, was all this just bait for the trap? She was really good bait.

"Superhot? Let's test that out." She came closer and kissed me gently on the lips. If she was bait for a trap, I was pretty sure I'd walk right into it. I didn't think I could help it. I felt like I did when I looked past the edge of a tall building and imagined how easy it would be to jump off and die. "So?" she demanded.

"Superhot. Total fantasy."

Helen looked me over carefully, gauging my reaction, and seemed dissatisfied. She said, "I brought the Doctor Who partly because I wanted a break from questions. I think you need some time to process what I've told you already. I thought you might enjoy watching these with me."

"Oh, yes, definitely." I was redirected back to the shows.

"If the show is as bad as I remember, I don't promise to watch more than an episode or two. Maybe we can rag on it together?"

"No, the eleventh doctor is the best! The first episode will blow you away: tight writing, insane acting and dramatic twists galore. The first ten minutes are a sci-fi *tour de force*. Plus, the doctor's new companion goes from being this totally chill Scottish girl to being this crazy, sexy madwoman, who sparked a whole Internet argument over whether Doctor Who was objectifying women. Let me tell you, I objectified her." Helen looked amused, fortunately, rather than annoyed. "This boxed set is awesome. We can watch in hi-def even though our streaming sucks. Where'd you get these?"

"Zachary from the Anime Club loaned them to me."

Zachary from Anime Club was mildly autistic and would completely freak out if anyone else touched his property. He was somewhat unpopular in the club for being unwilling to trade graphic novels with anyone because he said they creased the spines. "I didn't think Zachary would loan anyone anything ever."

Helen looked a little guilty. "I might have used a little girl power on him."

Of course he loaned them to Helen, I thought wryly. "Did you bat your eyes at him?" I asked sarcastically.

"Something like that, yes."

"Using your sex appeal is not 'girl power.' You can't call it that." I thought Helen's attitude was outrageous.

"Sure, it is. I'm a girl, and it's my power," she insisted.

"I don't think you're allowed to co-op an empowerment phrase from the women's movement and make it about manipulating males with sex. 'Girl power' is about what girls can do themselves."

"Alex, you sound like quite the little feminist." Helen sounded amused.

"I *am* a feminist. There's nothing wrong with that. America is about equality." I was defensive because I'd heard too many people treat feminism like a dirty word.

"And yet you see women as objects for your lust." She raised an eyebrow at me.

Ouch. "Sometimes," I admitted. "I try not to."

Helen laughed. "Horny feminist."

Her teasing hurt. Banter is like anything else, I supposed: it's all fun and games until someone gets hurt. I knew I was a ridiculous bundle of contradictions. I knew it was absurd to simultaneously objectify women and favor treating them with dignity. I was sensitive to the problem, but it was painful to have Helen rub my nose in the fact that I was part of it. I was a pig. I knew the truth of that deep in my bones, but it hurt more to have Helen know it.

I muttered, "Guilty as charged," and turned away to go to the basement.

Helen followed me. Once we were downstairs, she took my arm to get my attention. I didn't want to meet her gaze, but when I did, I saw only concern. "Alex, I'm sorry for saying that. It's true, and you're hurt more than you should be, but I didn't say it to be mean. I meant it as a joke, and you're taking it too seriously. I think it's great that you call yourself a feminist."

She looked down and continued more quietly and more slowly. "And I shouldn't have made fun of you for looking at women with desire—not when I'm hoping you'll look at me that way. When I look at you, I'm starting to feel... Well, let's just say I'm having feelings I've never had before."

I found that hard to believe. The world is full of attractive men, and she'd been living in it for a long time. I was nothing special to suddenly spark her interest.

Helen seemed to sense my skepticism. "I couldn't bear to be touched when I was seventeen, and even when I got over that, my attempts...weren't successful. I used to think I wasn't interested, but now I think maybe I hadn't found the right match." She looked at me.

I got it. I got what she was saying. I thought her attempt at empathy was sweet—and kind given how I'd overreacted to being called out for hypocrisy. She might even believe what she was saying, but I just couldn't. I knew how strong the physical desire I felt for her was and how difficult it was to behave appropriately around her. My libido didn't seem to have an off switch or even a brake when it came to Helen; the only way I could slow it down was to take away the fuel. I didn't think it was the same for her. I found it very difficult to believe that she felt any physical desire for my body comparable to what I felt for hers—except maybe for my blood. That time in the basement when she'd gotten carried away, that could've easily been me if we'd been kissing. She was the one who set the limits when we kissed. At least she would've been if I hadn't been so scared of her that I never tried anything. Eventually she'd see through me and be disgusted.

Helen seemed to divine my thoughts and contradicted them. "I do feel desire for you, Alex, at least as much as you do for me."

"See, I just can't believe that." I tried an experiment and ran my hand gently up the length of her arm. She closed her eyes. When I got to her shoulder and neck, she tilted her head to expose them more. She leaned in as I stroked her cheek. "Helen, if you were doing this to me, I don't know that I could refuse you anything you asked."

"What makes you think that I could refuse you?" she asked. Her voice was husky.

"You're saying you couldn't?" I didn't believe it.

"Alex, right now what you're doing feels so good that I'm seriously considering demanding that you not stop until we've done more than makes any kind of sense considering that Simon and your parents are upstairs." She was leaning into me.

I took my hand away and kissed her once quickly. "Good point. Let's watch Doctor Who." While the program was on, I thought about the difference in the way I felt about myself after what Helen had just said. I wasn't such a disgusting creep for wanting sex if Helen did too, and I had some choice. I wasn't a loser who couldn't get lucky with his own girlfriend. Instead, I was like a boy waiting until Christmas morning to open his presents. I was waiting until the time was right.

After the show was over, Helen admitted that it was a lot better than the Doctor Who she remembered, which seemed to be Tom Baker because she mentioned a scarf. I agreed that the show had come a long way. I realized that her life was longer than the whole run of the show. I had so many questions.

"Are you going to start grilling me now? I realize that you have a lot you must want to know, and I do want to tell you, but maybe your parents' basement is not the safest place for secrets."

"Helen, this is a two-way street. Maybe there are things you want to know about me." I couldn't imagine what, but I had no deadly secrets that couldn't be shared in the basement. "You can ask me anything. I mean *anything*," I said, not even sure of what I thought she might ask. I just wanted to reciprocate since she'd shared her big secret yesterday, and I didn't have a big secret to share.

"Well," she said hesitantly, "I do have something I really want to know right now, but it's a personal question and a bit rude to ask. The last thing I want to do is embarrass you." She paused, as if giving me a chance to stop her.

I had absolutely no idea where she was going with this. "Anything," I reiterated.

She seemed to make up her mind. "Okay." She took a deep breath. "It's just that I've noticed that you don't react to my attention the same way other boys do."

At first, I didn't get what she meant.

She paused and then continued, "I thought you did. You look at me intensely, breathe heavily and perspire." She suddenly seemed embarrassed as if she might be offending me. "Just a little bit perspiration, mind, just enough to smell really delicious."

"I still have no idea where you're going with this." I was afraid I was being obtuse, correctly as it turns out.

"It's just that when I decided to be your girlfriend, it never occurred to me that you might not be interested in me *as a girl*." She wasn't looking at me at all. "I mean you say you objectify women, you look at me all the time, and you agreed to be my boyfriend quickly enough, but you don't—I really can't believe I'm saying this out loud, but I really do want to know why—you don't have the usual, er, masculine physical response."

I'd been slow to get what she'd meant, but now I couldn't believe where I'd stupidly led this conversation. Naturally she wanted reassurance she affected me as much as she'd shown me I affected her. I had no idea how to do that without admitting too much about my private fantasies about her. With no ready answer, I froze.

"I overlooked it at first," she went on. "I've spend a lot of years in high school, so avoiding noticing that kind of reaction has gotten to be second nature to me."

How much of the truth could I share before she got disgusted?

She looked at me quickly, a brief searching glance. "In my experience, for most young men, if I so much as smile at them, talk to them, brush them gently with my hand—well, they react. You never have, including just now when you were touching my face, even when I told you that I was considering demanding you not stop."

I realized with surprise that this was probably technically true as long as we restricted ourselves to talking about the times when I was actually in her presence. All the hormone-fueled fantasies I'd indulged in had happened at a safe distance. So, I thought with relief, I might not have to admit just how inappropriately I'd behaved in my imagination.

Helen looked genuinely worried. I tried to think to think of the right words. I wanted the words that would assure her that she was everything I'd ever wanted in a girl. I wanted the words to forcefully reject the notion that knowing the truth about her made her undesirable. I wanted the words that would convince her that despite my geeky appearance and unimpressive intellect, that I was somehow special, somehow different from other shallow, superficial boys that just wanted her for body—while still confessing that I did want her body. But my cursed too-slow brain couldn't come up with any of the right words. The moment grew even more awkward.

"Sure, initially it was refreshing. I mean, you were quite the gentleman. I thought you must be really sweet." She snorted. "Then, I started to wonder, why you only looked at and touched me so carefully. I even had a brief moment when I considered whether you might be gay."

I spent a weird moment trying to imagine a straight man that wouldn't want her. My dad, I hoped.

She still wasn't looking at me. "I can't tell if you're actually attracted to me or if you just say that you are. We can take our time. You don't have to feel *that way* about me right now—or even for many years. I'd just like to know if a romantic relationship is ever possible. I'm older than you, and I think long-term."

I was hoping it wouldn't be too long-term. I kind of wanted a romantic relationship right away, but I was too scared to say anything.

She set herself up straight, shoulders square, looking away so I could see her profile. "Look, I see how my being undead could be a turn off."

The absurdity of that startled me out of my verbal block. "You're not any kind of dead! You're so alive! Your every movement is a song of grace." God, I couldn't believe how corny that sounded when I said it out loud.

She cocked her head, still without looking at me and said, "'Song of grace,' huh? Keep talking. I'm listening."

I took a moment to gather my thoughts, to try to express what I felt. "When I watch you move, like at the restaurant, I feel passion, maybe more than I show at the time."

"Very pretty," she said not unkindly, "but I think you are, if not begging the question, certainly avoiding it. I was asking why you don't *show* it." She gave me a little quirk of a smile.

"Oh, that." Well, here I was on safer ground. "That's because I am terrified of you in person. Sometimes." I tried to make it sound funny by adding, "It's a real mood killer."

Suddenly, she was looking straight at me, intently. That was frightening enough, but then my mind chose that exact moment to show me the memory of how it felt when she dislocated my arm, when she held me down in the basement and when she made me believe she was a vampire. My mouth got dry, my pulse sounded in my ears, my hands felt cold—and whatever interest all this talk might have engendered died in a spike of adrenaline.

"You fear me." She said it like a revelation. "Right now, you are afraid. A minute ago, you weren't, but now you are." She paused for a moment, processing what she thought.

"Alex," she said. She took my hands in hers, leaned in close to my face and stared directly into my eyes. I stopped breathing at the intensity of it all. "Don't be afraid of me."

She held my gaze with fierce sincerity, so close the breath from her words entered my mouth.

At that second, I stopped being afraid of her. None of her mysteries mattered. My body relaxed as I let go of my worries.

I realized how close we were. My hands were still in hers. Her exquisite face was next to mine, and I could see her skin down her neck to the perfect curve of her chest. Suddenly her clothes looked very thin, and I wondered what it would be like to touch her through them. I wondered how I was going to manage to keep myself from trying to do that and whether she really would be angry if I did. My body reacted.

Helen started laughing. Really laughing. I mean, it sounded truly joyful, and it broke the tension and all that, but she was still laughing at my expense. I was pissed—and also completely mortified.

"Stop that!"

"Sorry. It's just that you're so easy to read," she said wiping her eyes. She added sweetly, "At least now I know that my body pleases you when I'm not busy terrifying you." She burst into laughter again.

"Very funny," I huffed, feeling my wounded masculinity.

Then a scary thought occurred. "Wait! When you told me not to be afraid of you, suddenly I wasn't. Did you use magic on me? Like vampire hypnosis or something? How did you make me do it? Lose all fear?"

"Oh, sweetie, the magic I used was being a girl." She wasn't laughing, but she was smiling. At least she hadn't said "girl power" again.

"Being a girl, that's not magic."

"Really?" she said, "How often have you said 'no' to a pretty girl?"

The door opened above us. Simon's voice came down, "Mom says you guys are watching Doctor Who. What episode are you on? Can I join you? Mom says you have to let me."

We couldn't talk privately after that. We got our next chance when I was walking her back to her house. Helen wanted me to sneak out of my house on Christmas Eve at two o'clock in the morning—technically, that was Christmas Day—and meet her. She was going to take me to a secret place she had discovered in an abandoned coal mine not far out of town. There would be no Simon, no parents, just us.

It was crazy. It was scary. It was sexy.

Of course I said yes.

I felt a little guilty asking Alex to sneak away from his parents. I tried to pretend that any girlfriend would feel guilty about getting her boyfriend to risk trouble with his parents for her—any good girlfriend, anyway. But I wasn't fooling myself. I could bury myself in my schoolgirl persona well enough that I really felt innocent, but part of me always knew what an adult would say. The adult part of me was pretty clear that separating the boy from his parents in the middle of the night was a child predator move.

I resolved to go slowly with Alex—and not take his virginity any time soon. I was glad he wanted me to because my hopes for a future together depended on it, but I didn't want to rush him into too mature a relationship. Maybe I'd wait until he was eighteen. As much as I wanted him now, I was old enough to wait until the time was right—however long that was. I was afraid that kind of thinking only made it creepier. An innocent would be swept away. Well, innocence could be dangerous. I wanted to be good, and I wanted to be good for him. I would go slowly.

Of course, what I wanted to ask him in the mine was the height of selfishness. No amount of innocence could disguise that. This was about my needs, not his. I was disgusted with myself.

I still hoped he'd say yes.

12. MINE

On Christmas Eve I felt like I was five years old again because I was so excited for it to be bedtime. The difference was that instead of this being in anticipation of unwrapping presents from under the tree, I couldn't wait to sneak out tonight to meet Helen.

There was a tiny voice whispering cautions in my head: "No one knows where you'll be. She's a vampire. What if she wants to kill you? Why does she want to take you to the abandoned coal mine?" However, the possibilities of that last one were so exciting that I didn't listen to the rest. I was going to sneak out to meet my girlfriend, who'd suggested that we meet in a private place. My imagination was just about ready to quit because it'd been working so much overtime.

Fortunately, my parents assumed my agitation was all Christmas related. We went to Christmas Eve services at Trinity where watched Simon play the shepherd. I say "the" shepherd because we didn't have enough children for more than one. He was elated because he'd finally been promoted from being the sheep. The angel Gabriel was played by a young woman—again, not enough children—who was really attractive despite being in her mid twenties, and when she declared herself unto Simon, I imagined for a moment she was Helen. I chided myself for impure thoughts, but I was just a mess.

When we got home and I said I was going to bed, my parents just looked relieved. I think they were glad because it meant "Santa" could come sooner, and they could get some sleep. I set the alarm on my phone for two o'clock in the morning with the alert on vibrate and put it in my pillowcase under my ear.

After the alarm went off, I snuck downstairs in the sweatpants and shirt I usually wore to bed. I figured if I got caught, I could claim to be sneaking a look at the presents. I opened the doors to the house and front closet as quietly as I could. I planned to say I'd wanted a look at the stars if I got caught then. I put on my winter coat and boots and went to meet Helen, shutting the door silently behind me. I chose the coat and boots only because I need to wear something over my sweats and they were handy in the front closet, but I didn't really need winter clothes. It'd been unseasonably warm all day, reaching into the sixties. It'd been raining all week, and this afternoon there'd been thunder. That was seriously abnormal for Christmas Eve in Pennsylvania. The air itself felt strange and unnatural.

Helen found me when I was about halfway to her house. Silently she led me out of town towards the mine.

She looked a lot better than I did—I mean, she always did—but she looked really good in a large red parka, black tights and grey Ugg boots. I wondered if those were still in fashion. I remembered an eighth grade girl who had gotten sent home from school for a dress code violation because she had worn a short winter coat and tights with fur topped boots. Another girl had called her an "eskiho," and Mom had yelled at me for repeating that. By contrast, Helen was actually quite covered up. Her parka went down to her knees, and the hood was deep and furred on the edge so you couldn't see her face at all.

In fact, her outfit struck me as weird. It just wasn't cold enough for her to need that parka, and she certainly didn't need that hood. Maybe she'd bought the jacket for Christmas, and then the weather let her down. None of which explained her having the hood up.

It took us close to forty minutes to get to the mine. I knew I'd need to keep an eye on the time to be back before anyone woke on Christmas morning. Helen had brought two flashlights and gave me one once we'd left the lights of the town behind. The mine was surrounded by an old chain link fence with a metal sign that looked like it said "Cypria." The paint had flaked off the whole right side of the sign. I pointed it out to Helen with my flashlight.

Apparently it was now safe to talk because she said, "The sign used to say 'Cypriot Mine Company.' They added the fence and sign long after the mine was closed to keep trespassers out. As you can see, it's not much good now." She indicated where the chain link had fallen from its frame creating a large gap through which we could walk.

"It looks like it says Cypria now."

Helen laughed. "Okay, that'll be our name for it then."

We found the entrance to the mine, but I didn't see how we were ever going to get inside. There was a Roman arch of grey stone, like a bridge sideways, stuck into the side of a hill. On the keystone of the arch was carved "B2." Underneath the arch was obviously the entrance, which was about eight feet wide and about the same at the highest point. However, a large slab of poured concrete sealed the entrance.

"How are we going to get in?" I asked.

Helen was undeterred. "The slab's loose. I can lever it open." She walked up to the side of the slab. I didn't see because her back was to me, but it looked like she just pulled a bit, and sure enough there was about ten inches of space between seal and stone arch through which we could slip.

Once we were inside, I saw a tunnel sloping gently downwards. I'd half expected to see railroad tracks, but there weren't any. Maybe this was just for people. I wondered how they'd gotten the coal out. The walls and ceiling were some kind of rough grey stone. At irregular intervals were pairs of wooden support beams against the walls, holding crossbeams across the ceiling. These seemed to be made of the trunks of trees, stripped of their bark but minimally shaped. The floor was flat and felt like hard packed dirt and gravel. It looked reddish in the flashlight's illumination, and I wondered if it was iron oxide giving it that color. There were broken scraps of wood and debris scattered on the ground.

It suddenly occurred to me the mine itself might be dangerous. I'd spent so much time worrying about what Helen might intend that I hadn't given much thought to the dangers underground. Since she seemed to know her way around, maybe I was okay with her guiding me. I guessed both questions came down to whether I trusted Helen. Either I was safe with her or I wasn't, and I'd already made my choice.

We walked for a while until we must have been pretty far underground, and the tunnel had curved around for a bit and began to widen. Helen stopped.

"Sit down," she said, so I did. "Turn off your flashlight and close your eyes." The floor of the tunnel was cold, but I was warm enough in my winter coat. She stood across the tunnel from me and turned off her flashlight, so when I turned off mine, we were in total darkness. I closed my eyes and watched the afterimage spots from the bright flashlights.

I heard the sound of her unzipping her parka, and a rustling as she took it off. That was exciting and unexpected. While the spots faded from my eyes, I wondered, what was she going to do?

"Don't open your eyes yet," she said. After a moment, she continued, "Alex, you know what I am, but I don't think you really believe it. It's like a game of let's pretend to you right now. I want to take our relationship to another level, but you need to understand the real implications of what I want to do with you. You need to make a commitment to me. I can't be some childish make-believe fantasy that you can put aside and go back to your real life. That's why I asked you here: to show you some magic your mind can't explain away as easily as a dislocated arm or a sharpened canine tooth. Now open your eyes."

I did. With her parka set aside, I could see she had worn just a short-sleeved, black scooped-necked blouse, along with her black leggings and boots. I barely noticed what she was wearing because I was lost in the wonder of her skin. It was glowing faintly in the total dark: a weak light came off her face, her neck, her collarbone and even her hands. A pale nimbus that cast no shadows surrounded her. The loveliness of her features was exquisite and overwhelming.

"You're an angel," I whispered. "A Christmas angel."

She smiled radiantly. Literally.

"Normally, I hate that reaction. I hate that this glow can be used by our kind to prey on the superstitious, exploiting their faith. But when you say it, you're just so adorable I can't help but smile." She mused for a second. "I think it's because you really see me like that. That's how you think of me in your own mind." She looked at me tenderly, but then her expression hardened.

"Alex, I'm no angel. You need to know that. I've hurt others, and I'm capable of hurting you."

Caught in the wonder of her radiance, I did not think so.

"What are you thinking?" she asked.

"I was thinking that you glow."

"Obviously."

"Why?"

"It's not a traditional angel's halo, if that's what you're thinking. You'll notice my hair and eyes don't give off light. Still, you're not completely off track. Some vampires call it 'Lucifer's fire,' after the fallen angel in the Bible who was cast out from heaven and became Satan. It's one of the marks of our kind and something we need to conceal. We have to be careful about being seen in total darkness. It's too faint to be visible in any kind of light at all—even candlelight or starlight is enough to obscure it. Your eyes have to be completely adjusted to night vision to see it at all."

Her glowing skin was really cool, but it was hardly magic I couldn't explain away. "Helen, you know that they sell glow-in-the-dark makeup, right?"

Her glowing features looked at me in consternation. "It's not makeup. It's me!" She sounded indignant. "Look!" She pulled up the side of her shirt to show me that her hip was glowing too.

That instantly made my mind go in all kinds of inappropriate places. "I'm not doubting you. I haven't really doubted you're a vampire since you told me. I'm just saying the glowing thing isn't nearly as unambiguously magical as, say, casually moving the concrete seal on the way in here."

"Oh." Helen looked chagrined. "Here, I thought it was so amazing." She started to laugh at herself.

"It's amazing all right. Feel free to go ahead and show me as much of that glowing skin as you like." I was joking, mostly. Helen stopped laughing at herself and started laughing at me, which had been my goal.

"Aren't you cold, right now? It's not as cold as outside, but this tunnel can't be more than 60 degrees."

"Yeah, I'm cold." She laughed. "Seen enough? May I put my parka back on? It's comfortable for me underground, but I'm still a little cold."

I nodded, but she couldn't see me in the dark, so I said, "Yeah," out loud. She put the parka back on, but she left the hood down so I could see her glowing face. Neither of us turned on a flashlight.

After a while, she said, "I brought you down here for another reason as well. I want to offer you a choice, but I need to explain some things first so that you will understand the situation. I've already told you how important it is for vampires to keep the secret. I've also told you we are allowed to tell one human if and only if we guarantee that human keeps the secret, too. What I haven't explained is why that exception is allowed." She gave me a pointed look, like my mom's pay-attention look.

"There's a widespread folk belief among vampires that the blood of a willing victim is more sustaining than blood that's taken by stealth or force. The authorities frown upon this because for a victim to be willing, the human needs to be in on the secret. The practice is tolerated so long as the vampire stays within certain bounds: the vampire must have no more than one human at a time, closely monitored, and be ready and willing to deliver death without hesitation at the first sign the secret might be in danger."

Helen looked at me ruefully. "I'm skating pretty close to the edge of thin ice with you."

I thought about that metaphor. "Thin ice isn't a danger to someone who can't die. You're worried about me—because I'm on the ice with you."

"I *am* worried about you, Alex. I worry for both of us. I'm hard to kill, but I'm not deathless. If an inquisitor were to look closely into my relationship with you, such a one must not discover I'm not prepared to kill you. They'd kill us both. I'm breaking the rules unless I'm ready to end your life."

That was an uncomfortable thought.

"The belief in the potency of willing victim blood has given rise to a particularly loathsome kind of vampire predator. You know the story of Dracula, right? He makes himself this handsome figure of a man and seduces young women. I met a vampire like that once in Spain, who called himself Mateo. As disgusting as what I do is, he was so much worse. He was a charming Lothario who sought out women of the lower classes, wooed his way into their hearts and then drank them dry. He was a cunning, twisted serial killer who knew that no one in power would do anything about poor women who went missing."

Helen smiled grimly. "He didn't count on someone like me stopping him."

My mouth was dry. For the first time, I really believed Helen was a killer, too. "How did you stop him?"

"Oh, I didn't kill him myself, if that's what you're thinking—not that I would've regretted it. We aren't supposed to interfere with each other unless the secret's in danger. I just figured that someone who behaved as he did was sure to have violated secrecy in some egregious indiscretion, so I tipped off the vampire authorities. It turned out he'd done all sorts of madness, and they put him to death."

"Good! Think of all the women whose lives you saved." Maybe she was an angel, I thought. To those women, she was.

"Thank you, Alex. I'd like to see myself the way you see me, but you're so sweet and so blind when it comes to me. I stopped one killer, yes, but I'm part of a massive conspiracy with thousands of killers, and I keep their secret." She was silent for a while.

I realized she was blaming herself for all the people vampires killed throughout the whole world. What a weight of guilt! I thought of tenth grade English and Macbeth's "Will all great Neptune's ocean wash this blood clean from my hand?" I guessed that was how she felt.

After a moment, Helen continued her story. "Mateo believed in a legend, one that springs from the belief in the potency of willing victim blood. The legend said that once there was a vampire who was loved so perfectly by a human that she gave him all of her blood in fully willing sacrifice. She was so pure and so good and so loving that, the legend says, the vampire never had to drink blood again because the evil spirit within him was completely satisfied. Mateo wanted to replicate the legend."

Maybe I lack the maturity to handle heavy emotional situations, but I tried a joke. "So, you're saying that you'd never have to drink again if you could find and drink up Jesus Christ?"

She looked at me disgustedly. I explained myself, "You know, 'a perfect sacrifice for the whole world.'" She still looked disgusted. My joke had probably been in poor taste, but I doubled down. I put my hands up as if to ward her off. "I promise you that my blood is not anywhere near as good as Jesus's, which—if you want—just come on down to Trinity Episcopal on Sunday morning. We are literally giving it away."

Helen finally laughed. Whether it was at the joke or me, I'm not sure.

"I'm not expecting to find Jesus in you, Alex."

"That's a relief."

"Anyway, drinking Jesus would not be an option. I think you'll find that he loved and died for humanity, not for such as me. He cast out demons." Now she sounded sad again. Damn. "A relationship with me is dangerous. My parents know I've let you in on the secret, but even they don't know how much I've told you. I could be making a big mistake here."

Helen took a deep breath. "I might be about to compound that mistake with what I'm about to ask you to do for me. I told you all that I have tonight because it's very important to me that you understand the dangers involved in what I'm asking."

What was she going to ask me? I wondered. Of course I'd do it.

"I need blood every week."

The proverbial penny dropped. I got her drift. "You want to drink from me."

"Yes."

"Okay, do it."

Clearly she didn't understand that she could stop her sales pitch once she'd made the sale because she continued. "Normally, I'd been going into Philadelphia right now, but you know how I hate myself for doing that. That would be safer for you though. What if I'm tempted to drink more and more?"

"I trust you," I said, though I was starting to get cold feet. "Will it hurt?"

"No, not at all. I'd let the anesthetic in my teeth work to numb your skin before I drank. It might feel like I was one of those girls who gives her boyfriend a hickey."

"Disgusting," I said, and we both laughed at the irony. What she was proposing was way grosser.

"I would just take a pint. Like a donation to the Red Cross," she explained

"Okay, I've done that." I remembered it was no big deal. "My blood type was A positive. I drank juice afterwards." The nurse had made me drink the juice, but I wasn't faint or anything.

"Oh, we have Rh incompatibility. I'm A negative," said Helen.

"Is that a problem?" I wasn't sure what she meant, but I didn't want us to be incompatible.

"No, it won't matter for us," Helen said wistfully. "I can drink any type. It would only matter if... I can't... It just doesn't matter." Then she gave me a smile. "I can bring juice though."

I was feeling better. "Okay. Right now?"

"No, I want you to have time to consider. This is a big commitment."

I thought about that, a little relieved. Then, I admitted, "It's definitely not why I thought you asked me here."

"Why did you think I asked you here?" she asked surprised. Then, she got stern. "And why did you come, by the way? Have you no sense of self-preservation? A vampire asks you to sneak out of your home and meet her underground in the middle of the night, and it did never occur to you that you might die?"

"The thought did occur," I admitted, my mouth drying remembering the struggle I had had with my fears. "Ultimately, I decided to take a leap of faith and trust you."

"You gambled your life on me." It wasn't a question or an accusation. Helen said it like an observation.

"Yeah, well, I hoped maybe you'd asked me here for a different reason..."

Helen looked startled, then amused. "You silly teenage boy, did you sneak out here with me, potentially risking your life, because you'd hoped I make out with you?"

"Um, maybe." In my dreams, I'd actually hoped for a bit more.

She came over and put her face close to mine. "Maybe you'd hoped I was planning on making love with you?" It was a shrewd guess but not unkindly said.

"I'm taking the fifth on that one."

"How about this? Tonight I give you one kiss, for being a sweet boyfriend and for listening to all this. You get no more than one kiss tonight because I don't want to use undue influence to sway your judgment."

It was way too late for her to start worrying about swaying my judgment. I was long-gone on that score. I would've done anything she asked.

"It's your blood and your life. It should be your decision, something you want to do and not a trade for something else. Like this kiss."

She kissed me, once. Some kisses you never forget.

We needed to take a circuitous route back into town to avoid streetlights and detection. The memory of that kiss stayed with me as Helen and I walked, hand-in-hand, winding our solitary way back into town.

There was no excuse for my behavior with Alex in the mine. That I needed him didn't give me the right to ask him to meet those needs. People have a way of deluding themselves when it comes to getting what they want, and I was no exception. If I'd really loved him, I wouldn't have

asked what I did. It was selfish of me, but I hoped I'd be lucky enough that the two of us could escape the price.

When I came home that night, Mom saw me come in. Though she couldn't have read the guilt in my face, she could guess I'd been up to something with Alex, and it would've been obvious to her what I wanted from him—at least some of it. Tonight, she was right. She didn't say anything to me beyond a look. Perhaps I only imagined that she was reproachful. Generally, my mother was not judgmental.

But I was.

I'd already judged myself,

and I'd suspended the sentence.

13. INQUISITION

Needless to say, I was seriously underslept on Christmas morning. I kept yawning and rubbing my eyes, but fortunately my parents wrote it off to my being a teenager. We had a special breakfast of cinnamon rolls and scrambled eggs, after which we opened presents around the tree. Sometime midmorning Simon disappeared to play his new video game.

I took advantage of that time to call Jane to thank her for her present and to see how she liked mine. That was easier than calling Helen, who might expect some kind of answer for last night's question. I thanked Jane for the pocketknife multi-tool she'd given me. "I like all the attachments, like the screwdriver and scissors, but I can't find the blade."

"There isn't one," said Jane. "That's so you can take it to school. I bought it for you 'cause you're such a tool."

"Thanks. Did you like the book I got you?"

"*One Hundred and One Ways to Cook Broccoli*? What's the point? I already know the best way. I'll be sure to invite you over to try them all."

"Can't say I'm really looking forward to that."

"Should've got me a book of chocolate recipes then."

The rest of Christmas was all about family. We went over to Grandma Fulton's house in the afternoon. Usually, Grandma cooked, but mom brought a shepherd's pie she'd made earlier and heated it up in Grandma's oven. Grandma looked weak and spent most of her time in her chair. Usually, she drank a highball cocktail in the afternoons, but I noticed she was drinking plain water. Christmas felt somber.

The day after Christmas, I was free to go over to Helen's house. I had many questions, and Helen was willing to talk.

"What do you want to know?"

"Are your family all vampires?" I hadn't met them yet, and I was really curious. What were they like? I was scared to find out.

"Yeah. Some vampires live with a human, for the reason I told you on Christmas, but mine are all vampires. It's safe to talk here." I guessed she meant it was safe to talk because I was the only human in the house. That made me a little nervous.

I was also intensely curious about vampires. Helen clearly wasn't what I had thought a vampire would be. Since she was willing to talk, I took advantage. "Okay, I've got a whole myth vs. fact list to go through."

Helen smiled and indicated I should go on.

I started with the thing that was most obviously wrong. "First, sunlight doesn't burn you, so obviously that's a myth. Why do people say it?"

Helen considered for a moment before she answered. I wondered if that meant she didn't have practice explaining this to people. I liked that I might be one of the few—or the only one. She said at last, "There's myth that means a false belief and myth that means a traditional story. The latter are true, but they're metaphors. People fear the dark for good reason: they can't see danger coming. Vampires often hunt at night because it's easier to do so secretly."

That made sense. "So, you really are 'creatures of the night'—because that's when you hunt?"

"Exactly. When the sun rises, humans feel safe from vampires, and they are safer." Helen seemed to think that explanation sufficed.

It wasn't enough for me though because it didn't explain the stories. "I get that, but why is sunlight supposed to burn vampires?"

Helen tried again. "Do you remember that debate you had with Jon about goblins and trolls in Tolkien? Jon said that it didn't make sense that sunlight turned mountain trolls to stone in *The Hobbit*, but they fought at the battle of the Black Gate during the day in *The Lord of the Rings*."

Now she was talking my language. I got enthusiastic. "Because of the darkness that their master Sauron spewed into the sky!" I had argued that it wasn't a contradiction because the creatures had been protected by the darkness, so they weren't in the sun.

"I see you do remember," Helen said sardonically. "My point is that when people invent monsters they make them hate the sun, but they also understand on some level that monsters can come out in the day. They may even invent an Achilles-heel weakness, but people know that such weaknesses are subject to limitations."

"Do you have any of the traditional vampire weaknesses?" All the stories gave ways the vampire hunters could kill them.

"Well, the spirit that sustains us does get weaker in the sun. It's strongest underground, which is why we all need to spend a certain amount of time underground each day." I realized that Helen's affinity for my basement and the coalmine might not be just privacy.

I made another connection. "Is that why the stories say vampires sleep in their graves?"

"I assume so. That Dracula coffin-full-of-dirt bit would be useless on a ship though. The hold of the ship—below the waterline—works a little." I hadn't read Dracula yet, but I didn't want to admit it.

I had seen some TV shows though, and they had lots of tricks for killing vampires. "What about the other weaknesses: crosses, stakes, garlic, silver bullets?"

Helen smiled. "Should I be worried?"

I was so embarrassed. I'd gotten caught up in learning about vampires intellectually, and I hadn't remembered how Helen might feel about this topic. "No," I said earnestly, "I'd never hurt you." I wanted to reassure her that was the furthest thing from my mind.

She laughed. "I was just teasing. Of course you're curious. Well, crosses don't work and churches are no protection, but many vampires were raised in religious families and respect these things to a degree. A stake creates a serious injury in the heart and physically blocks repair—until it's removed. Vampires wither without food, and that can cause the stake to fall out. At that point, if a hapless human comes very close, the vampire may have enough strength to drain his blood and replenish his substance. Garlic just tastes nasty. Silver retards healing, so the bullet wound doesn't repair as quickly as it would."

Since I was a little grossed out picturing some of these things, I changed the topic. "How do you make a vampire?"

Apparently, I'd chosen the wrong topic. Helen hesitated. "I have issues talking about that one. The short answer is that you can drink a vampire's blood and have the evil spirit pass with it."

I wanted to know so much more. "But how—?"

"Enough. I'm not talking any more about that." Helen was curt.

Caught by my fascination, I'd missed her clear signal. "But—?"

Helen stopped me by putting up her palms in surrender. "If you insist on knowing the details, here's the catch." She got serious and looked me in the eye. "The transformation from human to vampire also changes gender. I was born a human boy, but now I'm a vampire girl. If you drank a vampire's blood, you'd become a girl. That's what I didn't want to tell you because I knew you'd freak out."

I was freaking out. "Whoa," I said slowly. I was having trouble imagining what this might mean for us. After I'd thought a moment, I asked, "If I became a vampire girl, would I still feel attracted to you like I do now? Would you still want me?" The catch was that I'd only ever want to be a vampire to be with her. If I became one and didn't want her anymore, the whole transformation would be pointless.

Helen smiled broadly. "Gotcha!"

"Helen!" I protested. I'd been totally suckered by her wicked sense of humor.

"I told you I wasn't going to tell you any more about transformation, so don't ask."

"All right." Message received. I changed the subject again. "What's the coolest thing vampires can do?"

"Fly. My family all flies, except me." There was longing in her voice. I could understand that.

"That's a bummer." I wondered if she felt like a caged bird.

"Yes, it is. You should see them in the air. It looks exhilarating. The freedom must be incredible. Of course, they have to be careful about not being seen. Still..." Helen sounded wistful.

"I'm sorry you can't fly." This took sibling envy to a whole new level.

Helen didn't seem too upset. Then she got a smug expression. "I do have one ability they don't have. Most vampires get one of two gifts: they either fly or have 'the eye.' The former is more common."

"So you have 'the eye'?" I didn't know what that meant though.

"Yes, most vampire families have at least one member like me because it's useful in keeping the secret. Also, most of our police have it." I wondered why that was.

"What can you do?"

"You know how when you try to lie to your mother, she makes you look her in the eyes and she can tell you're lying?" Sadly, all too well. I'd had to stop lying to my mother in middle school for that reason.

"Yeah." Oops, I realized, this could be a problem now that I was dating Helen.

"I can do that. Also, you know how when you are reluctant to do something that your father has asked you to do, he can stare you down and make you agree?"

"Yeah." I remembered the broccoli picking.

"I can do that, too." Helen looked a little smug.

"So, you have a built-in lie detector. I can see why that's useful for a police officer. What's the limit to what you can make people do when they're reluctant?"

Helen smiled at me. I don't think I would ever get used to that beautiful face and those beautiful eyes smiling at me. "Don't worry about that, Alex."

"Okay."

I went home for lunch because I hadn't told my parents I wouldn't be home, and I figured if I started blowing off meals without warning them, they might start limiting my time with Helen. I wanted to spend the afternoon with her, too.

Jane called after lunch. "Hey, you want to come over this afternoon and try out one of those broccoli recipes?"

"Sorry, I made plans with Helen." Thinking about vampires all morning made me ask, "Speaking of which, have you heard any more of that vampire story about Helen?"

"What are you talking about, Alex?" She sounded annoyed.

"The story. The one Mr. Miller told you." I was surprised she'd needed reminding.

"The only story Mr. Miller told us was a ghost story about Mary. You must be confusing me with some other girl." I got a sinking feeling in my stomach, and ended the conversation.

Back in Helen's room that afternoon, I confronted Helen about it. "Did you do something to Jane McCord's memory with that 'eye' of yours?"

"I have to keep the secret. It's for her safety as well as mine."

"So that's a 'yes,' then. Clearly, you can do a lot more with your eyes than my mom and dad! Tell me what you can do." Helen was silent, so I continued angrily. "Don't mess with Jane's mind! Memories are who we are. I don't want you changing her, making her into a puppet. Me, I'm signing up for this relationship, but she didn't agree to anything. Make me your puppet if you want, but leave Jane alone!" I was trying not to shout, but I might have gotten a little loud.

Helen looked increasingly angry as I spoke. "What makes Jane McCord so special? Maybe you'd rather be with her, eating broccoli! I am not making anyone into a damn puppet. What's wrong with you? I do what I have to do, no more."

"Is this how you took care of Reverend Brubacher? You made him forget everything?"

"Yes," she said, "to keep the secret."

"Speaking of which, you told me you've killed to keep that secret. I'm starting to think that I need more details about how many and who and why." I was sure she wasn't telling me some important things.

"I did what I had to do at the time, no more." Helen was insistent. "I don't want to talk about killing with you. You don't know what you're asking. I don't want to relive those memories. I don't want to burden you with them either." She made it sound like I didn't have the right to ask.

"You sound like Michael in *The Godfather*, when he tells his wife Kay not to ask him about his business. Am I as naive as she was if I believe you when you tell me you're not a monster?"

"I've never said I'm not a monster!" Helen shouted, but I couldn't tell if it was in anger or anguish. "I am a vampire. The most I can say for myself is that I don't regard humans as expendable. I take blood without killing. I only kill when I absolutely have to do so to keep the secret and avoid being killed by vampires. You are *not* naive when you call me a monster, but you *are* naive when you ask me to tell you about killing."

I wasn't going to be put off this time. "Educate me then. How do you live with killing?"

She seemed to deflate a little. "I don't know how to explain it to someone who has never had to do it. I try not to think about it. Truman lived with ordering two Japanese cities full of civilians vaporized, but I can't claim my actions saved more lives by stopping a war. Hercules could cleanse himself of the murder of his children by doing the twelve labors, but God hasn't told me what to do and didn't answer my prayer." Her words were full of anguish.

I had been bitter, but when Helen's anger turned into pain, something of her explanation started to penetrate. It was not so much her words as her struggle. I didn't think evil people struggled so much with moral choices.

Her last example distracted me into venting a pet peeve though. "It makes me angry when people talk about how great Hercules was. They just give him a pass on murdering his children and extensive philandering. It's infuriating there's such a double standard in judging Zeus's sons and daughters. Everyone from Homer to Shakespeare excoriates Helen of Troy for abandoning her daughter and husband. I don't see how she's a bad mother for leaving her princess daughter to be raised in the palace of the child's own father. It's not fair that she is so notorious for leaving a loveless marriage her father chose when she was faithful to the man she chose for herself until the day he died."

Instead of being angry that I gone off topic, Helen smiled a little wistfully and said, "I'm glad there is one Helen you will staunchly defend. It gives me hope that you might be persuaded to look past the faults of another."

I'd calmed down. "Helen, I am sorry. In my gut, I feel that you're good, or at least trying hard to be good, which is all anyone can say, really. It just scared me when I heard what you'd done to Jane because it highlights how little I know what you are capable of doing and what you might feel you need to do. I don't know the answers because you won't tell me anything."

Helen looked at me seriously. "I told you before. Vampire police take secrecy seriously. If the secret gets out because of me, they'd kill me. They'd hunt me down—we're all electronically registered now— and kill me. They'd kill you. They'd kill both our families. Our close friends. Everyone."

I shook my head, not in denial, because she had told me before, but in rejection, because I couldn't imagine it.

Helen saw through me. "You have to accept this reality. You're living in it now. Every single person who lived in this house in 1925 got killed because I got careless and let one person remember something. You know that."

I nodded without making eye contact.

Helen persisted. "Jane's knowing what I am risks you and everyone you love. The only way I could save myself and my family would be to kill you all myself."

I looked her in the eyes and let her see the fear and pain. "Would you really kill me?"

She looked down at her hands. "I don't know," she admitted.

"Jane?" I asked.

"In a heartbeat," she said.

She said it so easily, I thought. Then I realized why. "Because you've had to kill before."

"Yes," she admitted. "Thanks to my gift, I haven't had to do it very much, but I can't deny it's happened. Are you sorry I told you?"

"I'm not sorry I know the truth. Anyway, I asked for it." I thought about how I felt. "I hate that it makes how I feel about you so complicated when it used to be simple."

Helen smiled so wickedly for a second that I worried she'd read my mind when I'd had one of my lustful fantasies about her. I'd have to admit those weren't complicated feelings. Then she looked sad. "I am taking part of your innocence, in sharing with you my compromised morality. My whole life is a moral dilemma."

"Oh!" Her words had triggered a thought.

Helen looked at me intently. "Tell me what you're thinking."

"I was remembering that my English teacher at St. Augustine made us learn about stages of moral development created by a man named Lawrence Kohlberg, but—" I stopped, self conscious. Helen must know all these ideas already. As old as she was, she must have been to college. I must sound like a first grader telling her about the letters I learned to write.

Helen encouraged me. "I do know about Lawrence Kohlberg, but there's an idea in your head that's new to me. Anyway, I like hearing what you have to say. I want to hear your words. Go on."

I took a breath. "Okay, this guy Kohlberg would ask high school boys about an ethical choice. He told them there was a man named Heintz who could not afford to purchase a drug that would save his wife's life. Kohlberg asked the boys if Heintz should steal it. He ranked their answers on a scale of moral development. One of the most sophisticated, adult answers was that he should steal it because life is worth more than property." I paused to see if I was making sense to Helen.

She said, "I see the connection to me in that Heintz and I are both trying to protect our families, but I'm not merely stealing. I am killing. Who's to say which life is more valuable? That's why this story has never held any comfort for me. But you are thinking something more." She looked at me intently.

"My teacher told us that Kohlberg's methods and conclusions have been challenged as biased towards a Western perspective. She said Western societies tend to look at these choices as being made by individuals, but Eastern societies tend to emphasize social harmony and the good of the group."

Helen shook her head. "I don't think I'm good for the group."

She wasn't understanding me. "That's because you are so good that you actually think of humans as being in your group. But you're a vampire. That's your group."

Helen nodded agreement.

"Other vampires have imposed their ideas of social harmony and collective good upon you. They've created the system of laws that sets the parameters of your decisions, and you lack the power to change the laws."

Helen nodded again.

I tried an analogy. "It's like when my mom gets upset hearing about her tax dollars buying bombs that kill civilians in war. She goes to rallies, and she votes, but Dad tells her she can't change the world by herself."

Helen sat quietly for a moment. I felt bad for her.

"Helen, I'm not God, and I can't judge you, but I think you're judging yourself for the actions of the whole group and not just your own actions. I don't think you need to assume all that responsibility." Any more than my mom should, I thought.

"Alex, I don't even protest like your mother. I don't say a word." Helen was shaking her head.

"Right, because vampires would kill you. They're fascists. No big surprise there." Helen laughed without humor. I drove my point home. "You didn't choose to join this group, and it was already organized so that you didn't get a say in it once you did."

Helen seized that. "Why would *you* choose to join it though? By associating with me? You still have a choice!"

Did I still have a choice? "Haven't I joined already? You've told me your secret." Helen looked thoughtful, and I got worried suddenly. "You aren't thinking about making me forget, are you? I don't want to forget what you are." I was really upset by the possibility, and I knew I couldn't keep her out of my mind.

"No, I won't do that. I want you to desire the *real* me. I can't do that if I make you forget." Her reasonableness reassured me, and I calmed down a bit.

I felt sick to my stomach. "I hate it when we fight."

"As long as you remember fighting with me, you'll have proof that I'm not trying to make you into a puppet." Helen gave me a half smile.

That actually did make me feel better. I went home, not sure exactly what we had resolved, but sure at least that we had not yet broken up.

Why did Alex have to ask me those questions? Why did he want me to share those memories? I'd tried hard to cut the diseased memories out, to surgically excise them from my own brain, for my own health. I knew if I wanted to go on living, I couldn't afford to dwell on the negative. I couldn't afford to let my mind reel in endless circles of miserable thoughts. I'd thought I was more practical than this. I'd thought I'd let go of this part of my past. I'd thought I'd forgiven myself, or at least driven the memories so far back that they might as well have been forgotten. But here I was, remembering again—and wondering if I couldn't have done something different in Zinapécauro. I was pointlessly wondering what I could have done to change the outcome when I'd still had the chance. The memories came back fresh and vivid.

I wished Alex had never asked me those questions and dredged up these hated memories. Why couldn't he have just let me try to forget? My family had more delicacy than that; they never brought up the few times I'd had to kill. I felt sick to my stomach, just as I did all those decades ago. My thoughts had returned to the place I never allowed them to go any more.

I was stuck reliving my worst nightmare.

Remembering what I had done, I wondered if Alex would still want me if he knew. His words about my position in vampire society gave me hope that he might. More than that, they gave me hope for myself. I was starting to see a way to forgive myself for my role in the conspiracy. I could strive to make the best possible choices for myself, to do the least harm possible, given a larger reality that was outside my control. Recently, I'd prayed to God to let me be good and to let me have Alex. Was this the answer to both my prayers? Was this why God hadn't listened when I'd begged him to strike me down over the graves in Zinapécuaro?

I considered the possibility that I might have a future with Alex. I wondered what I could possibly have to offer him. If we stayed together long, I might give in to the temptation to make him like me. Then he might become a monster, too. That would be his choice, and I would not take his choices from him.

That reminded me that I needed to visit Jane again.

14. VISITING

Helen finally invited me to meet her family. I mean I'd been in her house several times, but either her parents hadn't been home or had been making themselves scarce. This time, Helen said she would introduce me. Also, her brother Julio was back from college, and his girlfriend Nabila was "visiting." I would get to meet them as well.

"Are you jealous that Julio gets to spend eternity going to college, but you're stuck in high school?" I asked Helen.

She laughed. "I don't spend 'eternity' in school! This is only my fifth time in high school. Most of the time, I'm pretending to be older than I'm pretending now."

"You're not really seventeen, like me? I thought that's when you said you were changed?"

"I stopped aging, not counting. I'm closer to one hundred and seventeen." I tried to absorb that. I knew it intellectually, but I didn't really feel it. I mean, she looked like a girl. Helen continued, "I usually live a few years with my parents after finishing school and then go off on my own for a decade or two. I've been a teacher, a nurse, a doctor and a salesperson." Helen's eyes twinkled when she added, "I was really good at sales."

"Wait, so you were a teacher and a doctor? Is that why you're such a good tutor? And could fix my arm?"

"Yes, I taught math for nine years, and I was a small-town general practitioner for a while."

"Cool, but I don't get it. If you don't have to be stuck in high school, why would you go? You're not really learning anything."

"I'm making connections, establishing myself in a community. You see, I can look much older by wearing different clothes and acting like an adult. But if I stay in a place for ten years where I started out claiming to be 30, well people are going to start to notice that I don't really look 40."

I was having a hard time picturing her even looking 30.

Helen seemed amused. "I've listened to a lot of envious thoughts from middle-aged friends. 'How does she do it?' 'What's her secret?' No one guesses the truth because no one really doubts my age. They all remember going to high school with me twenty years earlier."

"That can't work forever."

"No, late thirties is really my limit. After that, people start thinking it's uncanny. And my parents can't come visit me after a while because people would expect them to look much older than they do. If I want to see them, I have to go to them."

"Do you?"

"I do. Maybe it's because I've played the role so long, but part of me truly feels like they're my parents, and I'm their girl."

"You feel like a girl, you said. Is that why you can relate to someone like me?"

"Yes, and also..." She bit her lip and censored herself. I raised my eyebrows quizzically. She shrugged and said, "I see your potential. You know how parents fuss over babies, but young children think they're useless. It's because parents know that babies become people."

"So I'm a baby to you?" That hurt. Her face fell at my expression.

"See I was afraid you'd misunderstand. No, what I'm saying is that I already see the man you will become. That's what I see when I look at you right now."

"Oh." That was less painful. "I'd like to meet your parents."

A couple days later, Helen brought me over to her house. Victor and Marisol met me in the living room. Victor had the air of a distinguished Latin gentleman in his late fifties. He stood a slender six feet tall. Both his combed-back hair and his goatee were streaked with grey. His wife, Marisol, looked much younger, maybe late thirties. She didn't look like she'd ever been the beauty Helen was; her features were too strong for that. It was she who offered me a drink and served some finger food.

"It's with much pleasure I finally meet you, Alex," said Marisol.

"We know Helen has told you everything, so we don't need to pretend with you," said Victor. "We're as much her friends as we are her parents, and I can tell you that I've never seen her as happy as she has been since she met you. I'm glad for her."

"Thank you, sir."

Marisol added, "Helen's transition to this life was very difficult for her to accept, not like when I shared my spirit with Victor." Startled, I realized the Marisol was the oldest person in the room, that it was she who made Victor. "Since Helen has met you, I've seen more than acceptance in her. She has joy. Thank you for that, Alex." I was a little embarrassed and didn't know what to say. I think Helen rescued me by saying something funny.

After that, the conversation turned less personal. I learned that Victor and Marisol both worked as corporate representatives. They had large territories and often had to travel. I supposed that made hunting easy for them, but I didn't say anything about it. Helen had told me that none of her family killed to drink, at least not any more, but it didn't seem like an appropriate topic of conversation.

Julio and Nabila came down and joined us. Julio was a powerfully built, handsome young man of about my height, who looked like he was in his mid-twenties. I asked him if he played sports in college, and he laughed and said, "No, I'm always being recruited, and I always say no. I'm too good."

"Couldn't you throw a few games? Hold back a little?" I said.

"Nah, ain't gonna do it. If I play, I win, and I'm not supposed to draw that kind of attention to myself."

"That's my job. I draw attention to him," said Nabila. I saw that was no lie. If Helen was beautiful, Nabila was striking. She was at least two inches taller than Julio, proud cheekbones and glossy black skin. She wore her hair in a natural Afro with a pretty printed scarf worn as a headband. Her wide nose had a gold nose ring, and her teeth flashed white.

"Believe it or not," said Julio, "She can look like that on a college campus, and she fits right in these days."

"We both go to the University of Pennsylvania," Nabila explained.

"I wouldn't have been able to get in, it's so selective, but I've had Nabila tutoring me for the last sixty years."

Nabila just smiled and said, "It's nice to be able to go to the same school."

"How'd you meet?" I asked.

Julio got excited. "Oh, that's a great story. We were both hunting, and we accidently hunted each other! I didn't realize she was a vampire, see, 'cause I haven't got 'the eye' like Helen. Also, 'cause I'm not that bright. She don't have that excuse."

"I only saw your uniform," said Nabila.

"Yeah, vampires can't really serve in the army. Too many restrictions, gotta follow orders. How can you drink blood or get underground? Anyway, I was in North Africa in 1942 pretending to be in the army. It was better than hanging around in the United States and having everyone wonder why I wasn't serving. Also, I could drink people dry and everyone just blamed the missing on the war."

Julio seemed to remember his audience, and gave me an apologetic glance. "I don't do that no more, Alex. I was in a sorry state in 1942. I was so sick of my life I didn't care about anyone else's. Truth is, I was looking to die."

"You nearly did before I realized the soldier I'd lured to my room was really a vampire," said Nabila. "When I discovered my mistake, I was angry, but Julio just laughed. I almost killed him again, but he won me over to laughter."

"I did!" Julio bragged.

Nabila smiled at him. "We got along so well, we started hunting together. But we didn't feel like killing any more. We traded our own blood, even though we didn't have to because we're both vampires already."

Nabila turned back to me. "I loved Julio's spirit, and now we both share each other's spirits. 'Love is lak de sea. It's uh movin' thing, but still an all, it takes its shape from de shore it meets, and it's different with every shore.' Julio's sure right for me."

"Nabila, why do you sometimes talk like an American black person if you grew up in Africa?" She looked at me like I was crazy. I tried to explain. "You know, dropping 'g's, saying 'shore' instead of 'sure.' I mean, you're not from the South or the ghetto, so where did you pick that up?"

Nabila looked angry. "Mr. White Boyfriend, you're so ignorant, you aren't worth the time." She started to walk away. Then she turned back. "No, Helen says you're smart, so let me educate you. I didn't learn that bit of Ebonics from my mama but from a book. That's Zora Neal Hurston, I was quoting, and 'shore' was a pun. You hear me, wannabe college boy? English may be my fourth language, but I've been a white man's maid in D.C., in West Philadelphia and on the South side of Chicago. That real enough for you? You listening good? I'll talk any damn way I want."

Angry Nabila was really scary. I hoped Helen wouldn't be too mad at me for pissing off her once-and-future sister-in-law. "Yes, ma'am," I said.

Nabila looked closely at me, considering my tone. I think I had sounded appropriately terrified because she approved. "Good. You treat Helen right, you show me proper respect, and we'll get along fine." She turned to Julio and said, "When you're finished with that coffee, you better put the cup in the dishwasher." Then she left.

I turned to Helen. "I'm sorry I made your sister mad. I really didn't mean to."

Julio laughed. "That isn't mad. You haven't seen Nabila mad. In fact, I think she really likes you."

My eyebrows went up.

"Because she explained herself. Anyway, part of that was on me."

My eyebrows stayed up.

"See, Alex, I brought Nabila home to the United States after the war was over. In those days, an interracial couple was breaking the law in sixteen states down South, so we didn't live there of course. But even in the North where it was legal, people woulda noticed an interracial couple."

"People still do," I said, thinking of my grandma.

"It's not as bad now. Back then, it was practically screaming for unwanted attention, from both humans and vampires. I persuaded Nabila to pretend to be my maid—I'm the 'white man' she was talking about a moment ago. We lived in D.C. at first, and that was bad. We tried Philadelphia and then Chicago."

Julio seemed to be lost in recollection. Then, he went on, "Nabila's a proud woman, and it hurt her worse and worse to pretend to serve me. She understood it was necessary at first, but after the Supreme Court struck down the anti-miscegenation laws, she thought we could live openly as man and wife. I didn't agree and made her pretend for decades when she thought it wasn't necessary. She blames me, saying my liking for being served swayed my judgment. Sometime in the 1990s, I came around to her way of thinking, but these days she's not going to put a coffee cup in the dishwasher. So, some of that attitude you got was really backlash aimed at me."

I thought about my grandmother again, and I wasn't completely sure Julio and Nabila hadn't jumped the gun twenty years ago. I tried to apologize. "I'm sorry I stirred up old business. I really want her to like me."

"You didn't stir anything up," said Julio. "I told you she ain't angry. When she's angry for real, you'll know it. She's not resentful with the coffee cups. She's just reminding me that she's put ten thousand of my coffee cups in the dishwasher because she loves me that much. We are the center of each other's lives."

Julio patted my back. "Be careful there, Alex. With my sister, it's gonna be the same way: mate for life. One way or the other." He walked away.

"Whose life? Hers or mine?" I said to his back. He laughed.

"She said you was smart," he said without turning around.

Helen looked at me. "Well, that could have gone better."

"I'm sorry."

"It's not just you, I meant." She looked pensive. "I noticed my family all mentioned how they were created. I think they assume I'm going to make you like me."

"I'm not ready for that."

"I know, but I can see they've got you thinking about it." I couldn't deny it, so I stayed silent. "Alex, I think maybe the time has come to tell you about the worst day of my immortal life. I don't like to think about it, and I don't want to change the way you look at me." She swallowed. "But if you're even thinking about becoming like me, you need to know the consequences."

She squared her shoulders and beckoned with her hand. "Let's have this conversation in the basement. I'm going to need strength."

I wanted my family to welcome Alex, and I was glad my parents and Julio were trying to make a good impression, but really! It was all I could do not to tell them to shut up about sharing the spirit. Did they really think Alex and I were ready for that? They made it sound like it's always a love story. Alex needed to know the truth.

15. PAST

Helen's basement was incredible. Most of my friends with Victorian houses had nasty, dank basements, but this was a beautiful space, comfortably decorated. There were big comfy chairs and couches, a bathroom with a shower, and even a fridge with variety of snacks and beverages (no blood, thank goodness). The air smelled fresh and clean. The only unpleasant thing was the smell that proclaimed everything was new.

"This place is awesome."

Helen smiled. "My father redid it when we moved in. We spend a lot of time here, of course. It's much nicer than when I lived here before."

That reminded me of how long she had lived and how little I understood about her and her family. "When Julio was telling his story, he called himself a white man. I noticed that he and your parents all have lighter skin than you do. Why is that?" Suddenly, I was embarrassed. Maybe she was sensitive about race. "I'm sorry. I didn't mean to be rude."

"That's fine. I seem to remember my asking you a personal question or two."

I turned red, remembering. "Okay, but even if you answer mine, you still owe me because your question was way more personal."

Helen's eyes twinkled. "I'll have to find some other way to make it up to you then." She looked at the backs of her hands, and said, "I'm a little darker than both my parents and Julio because they have more Spanish ancestry than I do. I have more Native American blood. In biological families, that can happen by the roll of the genetic dice, but Julio and I were adopted."

"Who were your biological parents?"

"My father was a wealthy executive who worked for a company that mined silver. We lived in Morelia, which is a beautiful old, colonial city in Western Mexico. I'd love to take you there someday."

"I'd love to see it."

"We had a lovely house, with a small staff of servants. My father was a member of the elite—and he was white, with all European ancestors. My human life was a good life, and I was lucky—at least until I was seventeen."

"Your biological mother was Native American then?"

"Yes, I think so, but the picture you have in your head is not right. She didn't wear skins or live in a teepee." She giggled.

"Helen, no fair! You can't bust a guy for racism when he didn't say anything aloud." I heard myself say that and cringed. "Okay, maybe that's totally fair. Sorry. I'll try to think better thoughts."

"Hm, maybe I'd better be careful about replying to your thoughts. Besides making you self-conscious, I don't want to get into bad habits for when we're in public. Anyway, I think my biological mother was Mayan or Aztec or something. I don't really know as I never met her."

"She died when you were young?"

"No, she was my father's mistress. For some reason, he decided to raise me in his own household when I was too young to remember. His wife raised me along with her own four children."

"How'd he get his wife to accept that arrangement?"

"I have no idea. I couldn't read minds, then. He was rich, so maybe that's part of it. But Mama was always Mama to me. She treated me exactly as she did her own children. She loved me, and I loved her back."

"Wow!"

"I told you I was lucky. I think it helped that I was so beautiful. And Mama was a graceful and loving woman. I loved her, and that helped her to love me. Or, maybe it was the other way around.

"It was Mama who took me to the cathedral and taught me to love God. I was truly blessed and happy, even if I didn't always appreciate it, until I met the one who changed me."

I remembered that Helen told me she had been forced to drink that vampire's blood, and his evil spirit had passed to her. I realized I didn't really know what that meant. "You didn't really tell me very much about how you changed. What happened?"

"Ah, well, I don't like to talk about that much. It's an ugly story, but maybe you need to hear it before you romanticize vampires too much."

"Too late for that: I've already met you."

"Stop flirting and listen to my story."

"Okay." I'd really rather flirt than hear an ugly story about bad things happening to Helen, but I got the feeling she needed me to hear this.

"When I was seventeen, I was happy and loved, carefree and beautiful."

"Really? What's that like?" I never knew any girl my age who felt like that.

Helen laughed. "Maybe I didn't feel that way at the time."

She continued, "I went to a dance where I met a young man who flattered me and made me feel special. We looked terrific together on the dance floor: he in a tight black suit and I in a daring red dress. It made me excited. When he suggested that I come back to his room, I was ready to rebel against my parents and do it. I was a good Catholic girl, but I was so young and naive, I thought he merely wanted to kiss me.

"It was only a short walk through the streets to his room. He was staying in a basement apartment of a town house. We walked several steps down from the street and entered. Once inside, he lit a candle. I thought it was very romantic. Then, he said that his spirit was a strong one. It had never been shared, and he had chosen me, to give it to me. I didn't know what he meant, but I didn't object when he came close to me and put his hand on the back of my neck."

Helen paused for a moment.

I sensed the story was about to take a turn for the worse. "Helen, you don't need to tell me this." I wasn't sure I wanted to hear what happened next.

"No, I think I *do* need to tell you." Helen looked determined but tense. "You need to know why I call him the monster."

"He cut my neck with his teeth, and it really hurt. When I tried to scream, he put his other hand over my mouth. Between his two hands, I couldn't move at all. I could feel him licking and heard his slurping, but I couldn't move my head to see what he was doing. It was painful and terrifying because I couldn't move and could barely breathe."

Helen was shaking her head at the memory. "He didn't have to cause me pain or hold his hand over my mouth. His teeth had anesthetic, and he must have had 'the eye'—because I do. He just didn't care."

"What do you mean, he must have had 'the eye'?"

Helen explained, "Vampire gifts come of the evil spirit within us. He gave me his, so I have the same one. His spirit is now my spirit." She said it with a heartbreakingly resigned sadness.

"I don't understand. You don't mean you're like him?" I rejected the whole idea, angrily. "You're nothing like him!"

"I don't give it free rein the way he did, but I have exactly the same evil spirit in me as he had in him," she insisted. I didn't believe her, but I closed my mouth and didn't argue.

Helen ignored my skepticism and continued. "After he finished drinking, he pushed me down onto the floor. With one hand still on my mouth, he took his other hand and cut his wrist with his teeth. He said, 'Drink.' He forced my mouth open, but I still couldn't scream because he was making me drink his blood. I was so disgusted, I couldn't imagine anything more degrading than what he was making me do. Then, I felt myself start to change, and he said, 'I pass my spirit unto you.' He kept feeding me his blood until I passed out."

Helen shook her head. "I woke up with Victor and Marisol. Apparently, he had left me unconscious on their stoop, my red dress stained with blood. They took me in and explained everything to me. I would never again see Mama or Papa, but they adopted me, and now they are my mother and father. Sometimes I live with them as their girl. After a while, they go about their own lives, and I live mine for a decade or two. We always come back together. Eventually Julio joined us, and later Nabila. That's the way it's been for seventy years now."

"Did you ever see him again?"

"The monster? No. He passed his spirit to me."

I looked at her blankly.

"Drinking vampire blood turns humans into vampires only briefly. Then they die. What makes a vampire immortal is the evil spirit inside us. The monster wanted to die, so he gave his evil spirit to me. Then, he died, and I am the monster now."

"It wasn't your fault," I objected. "You can't blame yourself for what he did."

"That's why this's only my second worst nightmare," said Helen. "My worst nightmare isn't about what the monster did to me. It's about when I became the monster."

I shook my head, denying that possibility. I knew Helen's heart was a good one. She could never be a monster.

Helen's expression was bleak. "It was decades back when I was living in Mexico again. I had chosen to live in Zinapécuaro, a city not too far away from my original home in Morelia. I liked to walk the streets up the hillside to where there was a statue of Jesus and you could see the whole city with flat roofs of terracotta bathed in sunlight."

"What's terracotta?" I interrupted. I'd heard the word before, but I couldn't remember what it was, and it certainly didn't seem like anything I associated with roofs.

Helen smiled. "Reddish brown clay, like flowerpots or bricks. The roofs are made of overlapping tiles shaped like half pipes."

Oh, I'd seen that on houses in sunnier places. I nodded my understanding.

Helen continued. "One afternoon, I was walking home when I turned a corner and practically ran into a young couple with a baby in a carriage." She closed her eyes briefly and then steeled herself. "We all rocked back on our heels, finding ourselves so unexpectedly close. I looked into the man's face, only inches from mine, and saw a sudden look of horrified recognition in his eyes. Somehow, he knew exactly what I was. He shouted: '*Vampíro, voy a matarte.*'"

"What does that mean?" I asked. I didn't know Spanish and heard only the fury in her voice. I wondered if she had unconsciously mimicked the man's cry in her memory.

"Oh, sorry," she said. "It means 'Vampire, I'm going to kill you.'"

She continued, "Before I could react, he punched me. I was not surprised by the hatred—of course he hated me, given what he knew—but the force of his blow surprised me. Briefly I glimpsed a pattern of scars on the back of his hand before it connected with my face and broke my cheekbone. I hit the street hard with the back of my head."

I winced at that, but I found the sight of Helen's obviously perfect face reassuring. She must've magically healed. "What do you think the scars on his hand were?" I asked.

She considered. "Probably magic. I saw a similar pattern on the locks of Brubacher's church, and I couldn't get past the door."

I was distracted. "Mennonites can do magic?"

Helen shook her head. "No, I don't think so, not any more than anyone else. I think the minister back then—or maybe it was Brubacher—attracted the attention of the Order of St. Michael. They must've put protections on the church."

"Oh."

"I'm hoping it was the minister from before because otherwise we may still get a visit from the order."

"You're not still worried about that, are you? It's been over a month." It didn't make sense to me. Surely vampires merited a quick response. Otherwise, they'd be long gone. Or maybe they wouldn't. Helen's family seemed to stay in the same place for years.

"You're assuming they were sure. They may get a lot of false reports. They may have a backlog. Alex, if they do come, my family may have to disappear."

I hated that idea. "Will you take me with you?"

"No, and don't come looking for us. It won't be safe. Don't do anything to reveal your connection to us or that you know anything." She looked at me sternly.

I was getting anxious. "I can't just not see you again." I didn't want to picture my life empty of Helen.

She looked into my eyes and seemed to understand. Of course, she did, I thought sourly. She said, "Don't worry. I promise that if that happens, I'll wait until it's safe and get you a message. I'll give you some way to contact me, okay?"

I nodded, and she gave me a hug. I felt my tension drain.

Helen sat back. "Let me finish my story. You need to hear this. Maybe afterwards, you won't be so keen on vampires."

I shook my head. Never. Not if that vampire was Helen. Anyway, she certainly hadn't told me anything disturbing yet. I prompted her. "The man was beating you with his magic hand. Broke your face."

"Yes," she agreed. "He certainly had magic. Anyway, I levered myself off the ground and came at him with my hands and teeth. He deflected me though. It was like my strength was gone when he hit me. He began raining body blows on my torso like a prizefighter. I felt my ribs crack and a sharp pain on the right side of my chest." She showed me with her hands on herself.

"In that desperate moment, I wasn't sure I could win this fight, but I *had* to win. Who knew how much trouble he could cause knowing what he knew? I moved quickly and wrenched a metal rod out of the carriage. Apparently, unless he was touching me with his hands, my strength was unaffected by whatever magic he had. The metal rod was about as long as my arm and jagged at the end. I dove forward and thrust it up under his rib cage and into his heart. We both stood still for a moment, and then his body slumped to the ground."

Helen described it with a quiet ferocity. I didn't understand why she was so upset. "Helen, you had to kill him in self defense. He attacked you. That's not even murder."

"Maybe not, but what about his wife? It was her scream that reminded me. She had started screaming when I had grabbed the rod and the carriage fell, dropping her baby onto the street. I had to kill her too. I've told you about vampire law, so it was either her life or mine."

"What did you do?"

"I made the conventional choice: I chose me." Helen said it as though she wasn't sure it was the right choice.

"How?" Did I really want to know this?

"I grabbed her arms at the elbows and looked deep into her eyes. 'Feel no pain,' I whispered. Then—Alex, it wasn't pretty—I savaged her neck with my fangs, cutting her carotids in the process. My body craved her blood, both to nourish the evil spirit that would heal me and to provide substance for the flesh to be repaired. I drank the arterial spout in great sloppy gulps, as never before or since, getting blood all over my face and clothes. I drank and drank until the blood stopped coming because her heart had stopped beating."

I was horrified. She'd painted a picture with her words, but I was having trouble imagining Helen doing this. Maybe I just didn't want to believe her.

"I hated myself in that moment."

"Why?" I asked. I thought I knew why, but I didn't want to believe it.

"Because the murders and the viciousness of my attack confirmed my worst fears about myself. The mess I'd made disgusted me. Worse, I felt the blood doing me good, repairing my ribs, my shortness of breath and my broken cheek. It took time to heal completely, but already in that moment I felt strong, vibrant and vital. I never felt like that after my usual pint of blood. I could see why some vampires choose to drink their victims dry, and I hated that I understood them because I felt sure that I could not have done so if some part of me had not been just like them."

That was worse than I thought but not entirely unjustified. "I don't think so. You were trying to save the lives of your family and yourself. You were injured. You weren't doing it for pleasure."

"Thank you." She paused and took a breath. "Anyway, I got up from the body of the wife, full of hastily made plans for getting the bodies out of sight. I could close the man's jacket over his chest wound, stage him with an empty liquor bottle from the gutter, and bundle the woman and baby's bodies to take in search of a drainage pipe or trash heap. That would serve until night. I would also have to clean the blood of the woman from the street and hide the broken carriage. I went to get the baby's body."

Helen's voice rose in agitation. She was wringing her hands. "I can't talk about the baby! Please don't make me talk about the baby." She was pleading with me.

"Okay, okay," I said miserably. "You don't need to say any more." I guessed I understood. Helen calmed down a bit.

"Then I went home to my parents under cover of darkness. They saw the blood on my clothes, so when I said, 'Help me,' they came without question, and my father brought three shovels. We buried them on the hills outside of town. The soil was rocky, and the shovel twisted in my hand until I learned the trick of using the tip to lever each rock out of the dirt until everything was loose. I have never forgotten their faces."

Helen looked me right in the eyes. "Alex, this is my worst nightmare. This is what I try not to think about. This is why I call myself a monster."

It was an ugly story, but she didn't have any good choices. The girl I knew was good. "You are not a monster," I said.

Helen looked skeptical. What could I say to convince her of my faith?

"Drink from me."

"What?" Helen was shocked.

"Drink from me. What you asked me on Christmas? That's my answer. I want you to drink from me." I was sure it was the right thing to say.

I saw Helen's expression change from surprise to thoughtfulness. "Alex, if you can hear all that and still... Well, okay, maybe. Let's give it a month. If you still feel that way, I'll take you to the mine some afternoon."

"Why the mine?" It'd be a lot easier, and probably more comfortable in her room, I thought.

Helen squirmed a bit. "Well, it's underground, of course. And I don't think my parents would approve of me drinking blood in the house."

For some reason, that struck me as funny, and I laughed and laughed. Eventually, Helen joined in, but she might've been laughing at me.

Somehow, telling Alex my nightmares was easier than I expected. Perhaps it was because I'd been thinking about them so much recently that I was used to the horror. Perhaps it was because Alex didn't seem that horrified. I worried he was so smitten with me that I'd corrupted his judgment as well as his innocence.

But some of what he said made sense. Though I have the monster's evil spirit, I don't let it make me into him. It was self defense when I killed the man. I'm truly sorry for the woman, but my choice did save my parents, as well as Julio and Nabila. I didn't know enough to know whether I should blame myself for the baby.

Alex's offer to let me drink from him astonished me. Even given what I'd just told him, his faith in me remained unshakeable. Maybe I should have more faith in myself.

16. CONSENT

Helen led me to the mine entrance, and we chatted amiably as always, as though nothing special were about to happen. Helen wore a backpack, and I was pretty sure she wasn't packing textbooks and homework inside, but I didn't want to ask her what she was carrying. I figured I might not want to know.

When we got to the concrete seal of the shaft, Helen did her usual trick opening it, and we slipped inside. She turned on a flashlight and gave me another. It was less cold inside than it was outside, so our winter coats were keeping us plenty warm as we walked. Once we got to the bend in the tunnel, she said, "This is far enough. Go ahead and sit down."

"All right. How do you want to do this?"

"I've thought about that, but first I need you to say that I have your full and free consent to drink from you."

"You do. That's why we're here."

"Alex, you understand that you don't have to let me do this? I'll still be your girlfriend if you don't. I'm not pressuring you, right? You want to do this?"

"If I don't, you'll go to Philadelphia and drink from some other guy, right? His blood will be inside you, not mine?"

"I need to drink, yes. I could agree to drink from a woman if that made you feel better."

Strangely, it *did* make me feel much better to imagine that. I knew it shouldn't matter, that drinking blood was like eating for her. She was not cheating on me by going to Philadelphia. I realized I hadn't been being fair to her in my thoughts. I bit my lip. "But you want to drink from me, right? Not some stranger?"

"Yes, I want that, very much."

"Then, that's what I want also," I decided.

"In that case, here's how I want to do it. I'm going to drink from a blood vessel under your arm near your armpit. Don't look so shocked. I don't want to cut you somewhere visible. If anyone sees the incision, you can say you were trying to climb a chain-link fence and you slipped and cut yourself. If they ask why you didn't get help, you can say that you knew you weren't supposed to be climbing the fence." Helen had clearly thought this through. She continued, "Anyway take off your shirt, and wrap this blanket around you." She took a blanket out of the backpack. I took off my shirt and wrapped the blanket around me. "When I'm done drinking, I brought these wipes to clean up, and this antiseptic and bandages for your incision." She produced a small first aid kit.

"Okay," I said a little nervous.

She looked a little nervous, too. She took off her jacket and started to unbutton her blouse. "Fair is fair, so I'll take off my shirt, too—just my shirt. Let's cuddle up together."

Wow, I thought, right before my brain crashed. Once I'd rebooted, I said, "If I'd known you were going to do that, I'd have begged you to drink my blood weeks ago."

"That's exactly why I did *not* tell you. I didn't want this to be a *quid pro quo*. I don't want to be taking advantage of your desire for me. I'm hoping we both might enjoy this."

She took off her shirt, but she left her bra on, so maybe this was not my dream completely come true. She curled up with me under the blanket, and we kissed and snuggled for a bit. I'd never touched a girl like this before, and I couldn't believe the effect it was having on me. My senses were overloading. It must have made me stupid because I didn't filter the next thought that came into to my head.

"Helen, why don't you shave under your arms?"

She tensed up. "I forget what a modern boy you are. Does it disgust you?" She tried to move her arm from around me, but I held her hand, so she couldn't.

"No, I'm sorry. I didn't mean it like that. There's not very much, anyway." I was kicking myself for saying anything.

"That'll be the Native American in me. We're not very hairy, except on our heads." She sounded really self-conscious.

"Helen, I'm sorry. I like the hair on your body just fine. I was just surprised." It was true, but I didn't think she'd believe me. I tried to explain. "It doesn't seem to fit your image. You are friends with cheerleaders and prom queens. I would think they might tease you for being too natural."

Helen sniffed. "No, Alex, they don't tease me. Sometimes I fall victim to a friend's makeover plan, but I try to avoid it. I will shave my armpits and legs sometimes for a dance or something like that, but mostly I don't shave at all and wear concealing sleeves and dark tights." I realized that I had seen her wear these things without knowing why she was doing it.

"I don't have much of choice about body hair. When I was turned into a vampire, times were different. In those days, Mexican girls all wore full-length skirts and long sleeved blouses. No one shaved. The spirit that keeps me immortal tries to keep me as I was. It heals my flesh very quickly. Hair, it takes more time on, almost as if it's undecided how important it is. However, it all grows back within several days to exactly what it was when I was turned. I don't usually do anything about it because it's a huge pain to keep it up."

This was fascinating, but it didn't make sense. "I don't understand. Your mom cut your hair short in November, and you've been letting it grow back ever since."

"My mom cut my hair in November, and she's cut it every day since. She lets it be a little bit longer each day. It'll take a half hour out of every morning for another couple years before we can leave off."

I just stared at her. I'd heard girls complain about the time it took to get ready in the morning, but this seemed excessive. I made a face. She giggled a bit at my reaction, and then she sighed.

"My parents thought it was that important that I not look like Elias Brubacher's photograph. Now that the photograph's been destroyed, I'm really wishing they hadn't insisted on the haircut." She sounded rueful.

"I had no idea." I shook my head. I really should expect the unexpected from my vampire girlfriend, but I'd never once thought about hair.

"That's the general idea. It's much easier to let people think I prefer to be hairy than to conform to fashion and risk someone noticing shaved or cut hair that reappears as if by magic." I ran my hand over her head and realized that this hair would all be longer tomorrow morning—until she cut it again.

Helen felt a little stiff when I returned my hand to where it had been before. She laughed nervously, "I'm sorry, but you've made me a little self-conscious about my appearance. Now that you've found out my little flaw, I'm afraid that you are disappointed. I am trying to imagine myself doing all the work it would take to keep myself clean-shaven, and I am really not relishing the prospect. I'm not sure I'm willing even for you."

"Helen, you *are* perfect." She was not looking at me.

"It's sweet of you to say that." She clearly didn't believe me, and she wasn't making eye contact.

"No, I'm serious. I like your body hair." As soon as that came out my mouth, I was embarrassed to hear that it sounded a little too fetish-y.

"That's sweet of you to say, but it's a little hard to believe. If it's true, you're a little weird." Not as weird as you, vampire girl, I thought. She still wasn't looking at me. She asked, "Don't all guys these days want their girlfriends shaved everywhere but the tops of their heads?"

"I don't know. Not me." I tried to explain how I felt. "If you want to shave for a particular outfit once in a while, sure that could look nice. However, these tiny hairs on your forearms and the fuzz on your stomach and the nape of your neck—they're all beautiful to me. I would never want you shave them."

Helen was shaking her head in disbelief, still not looking at me, "You are so cute when you are trying to be nice to me. Weird but cute." She had a little half smile.

"I'm serious. When we first started dating, I thought you were like my own supermodel girlfriend." She looked at me and shook her head.

"You should stop while you're ahead," Helen warned.

But I wasn't trying to flatter her or insult her. I was trying to explain. "Supermodels aren't real girls to me. Sure, they look nice on a magazine cover, all glossy skin and perfectly angled cheekbones, but I want a real girl with curves I can touch." Helen was looking into my eyes now, fascinated. "I don't want someone who is all skin and bones—all shaved, painted, Photoshopped, plastic-looking skin and bones—who exists only in a photograph. Your curves and the hair on your skin are sexy to me because they mean you're a real girl with curves that can be touched. That's exactly what I want." Helen looked astonished but no longer doubtful. I wanted her to smile again, so I tried, "Plus, huge bonus for me, you're my girlfriend, and right now I'm touching you." She laughed.

"Thank you," she said.

"I believe the words you are looking for are 'you're welcome.'"

She got a big smile. "You are." She relaxed, and then she kissed me.

After a few minutes, she asked, "Are you ready to do this?"

I didn't feel entirely sure, but I'd already agreed, so it was time to deliver. I tried to sound confident. "Yes, I'm completely ready."

Helen contorted herself around so that her top teeth could clamp on the underside of my upper left arm. She used one of her sharp canines to prick my skin. She must have used the anesthetic she promised back at Christmas because the area went a little numb, and then I felt a tugging as she punctured the skin and blood vessel. I thought to myself: don't look, don't look and you really don't want to look. Then, of course I looked.

It was pretty disgusting. I could tell that Helen was trying to drink from me as neatly as possible. She had her lips locked tight around my skin, sucking. However, she had to swallow periodically, and whenever she did a little blood would escape past her lips and get smeared around on my arm and her face. It was making a mess despite her efforts, and the whole thing was making me grossed out and a little queasy in my stomach. I wasn't sure that it had been such a good idea when Helen told me to eat beforehand.

The whole thing lasted a little while. Afterwards Helen sat up and wiped me off with the wipes from the backpack. First she wiped the wound on my arm. Once it was clean I could see that it wasn't much bigger than the hole the needle makes when the doctor takes blood for a test. Helen took a disinfectant wipe from the first aid kit and wiped the area again. Then she clamped a gauze pad down on it and used surgical tape to keep it in place. Only once she was done did she use the wipes to clean the blood from her face.

I was worried by the serious expression of concentration she wore throughout this whole procedure. Was she sad for some reason? Was my blood not good? At this point, I wasn't sure if it would be more farce or tragedy if it turned out that my blood had a revolting taste. She had tasted it before in my basement once, so that couldn't be it, could it? I was sure I had stayed away from garlic.

"Here, drink this," Helen said, handing me a juice box. "I drunk about a pint, the same as a Red Cross donation. This might help you from getting dizzy. Don't stand up right away either."

Then, a much more terrible thought occurred to me. What if Helen was like one of those guys who go around seducing inexperience virgins with lots of attention, all of which suddenly ceases as soon as they get their way? I worried that the next thing Helen might do was look me in the eyes and tell me to forget everything, even my broken heart. I avoided eye contact.

"I'm suddenly feeling very sleepy. I'm not sure why. I don't usually react to blood this way. Anyway, I think I'm going to curl up here in the mine instead of going home. You don't need to worry about leaving me here; you know I can protect myself, not that I'm likely to be disturbed. My parents know I might stay out all night. Anyway, as soon as you're sure you're not dizzy, you can put your shirt back on and go home. I always leave the seal cracked when you're in here with me, to keep the oxygen flowing through the vent that serves this spot. Here's the key to my car. You can leave it at my parents' house."

I took a moment to appreciate how much more thought and organization Helen had put into this expedition than I had. I hadn't even considered the possibility of suffocating in the mine. Still, she wasn't reassuring me.

"You're sending me away?" I tried to keep the hurt from my tone.

"I just thought you wouldn't want to get in trouble with your parents for missing dinner, and it'll start to feel cold for you here in the mines. You're certainly welcome to stay, but I may sleep until morning. I'm half asleep already."

The whole experience was all suddenly too much for me. Shirtless and bandaged, having just watched Helen drink sixteen ounces of my blood and completely insecure of her feelings for me, I felt so vulnerable it was all I could do to keep from bursting into tears. I didn't want to walk back down the tunnel in the late afternoon dark alone, find my way to Helen's car—which I'd never driven—and navigate back to her house. I realized how much I'd let Helen do for me and felt like an incompetent child. She was more than a century older than I was, and I worried that I must seem like a child to her. Why would she want me for a companion—except for the blood I had just given her? Was this all a clever manipulation? Tonight I'd practically begged her to do exactly what she'd forced me to do when I hit my head in the basement. Did she really care about me at all?

"Was I good?" I couldn't stop the trembling in my voice. Would I ever learn to stop asking questions for which I lacked the courage to face the answers?

"Alex, what's wrong?" Helen sounded really concerned. "Look at me." I refused to look. I was afraid to replace pain and uncertainty with the certainty of oblivion.

"I'm afraid my blood was a disappointment to you. After all this anticipation, you feel let down, and that's why you're sending me away."

"Oh, Alex, no!" she said, sounding distressed. "Drinking your blood was the best experience I've ever had. I can't even begin to describe it—because you've no frame of reference. Maybe, well, it's like I've been surviving on morsels of stolen stale bread and sips of tepid water, and you're a whole Thanksgiving dinner. If I'm sleepy, it's only because I'm intoxicated with rich wine."

"I didn't drink anything tonight," I said sullenly.

"I know. Alcohol in the blood tastes disgusting. Sometimes I've staggered away from my victims because of the amount of alcohol in their blood. Fortunately the spirit heals me of the poison quickly enough. I only meant I'm overwhelmed by the intoxicating feeling of joy and satisfaction your blood gave me. I drank only what I usually do, but already I'm full beyond my capacity. I'm practically ready to pass out."

"I'm glad it was good." I wanted it to be good. I wanted her to care about me like I cared about her. Then I wanted my blood to be good, so I could let her drink it to show her how much I cared.

"Look at me," she said, grabbing my chin. She easily forced my head around, and looked into my eyes, now brimming with tears. I was ashamed of myself. I'd asked for this, so why was I fussing?

"You're crying," she said, horrified. Then she stared at me intently for a moment, and suddenly huffed, frustrated. "I can't read you when you're crying," she admitted. She bit her lip. "My dear, dear

Alex. You have it all wrong. I like being with you, just for yourself. I'll never drink your blood again if that will convince you."

"You'd do that for me?"

"I *told* you that before I drank. I told you I'd be your girlfriend no matter what."

I knew that she had. Why was I so insecure? "I guess I had trouble believing that."

"Believe it," she said. "I will never drink from you again if you think that letting me drink is a condition of our relationship."

I processed that. Then, I relaxed with relief. "Then I am truly glad you liked my blood. Drink it whenever you like." My tears had now become ones of joy.

Helen stared at me intently, looking wide-awake no matter what she'd said about being sleepy. "I don't want you leaving me like this. Stay with me for as long as you want. I really must sleep soon, but I don't want you to leave me unless you want to. If you get grounded, we will put a brave face on it. I'll let everyone at school think you had your way with me, and you'll be more popular than ever. I don't want you making some walk of shame down this tunnel. Don't leave me until you're sure that I'll be there for you tomorrow." She yawned, her wakefulness apparently at its limit. "I will be." She said it with her eyes closed, curling up on the floor with me. Then, her face went slack, and she was asleep.

I looked at her apprehensively, feeling intensely but unsure of what I was feeling. My ancient immortal girlfriend, who usually looked seventeen, looked like a small child in the innocence of sleep. At the corner of her mouth was some dried blood of mine that she had failed to wipe (it's not like she had had a mirror). My initial disgust at what we'd done was fading in light of her expressed feelings. If I was a feast after a famine to her, that was no less than what she was to me. I'd been lonely, and she'd offered me friendship. I'd needed help, and she'd not stinted to help me in more ways than I could remember: with school, with friends, with trust, with confidence.

She was beautiful to me. Even though she'd not put her shirt back on and had explicitly authorized me to touch her, I felt only concern that she'd be cold and wanted to wrap her in the blanket. What had muted my outrageous lustful hormones into this tender solicitude? When I tried to put the blanket around her torso, I realized she'd clamped her hand around mine in a tight grip. I had to pry her fingers loose before I could use my hands to cocoon her in the warm fabric.

I consulted my feelings as I watched Helen sleeping. I came to the conclusion that I wasn't in any way disgusted by what she'd done. She said my blood had given her joy and satisfaction, and I earnestly longed to do that for her again. She'd proven to me time and again that she cared for my wellbeing, and while she'd admitted and explained her needs, she hadn't made my fulfilling them a condition of our relationship. I'd done that willingly because I wanted to be as important to her as she was to me.

I had total faith in her promise to be there for me tomorrow. I knew she would be. I felt a moment of pure bliss.

The next moment I felt a white-hot burning rage. If it had been a difficult journey for me to accept what had happened between us, what must it have been like for her when the monster took her blood by force? Even when Helen had taken advantage of my ignorance and licked my wound, I'd trusted her on some level not to go too far. She'd stopped, and my faith had been justified. Now that I knew the bliss of freely giving what had been ripped from her by force, I shook with anger at Helen's maker.

I rejected that notion as soon as I thought it. He hadn't made Helen: Helen had made herself into his opposite. He'd been Helen's nightmare, and now she was my dream. Sustained by my dream, I got up and put my shirt and jacket back on. I walked down the tunnel and felt no fear because I wasn't alone. I'd never be alone. I went home, and that night I slept the happy sleep of those who feel loved.

The Greek gods were said to eat and drink ambrosia and nectar, which made them immortal. The blood of my victims had kept me immortal for over a century, but never seemed like the food of gods—until I drank from Alex. Its effect on me was so powerful that I could barely shake off its intoxicating sleep for long enough to reassure him. Then, I sank into a dream where I held his hand and guided him home. In the dream, his home was paradise, and for the first time in my long life, I felt like I belonged there.

17. CANCER

No one noticed if I was touching my left arm more than usual the next day. No one asked where I'd gone with Helen the day before. Even I didn't care.

A bleary-eyed Simon came and woke me. "You gotta come down, Alex. Mom's completely lost it."

When I went downstairs, I could overhear mom talking on the phone, "...and kids are definitely okay? ...Twelve and seventeen. ...All right. ...When do visiting hours start? ...I'll check with the nurse on the floor." When she hung up, she burst into tears and put her head on Dad's shoulders. "Oh, Joe, I don't know what I'm going to do without her!" She was sobbing, and Dad put down his cup of coffee on the counter to pat her on the back.

"We'll take this as it comes. Sarah, here's Alex."

Mom sniffled and turned around. She looked at my brother over my shoulder and said, "Simon. Clothes. Now!" Then, she turned to me. "Alex, honey, Grandma took a turn for the worse. She's in the hospital, and she's asking to see you children. She's not expected to live more than a few days." When she said that, her voice broke, and tears started down her cheeks. In a moment, she was sobbing again.

Dad said, "Alex, you need to get dressed. We're driving to the hospital."

When we got to the hospital, Mom and Dad went into Grandma's room first, so Simon and I kicked our heels in the waiting room. He started playing games on his phone, which made me angry at first, but then I thought, maybe he just can't deal. I wondered if I should take out my phone, too.

Mom came and got us. She said that Grandma wanted to see the two of us, but they'd just given her morphine, so the visit would have to be short. For Simon, it was. He took one look at Grandma and ran out. I tried to be brave, but I felt like crying. Grandma was lying on a hospital bed, in one of those thin gowns with ties at the side, attached to a whole variety of tubes that I assumed were keeping her alive. They weren't doing a very good job. She looked like she had sunken in on herself. Her skin looked fragile, and she couldn't lift her head.

"Hi, Grandma," I said, and then I choked up.

"I'm so glad you came. I wanted to say goodbye to you." She spoke so easily I could close my eyes and imagine she wasn't sick.

"I don't want you to say goodbye. I don't want you to die." I was nearly in tears.

"It's all right," Grandma said. "Death isn't a tragedy when you're old. I lived a good life with Bob, and I've enjoyed watching my children and grandchildren grow up." She tried to shift herself in bed. I reached over and helped her, but she didn't seem any more comfortable. "I'm proud of you, Alex, and I would've liked to see you graduate and go to college and get married and all that, but I'm sick now and tired. It'll be a blessing when the Lord calls me home. I won't have to bury my children or any more of my friends. I'm ready to go."

Tears streamed down my face. I didn't sob, but I couldn't stop the tears.

Grandma noticed. "I see you're not ready to let me go yet, Alex, but you don't have to. The memory of me will always be with you. At all those important moments in your life where you miss me, I'll be there." Her voice was getting quieter. "You'll hear my voice whispering in your head because my spirit will be inside you. It was like that for me after your grandfather died. He's here now, I think. He's so proud of you. He's glad you have been able to spend so much time with me, keep me company, after he passed..."

She drifted off from the morphine.

We went home that evening and ate a miserable meal of take-out food. In the morning, no one had to tell me that my grandmother had died. I heard my mother's wail of pain from upstairs. I went down the stairs and peeked into the kitchen to see that Dad was standing by the phone, comforting Mom again. I was also hurting, but I didn't want to intrude. I went back upstairs.

No more genealogy with Grandma, or gardening with Grandma, or trips to the graveyard with Grandma, or Christmas with Grandma. I remembered that when I was little and would sleep over at her house, she would read to me and sing a song for me before I went to sleep. I cried.

Simon came upstairs and told me we wouldn't be going to church. Mom and Dad had lots of arrangements to make, so Dad suggested that we stay out of the way until lunch.

I got dressed and went over to Helen's. Her mom answered the door and invited me in. When Helen came down, she took one look at my face and brought me to her room. She sat me down on her bed and held both my hands. "I can tell you've been crying. When I saw that you'd gone, I'd hoped that meant you were okay. I'm so sorry. I won't do this with you if it makes you sad."

Friday afternoon already seemed like such a long time ago to me that it took me a moment to understand what she was talking about. "Oh, no, I'm not crying about that. Friday was good. It made me happy to do that for you. Drink from me any time you like."

Helen sat back. "Wow, that's very accommodating of you. But what's this all about then?"

"My grandmother died last night."

"Your mom's mom, the one I met? I'm so sorry. You seemed really close."

"We were." Helen had her hand on my back, but my chest was still tight. My head hurt. "My mom's a wreck. Dad's helping make arrangements. I don't know what to do."

"I'm here for you, Alex."

"Can you make me forget this pain?"

Helen looked sympathetic, but said, "I won't do that. Your grandmother's part of who you are. If you forget her, you'd lose that part of yourself."

"I don't want to hurt like this."

"I don't want to see you hurting. But grief is something you have to do. Sometimes love is painful. Sometimes it requires a sacrifice. You loved your grandmother, and she deserves your remembrance."

I sobbed a bit. I did love her. Helen was rubbing my back. I turned my face to hers and kissed her. It was a fierce demanding kiss, and she responded by kissing me back. I held her shoulders and leaned her back onto the bed, still kissing her. I wasn't even thinking about what I was doing. Later, I was a little ashamed to realize that I hadn't asked her first, but Helen didn't resist in any way or use any of her great strength to stop me.

Instead, she let me break the kiss when I needed air, and she put her head on my shoulder and quietly said, "Well, that's twice you've surprised me this morning. What's this all about?"

I was breathing heavily and trying to think. Thinking had become hard, and so had other things. "It's about how I feel about you. I—I want to make love to you." I was embarrassed by how audacious a request I had made, and I was both eager and terrified for her answer.

"I want to make love to you, too," Helen said, holding me tightly against her. She had to have felt how excited I was. Then, she gently sat up, so that I sat up, too. "Are you ready for this in here?" She put her hand on my chest over my heart. "Your grandmother just died." I didn't want to think about that. "If you truly need this, I won't deny you any comfort I can provide. We can take off our clothes and get in this bed right now. My parents won't come barging in. But this is not what I had in mind for our first time." Her words were exciting because they were saying "yes," or at least not saying "no." A minute ago that would have been enough. However, I heard in her tone resignation, not enthusiasm, and to my surprise that wasn't enough for me.

Helen went on. "I want it to be special, something we've waited for until we're sure that we're doing the right thing. I know I'm long past ready, but I'm not sure that you are. I don't want to take your virginity until I know it's right for you."

I thought about what she said for a minute. "Okay. I think that's what I want, too." I pulled back a little from Helen. I put my legs up in front of me and wrapped my arms around my knees. "Don't take this the wrong way, but I need not to be touching you right now. My body's gotten a little carried away." I avoided eye contact. My body had been swept by both sadness and lust, and I felt sick to my stomach.

"Look at me, Alex." I did. She gazed into my eyes, and said, "It's okay what you are feeling. It's human. You don't need to be ashamed."

We sat quietly for a while. I wondered about when she might think the "right time" was. Then I thought of something else.

"You said you didn't want to 'take my virginity' until it's right for me. That was your phrase, 'take my virginity.' That means you have experience, right?"

"Does that bother you?"

"Not really. I know you're a lot older than I am. I guess I figured you would have had dozens of lovers by now."

"What!" Helen looked offended. "What kind of girl do you think I am?" Unfortunately, since I was looking her in the eyes, she knew exactly. "Oh, I see."

I tried to explain myself better. "I know you've had lots of lives, and there would've been lots of willing men. I wasn't judging you. I was just hoping you'd let me be one of them."

Helen pressed her lips together and narrowed her eyes. "You thought I was a bad girl, and you liked that," she said dryly.

I didn't think about girls like that, and I tried to defend myself. "No, that's not fair. I don't think it would make you a bad girl if you had had dozens of lovers. You've lived so long, it would be natural. No one would judge a *man* for that." I didn't think it was fair to judge girls for wanting and doing what boys did—unless it was bad for both. I hoped sex didn't fit into that category because I certainly wanted that.

Helen's face relaxed a little. "Okay, I won't take offense then." She added pointedly, "But I'm an old-fashioned girl."

Despite what I'd just said, I'd also sometimes wondered if Helen was a virgin. I confessed, "I did think maybe I was wrong about your experience. When you told me about the monster, I thought he might've turned you off men. Then, you told me you feel like you've been frozen as girl and I was making you feel new feelings. I thought maybe we could be a first for each other."

Helen smiled. "Actually, that's kind of sweet. It's not that far from the truth. I've only been with two men, and neither of them made me feel what you do."

I guess talking about sex had made me dumb because I said, "Who were they?" I really didn't want to know.

Helen smiled. "Your second guess wasn't that far wrong. The monster did turn me off men for many years. I didn't trust any man. But after a number of decades, I grew curious. I could see that many women enjoyed the company of men, and I wondered if I was missing something. I allowed myself to be seduced by a very handsome, very smooth human man, whom I met at a club. He was demanding and rough and selfish, and I didn't enjoy it at all."

"I'm sorry," I said. I didn't know what she meant, but I hoped I could be better. I was suddenly afraid I'd be a bad lover. I had no idea what was involved beyond the basic mechanics, so how would I know if I could be a good one? I wanted to be a good one for Helen.

"I didn't try again for a long time. My parents' example changed my mind. They loved each other. I saw how Mom felt about Dad's attentions. I wanted that for myself, so I looked for someone better."

"Did you find him?"

"I did. Well, I found someone better than the first, anyway. I met a sweet man who had been widowed with three children. He needed me. He was so grateful for my love that he never questioned my quirks: I needed a nightlight, and I had to spend one night out a week without him. Oh, that poor man! He thought I was cheating on him, but he accepted it like a martyr because he felt he deserved it for choosing someone so much younger." She shook her head, smiling a little sadly.

I thought about why Helen would let him think something so hurtful, but then I figured it out. "But you weren't cheating. You were drinking blood, right? So, he wasn't in on the secret?" She'd have had to let him believe something to keep from asking questions.

"No, he never knew." She went on blithely, "Anyway, I was happy to meet my husband's needs in bed because I loved him, but I never felt the desire for him that he felt for me. That's why there was never anyone after him. I assumed that's the just the way I was until I met you."

"Wait, wait, wait." I was horrified. "You're married?" This upset me the way nothing else she'd ever told me had. It had come up so suddenly, and I'd never even considered the possibility. How could I ever be to her what she was to me?

"I'm a widow. My husband died a long time ago." Helen said it quietly.

"How can you never have told me this?" She should have. "Here I am thinking you're the one for me, but you already belong to someone else?" I was so angry I was already off Helen's bed and standing by her closed door.

"Marriage wouldn't make me someone else's property." Helen sounded angry this time.

"Don't. Just don't. Don't make it sound like I'm trying to impose some ancient view of marriage on you. You're telling me that you stood before God and your families and pledged yourself to each other for all eternity. You made me feel special, like you were choosing me, but you already chose someone else!" I was shouting.

"I stood in front of a town clerk, and I only pledged myself until death. My husband died more than half a century ago!" Helen was almost as mad as I was.

"Did you kill him?" I said viciously.

That's when Helen slapped me across the face, like they do in movies. As angry as I was, that was like a bucket of cold water over my head. I'd never actually been struck intentionally. Jimmy and Jon might rough house, but they didn't fight. My eyes filled with tears, and I felt like a giant baby. I knew I was being immature, but I was so upset by Helen's marriage and so angry that I didn't know how to back down.

"How dare you?" Helen was fierce. "I loved that man. He may not have made me feel crazy sexy good like you do, but he also never made me so angry I could bite—like you are doing right now, God damn you."

"You're the one who's damned," I said.

"You'd better leave," said Helen.

"Okay, but before I do, tell me one thing. Tell me that I don't look like this husband you love. Tell me that I'm not some sick attempt to recreate a lost marriage. Tell me that."

"That's not the one you look like," Helen said bitterly.

"What? What does that mean? I look like someone else? Who?"

"You look like the monster."

"I look like *him*?" I was aghast.

"You could be twins."

I was shocked beyond words. I stood for a moment looking at Helen in anguish. "I don't know what's going on here," I said at last. I burst into tears and ran from the room.

When I got to my house, my father saw me on the way upstairs. Some time later, my mother came to my room. "Alex, what happened?"

"I had a fight with Helen."

"Oh baby, I'm sorry." Mom looked sympathetic.

"I'm so angry with her." I was shaking.

"Anger is a part of grief. Did Helen really do something bad, or were you just angry?"

I opened my mouth to say what Helen had done, and then I closed it again. That gave me time to wonder. "Maybe I was just angry."

"Wait until she cools off then, and apologize," Mom suggested. "She may understand that you weren't yourself this morning."

"Okay."

Once Mom left, I texted Helen, "Is it all right if I come over this afternoon to say sorry for overreacting?"

She texted back, "Is it all right if I'm still mad at you because some of the things you said are inexcusable even by grief?"

That pissed me off, so I turned off my phone for an hour while I tried to do homework. I finally cooled off and texted back, "Yeah."

She responded immediately with "At one o'clock then."

I was prompt. She took me to her room, sat down in her desk chair, and prompted, "Well?"

"I'm sorry, Helen."

"For what specifically?"

"Whatever you want." Helen didn't say anything. I tried again, "For being a jerk?" That usually worked with Jane, but I still got nothing. I thought back to our argument. "For suggesting you killed your husband?"

Helen closed her eyes in pain, and said, "Yeah, that." She added, "I loved my husband, and I already feel disloyal to his memory for letting you know how much more I feel for you. I will not let you desecrate his memory."

"I'm sorry. I was kinda torn up inside this morning—still am really. I'm still weirded out that I look like the monster."

"You're weirded out! Imagine how I felt seeing you!"

"Well, that's just it. I don't get it. Why would you want to look at me?"

"The shock made me notice you. Really notice you. But you are not the monster, Alex. You are a sweet boy, and you will be a good man. He just looked like what you really are."

"Oh." That made me feel a bit better.

"You got angry about my husband and—said what you said—before I mentioned that. Why did you?" Apparently I was not yet off the hook.

"I'm sorry. I don't really get how you feel about your husband. I've never had that kind of relationship." She looked so young, but she had so much experience. "God, you're so much older than I am. What do you see in me?"

"That's two different questions. As to my age, I feel both young and old. Part of me is like Peter Pan, never growing up. I act the role of a girl, and I've internalized it. Another part of me has grown up. That part has decided I want to change, and I want you to be a big part of that new life."

That sounded good, but I wasn't sure if I could deliver what she needed. I tried to make light of it. "So, if part of you is like Peter Pan, do I have to worry that you're going to disappear back to Neverland and leave me heartbroken, like Wendy?"

Helen's lips quirked in a half smile. "What and leave you and Jane together? Do you think I will come back for your son?"

"I keep telling you that Jane and I are just friends!"

Helen's smile became ear to ear. "Good news for Jane's son, then." I ignored her.

"You didn't answer the second question. What do you see in me?"

Apparently Helen was still in a playful mood. "Very perspicacious of you," she said.

"Stop teasing me with your vocabulary. You know I'll just look it up on my phone later."

"Nah, you're too lazy." I went to get out my phone. "Stop, you'll miss the answer, and you might want to hear this. I want you to be part of my life because, in no particular order: You make me think and you make me laugh." Did I? She did the same for me.

"You are arrogant enough to meet me as an equal and humble enough to back down when you're wrong." Was I still arrogant? Maybe I was, to think I could be Helen's boyfriend. I hoped I knew when to back down. If I were with Helen, I'd probably have to a lot.

She made sure she had my attention and continued, "You are handsome when you're not being goofy, and you're plenty goofy, which is good because who wants handsome all the time?"

"Um, everyone?"

"No," she dismissed me. "It'd be distracting. Let me finish. You love justice and compassion. I admire the former but need the latter." She looked at me to make sure I was following her.

"Above all, you have a genuinely loving heart with a giant blind spot when it comes to all of my faults." She smiled at me fondly.

I smiled back. "You don't have any. Except maybe that you yell at me sometimes."

Helen kissed me and made me forget everything but the taste of her lips.

It's okay though because her eyes were firmly closed and I remembered everything else later.

"Are you sure this boy is old enough?" asked Mom.

"You heard us then?"

"Querida, anyone in the house could hear this morning. You two were quite loud."

"He was just upset because his grandmother died."

"He also seems to have some romantic ideas about marriage, and he puts you on a pedestal."

Yes, I thought, I love that about him.

Mom looked at me shrewdly. "I see I'm not telling you anything you don't already know. Just think about what you're doing to him, and be careful."

"When did you start reading minds?"

"Sometimes you make it easy."

18. MEXICO

At some point, Helen asked me if I had uploaded the headstone photos we'd taken at the graveyard back in November. I was a little ashamed to admit that I hadn't.

"You know, with your grandmother gone, you could take over her work on the family tree. It could be a way to honor her. What do you think?"

"That'd be awesome! It might be lonely though, without her."

"What if I helped?"

"You would do that? It can be pretty tedious, and they aren't your ancestors. I can get a little obsessive when I'm doing research."

"I think I'd like to see you work."

"Well, I should start by uploading those photos. Then I should check the tree for messages."

Helen and I spent a couple of hours on the family computer. She was amazed by the way I could tap the keyboard and bring up copies of handwritten records from hundreds of years past. I told her various stories from my family's history.

With her finger on the screen tracing the curved handwriting of an old baptismal record, Helen asked, "Would you mind if I used your grandmother's username and password tonight?"

I looked at her blankly. It was weird that she would want to work on the tree without me.

She noticed my confusion and explained. "I'd like to do some research of my own, about my own history."

"Oh, okay."

"Don't worry. I'll keep everything encrypted and anonymized."

"That seems totally unnecessary. It's an Ancestry account. I don't think using someone else's account is a high priority for criminal enforcement."

Helen looked at me strangely.

"What I am I missing here?" I asked.

"Remember how I left that woman alive, and the Williamsport vampires slaughtered everyone she knew?"

"How could I forget?" I said. I wasn't being truthful though. Helen was so sweet I was always forgetting the danger. I think Helen saw through me.

"Should the police ever consider me a danger to the secret, protocol is to find any humans I've told and kill them and their entire families. Your grandmother's login gives access to information on over six hundred living relatives."

I looked at her in horror. "Would they kill them *all?*"

"Probably not," she said. "The usual is just immediate family and frequent contacts. However, I don't want this information on my computer. I don't even keep your number in my cell phone."

"Thanks, I guess." But I worried.

I was a little preoccupied at dinner imagining everyone in my family from fourth cousins on down being sucked dry by murderous vampires. Even though my mom was still distracted by trying to manage her mother's estate and do her own job, she still noticed enough to ask me what I was thinking. To distract her, I told her about the work Helen and I had done on the family tree that afternoon. Mom's eyes shone. "I'm glad you're doing that. My mother would've been happy to know that you're continuing her work."

I swelled with pride at the thought.

About a week later, Helen came to me with a proposal. She wanted me to come on a trip with her to Mexico over Easter break. She was really excited to show me her hometown of Morelia.

"I'd really like to go," I said. Morelia sounded like a beautiful place, and the weather would be a lot nicer. Plus, I'd be with Helen. I tried not to get my hopes up because I was sure to be disappointed. "I don't think my parents are going to go for that."

"Why not?"

"You. Me. Mexico. Spring break."

Helen looked a bit disgusted. "You have the wrong idea. It's not that kind of trip."

"It's not me that'll have the wrong idea," I protested. "It's my parents."

"We won't be going by ourselves. My whole family will come. It'll be educational."

"That might work. Why the sudden interest? It's only like three weeks away."

"Talking to you about my past has made me nostalgic. I want to share it with you.

"Okay, let's see if my parents go for it."

Surprisingly, they did.

They thought it seemed a little hasty, but Helen presented it as a long-planned family trip to which her parents had agreed to add me because she'd begged them to have a friend her own age. My father pointed out that it was a good thing that Grandma Fulton had paid for us all to go to the Bahamas when I was fourteen, or I wouldn't have a passport, and there was no time to get one. That almost started a family argument because Mom remembered that you don't need a passport for Mexico. Apparently, she'd had a spectacular Spring break trip there when she was a sophomore in college, and she had only a driver's license. Dad said the rules had changed five years ago, and people came to the post office all the time now to get passports. Also, he wanted more details about this "spectacular" trip of hers, and why was she blushing? I left them alone at that point.

Before I got permission, my mom needed to talk to Marisol, of course, to make sure we'd be properly supervised. Marisol told her I'd be rooming with Julio, so I wouldn't cost any extra. Helen would be rooming with Nabila. Mom offered to pay for my plane ticket as well, but Marisol refused saying they were glad to have me as company for Helen. Once reassured, both my parents thought it'd be a great travel experience for me. They'd miss me at Easter, but I promised to see if I could go to Easter services at the cathedral in Morelia.

I was excited, and Helen even more so. She kept telling me about records of her old life she'd found on Grandma's account. There was so much more offline, she'd said.

That made me suspicious. "I'm not going to spend the whole time in dusty libraries while you look up old records, am I?"

"No, I want to show you the places. The city was old when I lived there, and much of it hasn't changed since colonial times." She cocked her head. "Maybe some records."

How could I resist her when she was trying to be cute? "Okay," I agreed. "Is there anything special I should know about traveling with vampires?"

Helen looked like she was struggling with the urge to tell me some joke. She lost the urge. "Bring iron vitamins," she said giggling, "for your hemoglobin. Don't want to get anemic."

"I can see you think that's a joke, but wouldn't it be a good idea? Will you be drinking from me on the trip?" It'd been a month, and she hadn't done so after the first time.

"No, I'm good. Your blood's amazing. The effect has really lasted."

Another thought occurred. "Will Julio or Nabila need to drink from me?"

"No!" Helen was surprisingly fierce. "No one drinks from you but me."

"That's a relief." I hadn't really wanted to share with anyone but Helen. I hadn't been sure of what was expected though.

"That reminds me," Helen said. "There's one thing that might be useful to you. In the unlikely event we meet with other vampires in Mexico, there's a sign you can make. It proves that you are allowed to know the secret." She showed me a series of seemingly random fidgets, including stroking the throat with thumb and forefinger, pulling the ear and touching below the eye with the opposite hand. She had me practice until I'd learned it.

"If you do that in front of a strange vampire, he or she will ask you for a name. Say María Helena Morales."

"That's your birth name, right?"

"Yes. You probably won't ever have to use this because I'll be with you, but if you and I were separated, this would keep a strange vampire from drinking from you or deciding you know too much." That sounded good to know.

When the first day of Easter break came, I was packed and ready to go. My parents kissed me goodbye. The four Garcías, Nabila and I spent nearly a day with parking lots, airports, planes and shuttle busses.

The one big surprise came in Mexico City when we changed planes. "My parents aren't actually coming with us," Helen confessed. "They are going to have a romantic vacation for two. Only Julio and Nabila will be coming to Morelia with us."

"My parents wouldn't have agreed to them as adult supervision."

"I know. Hence the subterfuge."

I raised my eyebrows.

"Well, Mom and Dad don't exactly approve of this trip with you. They agreed to let me, but they're not going to come along."

"I don't like lying to my parents."

"Alex, they also wouldn't have agreed to let you come if they knew I'd drunk a pint of your blood."

"True that." I spend a moment trying to picture how my parents would react to that piece of news. At the very least, they'd take out a restraining order against Helen.

Later, it turned out we weren't really staying in a hotel. Helen had rented a house outside of town. When she picked up the keys to the house from the agent in town, she'd put on a scarf and an attitude that made her look a lot older. Honestly, I don't know exactly what it was, but suddenly Helen looked like an adult to me—maybe twenty five or thirty. When she saw me being weirded out, she tossed her five inches of hair and giggled. She was my girl again.

The house she rented was freaky to me. All the houses in the suburbs had tall, mismatched walls interrupted by colorful steel panels or gates. The streets were just walls with doors in them—small ones for people and large ones for cars. The walls were often topped by chain link or razor wire. You couldn't even see the houses. When Helen opened the door in the wall with her key, it led to a well-kept green grass yard and lovely, compact house. Julio brought the car in through the gate.

When we brought our luggage up to bedrooms, I got another shock. Helen pulled me aside and said quietly, "Julio tells me that there is no way he's not going to share a room with Nabila. That means I'm sharing with you." My heart rate picked up about 30 additional beats a minute. Helen fixed me with a no-nonsense stare. "This does not mean we'll be having sex. I don't think you're ready for that. Can you handle sharing a room with me on those terms? 'Cause otherwise I can tell Julio I'll be rooming with him and Nabila."

"No, I'm good." Sharing with Helen was preferable to being alone, even if there were limits.

The next day, Helen took me on a walking tour of the town by herself. I don't know where Julio and Nabila were. We could walk into town. It might've been a mile or two. The weather was warm for April, but not as warm as I would've expected at this Southern latitude. Helen explained that was because of the high elevation.

The center of town was amazing. Helen called it "*el centro*." All the buildings looked centuries old, some dating from shortly after the conquest. The cathedral was beautiful. Helen even took me inside. She cried for a moment and said she remembered what it was like to love God. I wondered if that meant she didn't hate God anymore.

We ate lunch at a café across from the cathedral. I tried to order a beer, but Helen nixed that idea. Sometimes I thought Helen and I didn't need adult supervision because she *was* adult supervision. I made the mistake of mentioning that to her. She pulled herself up all stiff and said haughtily, "Fine. Order whatever you like. I reserve the right to dump you when your brain doesn't develop."

Shit. I'd pissed her off, and she had a point. "Actually, I think I'd rather have a Coke."

Helen had the grace not to triumph over me. She nodded gravely and ordered for us both in Spanish. She wiped her mouth with a napkin, and I suspected her of hiding a smile behind it. I pretended not to notice.

Walking down a street later, Helen pointed to an old hotel and said, "That's where the dance took place where I met him. She walked with me a short distance to an old town house and said, "That's the place where I was changed." For a moment, I could picture the story she had told me vividly. Then, I thought about what this must be like for her, and I had a disturbing thought.

"Helen, I look like him, right?"

"Yes, you know that. I confess I hadn't meant to tell you, but I was angry. That's not still a problem for you, is it?"

"I was just wondering what this was like for you. Here you are walking from the place where you met him to the place where he...did what he did...with someone who looks just like him. Are you reliving the experience? Why would you want to do that?" I was worried that maybe she was using me to take the venom from the memories. Was that why she'd chosen me? Because I looked like him?

"Alex, I've admitted you look like the monster. I didn't mean to, but I did. I thought you were okay with that? Are you really?"

"Yeah, totally." Of course I wasn't. The whole thing was bizarre.

That wasn't acceptable. "Look at me, Alex." I didn't want to. Helen stopped walking. "Look at me," she repeated.

I gave in. I looked her in the eyes.

"Oh," she said. "I see." She thought for a moment. "How strange," she said. "You're worried that I chose you just because you look like the monster. But the truth is you don't look like the monster to me anymore. It's so weird. The monster looks like you."

"What?" I said.

"In my memories, the monster looks like you, not the other way around. It feels like a trick, like the monster is wearing an Alex disguise."

"I don't get it."

"I don't either. I thought memories were immutable. Now I feel like the reason I trusted the monster is because he looked like you. Because he looked like someone I..." Helen tapered off. She looked at me accusingly. "How did you change my past?"

I shrugged and put up my hands. "I'm just seventeen."

Helen looked mollified. "I know. I'm sorry. This is about me, not about you. Don't worry about it. I'm good."

Strangely, I was too. If the monster looked like me, that was on him. I was myself, and that was okay with me—and with Helen. He could go to hell. He probably had.

Much later, I realized Helen probably only noticed me in the first place because of the way I looked. Being magical herself, she tended to expect magical reasons for things. It occurred to me she'd met a large number of boys in her long life, and she picked me out because I looked like the monster. Perhaps my appearance was not so much of a coincidence. I'd started noticing any girl that looked even a little bit like Helen. If I kept looking enough, would I find one that looked exactly like her? Lots of people look a little bit alike, but if you look long enough, maybe it's inevitable you'll find two that look exactly alike.

And did we look exactly alike? Maybe she didn't remember him as well as she thought. It'd been a century since she'd seen him, and her memories might be different now. That happened to me all the time. I'd changed a lot in the past year, and I looked at my whole past differently. Helen had been unchanging for so long, maybe she forgot that. In that respect, maybe I *had* changed her past: not the way she would—with memory altering magic—but by changing the way she felt about my appearance retroactively.

That's the best explanation I had, but with Helen of course it could be magic.

That night, I kissed Helen in our room. All we did was kiss, and I wanted much more, but it still felt like enough. I fell asleep feeling loved.

The next day, Helen asked me if we could take a side trip to Zinapécuaro. "Why?" I asked. "Isn't that the place of your worst nightmare?"

"Yes, but I'd like to find out what happened to the baby."

I was puzzled. "I don't understand." She'd killed the baby, hadn't she?

"I'm haunted by the baby," she explained. "I want to know what happened to him."

I didn't get it. He died. "Didn't you tell me you buried him with his parents?"

Helen looked a bit uncomfortable. "I actually didn't. I was too upset to talk about the baby."

I remembered that. I realized I'd just assumed. "So what's the story?" I wondered what could be worse for her than the baby's being dead.

"When I went pick up the body, I found out the baby was still alive," Helen said.

"Thank God for that, right?" That had to be better than she'd killed him.

Helen shook her head. "I don't know that this baby had much to be thankful for. I'd just killed his parents. He'd hit his head hard on the pavement, and there was a big dent in the side of his skull." That was an upsetting image. I didn't know if the damage to his head would leave him disabled.

"My heart went out to this tiny child. When I picked him up, I realized he couldn't be much more than three kilograms—about seven pounds. He was practically a newborn. That gave me an idea. Perhaps I could save him. He was too young to be a witness, so I wouldn't be breaking the law to give him a chance."

"Did you call 911?" That's what I would've done.

Helen smiled. "Modern child! We didn't have anything like that back then. Also, I didn't want to involve the human police."

Helen described how she'd soaked the baby and her skirts in blood of the parents. I didn't want all of the details, but I knew if I complained, Helen would insist I face the truth about her.

"I took the baby to the Sisters of Mercy Convent. I used my seventeen-year-old appearance to make a scene. I banged on the door and wept. I told the sister who answered that I couldn't bear the shame of being an unwed mother and threatened to kill myself—or the baby—if they wouldn't take it. The sister saw the blood on my skirts and assumed I'd just given birth to the child. She saw the damage to the child's head and took him from my hands immediately." Helen nodded.

"That's what I'd hoped for. I ran away once she was holding the child. Given the opportunity, she would've tried to convince me to raise the child myself. I knew the mother superior was a woman of good sense. I was determined that the baby would have a chance, and I trusted them to do well by him. I never found out what happened."

I wasn't sure why this bothered Helen so much. "Why do you want to know after all this time?" Surely it didn't matter that much whether she'd killed two or three? It was still multiple homicide. I felt guilty immediately for thinking something so stupid. Of course it mattered. To the baby.

"I'd like to know he was okay." Helen sounded hopeful.

Of course she would if that's how it turned out, but... "What if it's bad news?"

"I'll have to deal." She sounded committed. Well, since she'd learned to cope with the death of his parents, she could learn to cope with this too. Or, had she coped? I remembered it was her nightmare.

I foresaw tedious hours in records repositories, but I understood this was important to Helen. I wanted to know the baby turned out okay, too. Babies should have a chance.

Helen went to tell Julio and Nabila. We set out midmorning for Zinapécuaro.

The third time Julio was pulled over by the national police, Helen lost patience. "Dammit, Julio! Can't you drive the speed limit?"

"*Calmate, hermana.* If you didn't want police attention, you shouldn't have rented such a sweet car." It's true that Helen had rented a lovely red Mercedes four-door, but I hadn't noticed Julio speeding particularly. Helen stepped out of the back where she was sitting with me, and spoke to the officer. He let us go. After that, Helen insisted on driving. Nabila just smiled throughout the whole situation.

The roads were scary, police notwithstanding. The terrain was mountainous, and the roads were all switchbacks and blind curves. I was grateful when we got to Zinapécuaro. Helen was not sympathetic. "Don't you trust my driving?" she asked.

"Certainly I do," I said. "It's the trucks coming around the blind curves I don't trust."

When we arrived at Zinapécuaro, I got the impression of a much smaller town than Morelia, situated in a valley. Helen checked us into a total tourist trap of a hotel on a hill outside of town. It had two stories of rooms spread out around a pool. I had brought my bathing suit because my mom had told me to, and it was so hot I was all for a dip. Helen joined me in a demure all-black one-piece that nevertheless looked amazing on her. When we got back to the rooms, Julio pulled out a pack of cards and said, "What da ya say the four of us play a game of strip poker?"

Helen looked five kinds of evil at him and said something in Spanish that I didn't catch. Nabila, however, spat out the Coke she'd been drinking, and laughed. "Come, lover," she said to Julio, "I think we're not wanted."

Helen and I slept in the same bed that night, but nothing happened. Helen let me hold her, but nothing else. I didn't complain. I didn't get much sleep either.

The next morning, maids looking to clean the rooms woke us. I tried the limited Spanish Helen had taught me on them, and they just laughed.

Helen woke and spoke to them, and they left. "What are we going to do today?" I asked blearily.

"Let's go visit the Sisters of Mercy."

"Okay. I could use mercy." I closed my eyes against the sun.

"Very funny." Helen didn't seem amused.

Neither was I after spending nearly two hours in a convent listening to Helen converse in a language I didn't understand. She seemed to make a large donation in cash. At first, I was inclined to be judgmental: what kind of nuns took bribes? Then, I reconsidered. Who was I to judge these women of God? Their lives and their good work needed financial support. Helen always seemed to have plenty of money. Maybe this was like a tithe for her.

Finally, Helen explained to me. They had opened their records to her. She was ecstatic. Not only had she discovered the baby she left ("*el bebé abandonado*"), but she'd discovered he'd survived. Apparently the dent in his head went away pretty quickly—the nuns said infants' skulls can be soft and pliable. Within a month, he'd been claimed by monks from a religious order. They'd told the nuns that his father had been a security guard for them. He'd gone missing the day of the baby's arrival, and they believed that he'd been murdered.

Helen raised her eyebrows significantly at me when she told me that part of the story.

I started to ask, "Was it...?"

"Yes, it was the Order of St. Michael. The nuns said they claimed to be 'dedicated to fighting the spiritual forces of wickedness with the spiritual forces of God.' They took the baby to their chapter house to raise."

Helen was too excited to let me ask any questions. She was practically jumping up and down. "I haven't told you the best part!" she said. "He's doing very well and is living in Zinapécuaro today." Helen's excitement was infectious. I was happy for her.

We returned to the hotel. I went swimming, but Helen stayed with her laptop computer. When I returned to the room, she announced triumphantly she had located the grown-up baby's house.

"Let's go there tomorrow," she said.

I agreed.

I fell asleep looking at Helen talk on the phone in a beautiful pale blue nightgown. She was speaking Spanish, and I didn't understand her words. What I did know is that I needed to learn Spanish because that was the language of Heaven, and I needed to know what my angel was saying.

"Mama, he encontrado el bebé que pensé que había matado. Por favor, ven acá."

"Hija, eso esta en el pasado. ¿Por qué es esto importante ahora?"

In the background, I could hear my father Victor. "What does she want?"

"Us. To come."

"Why?"

"Because her slain baby lived and has a house in Zinapécuaro. She wants to visit."

"Better left alone," said Dad.

"Claro que sí," *said Mom,* "pero ella no puede."

"Podemos," *he said.*

"De veras," *Mom said. "Helen, I am glad for you, but we won't be coming. Before you visit this man, ask yourself if this is a good idea. If he has lived without interference until now, isn't he better left alone?"*

"Necesito conocerlo."

"¿Es esto sobre tú o él?"

"No lo sé." *I truly didn't know.*

19. DANGER

The next morning, we repeated the scene with the maids waking us up. Julio and Nabila joined us for breakfast, but then they planned on going on their own to explore the town. Helen was eager to check out the house she had discovered in her research the day before.

She put on an outfit I'd never seen. It looked a lot like what I'd seen locals wearing the day before. Except for her short haircut, Helen looked like she could be a native. Then I felt stupid because I remembered she was one. I looked at my own outfit of tight jeans and shirt worn loosely over a T-shirt. I'd planned to be able to take off the outer shirt if it warmed up in the afternoon sun as it'd done the day before.

"Should I try to blend in, too?" I asked Helen.

She smiled and tried not to laugh. "I don't really think that's possible. Everything about you screams *Norteamericano* and *turista*."

My Spanish lessons had gotten me that far. "You're North American, too. Mexico is on the same continent as the U.S." Helen just shook her head, smiling.

"If I look like a tourist, then what good does it do for you to look native?"

Helen stopped smiling. "I thought there might be a situation where I might need to get local people to talk. If that happens, I might send you out on your own for a while."

That didn't sound like a lot of fun. Helen seemed oblivious to my glum reaction in her excitement to get going. I tried to be happy for her. I could tell it was important to Helen the baby lived. If he was doing well, maybe that would help her forgive herself for his dead parents.

We left for the house. We walked down from the hill where the hotel was located through streets where houses became closer together. Helen explained to me that we would actually have to walk through the center of town because the person she was looking for lived on the other side. We passed by a large square plaza she said was the zocalo.

The place and its people looked really poor to my American eyes. I'd thought that Minersville was economically depressed, but I now saw everything is relative. I'd always compared Minersville to rich places I saw on television. Compared to Zinapécuaro, Minersville was rich. At home, the clothes were sturdy and clean, the cars were generally under ten years old, and the houses followed zoning rules (and usually didn't have scavenged construction supplies leaning up against them). Zinapécuaro resembled Southern California in the style of the houses, but it was like a poor cousin. The prevalence of graffiti and the number of buildings with high walls, barred windows or spiked iron fences made me nervous. I hoped Helen wouldn't leave me alone. I wasn't kidding myself that I was going to protect her. It would definitely be the other way around.

Something about actually being in Zinapécuaro and seeing the way people lived here made it seem like I'd been transported into the past. Every once in a while, I saw a person with a cell phone or some house built in a modern style, but mostly the place looked like it might have looked decades ago when Helen had lived here. It was easier for me to imagine the couple Helen had killed. Part of me hadn't truly felt the reality of her crime before. Intellectually, I could excuse it as self-defense and just part of Helen's terrible secret reality, but it was hard not to picture the lives of the people we were walking past. Helen had suddenly had to kill two such people, just walking through the streets like we were doing now. I couldn't imagine it.

Eventually we got to the right street. Helen pointed out a one-story, tan masonry house. It was surrounded by a couple of trees and a four-foot brick wall, capped with cement full of shards of broken glass. Since the wall was so low, I wasn't sure how effective an anti-burglar measure this was, but those wicked looking daggers of old bottles did send a strong message.

Helen stopped suddenly. "Alex," she whispered, "I want you to pretend you don't know me. Take out the map we got at the hotel and study it like you're lost. Now."

"Why?" I did as she said.

Helen stopped and fussed with a shoe. Without looking at me, she said, "That house has protective markings like the ones on Brubacher's church. I see the sign of the Order of St. Michael, the letter "M" with a line showing the angel's sword. This is a dangerous place. For me, not for you. As a tourist, no one in that house would care about you. As my companion, you might be in trouble."

That made sense to me. She could fight or run better if she didn't have to worry about me. The part that didn't make sense was that we weren't *leaving*. This felt like looking for trouble. "What are we doing?" I whispered urgently.

"I'd hoped to meet this man myself, but if the house is protected by the order, it's unwise for me to be here at all."

"Right, let's go." I was starting to feel panicky. I risked a quick glance at Helen. She was taking a large envelope out of her bag. It was some fancy stationary with a single name elegantly written in script on the front.

"I want you to go instead. You're human. You should be perfectly safe. Give this envelope to him." She handed it out towards me.

"No, Helen," I hissed. I didn't move to take the envelope. This was an exceptionally bad plan. Of course, I realized now I hadn't had a good idea of what would happen when we got here. Clearly, Helen had come prepared.

"It's a confession and an apology. It doesn't say anything about vampires, but it says where his parents are buried and it includes money for a proper memorial." I didn't take the envelope. "Please, Alex, this is important to me." She looked at me with pleading eyes, and I gave in.

"What do you want me to do?"

"Just go knock on the door and give this to whomever answers. Don't linger. Turn around and walk straight down this street for several blocks. I'll meet you."

Reluctantly I accepted the envelope.

Helen left me, and I faced the house. There was a low wooden gate in the wall, and I realized that it had a simple latch that could be worked from the outside. Looking at the glass shards embedded in the wall, I really didn't want to touch that latch. I almost turned around to chase after Helen without making the delivery, but I didn't want her to think I was a coward and suspected she'd make me come back anyway.

I opened the latch and knocked on the brown wooden door. The man who answered the door was short and squat with powerful arms, close-clipped dark hair and a thin mustache.

"*¿Qué quieres?*" he said.

I didn't know enough Spanish to answer him, so I used a stock phrase Helen had taught me to tell him: *"Lo siento. No hablo Español."* I'm sorry. I don't speak Spanish. Then I said, "I'm supposed to give you this," and handed him the envelope.

He took it with a powerful hand. I kind of freaked out when I saw the pattern of scars on the back of his fingers. I realized this man was a vampire fighter just like his dad had been. I didn't want to mess with him, and I was terrified. I stammered out a foolish, "That's it. Thanks. Goodbye."

I turned around and walked away quickly. I looked once over my shoulder and saw the man staring after me, but he hadn't moved to follow. Then he shrugged and turned to go back inside his house.

I didn't walk straight back to Helen. That was probably stupid because I could've easily gotten lost on those streets in Zinapécuaro—everything was unfamiliar, and much of it looked the same to me. However, I was worried that if the man came after me, I'd be leading him straight to Helen. I was sure they'd fight to the death, history tragically repeating itself. That would defeat the whole point of this little trip—if there had been a point. So I took a roundabout route, circling back to make sure I wasn't being followed. I wasn't.

When I eventually turned a corner and spotted Helen a block away, I breathed a sigh of relief.

Then, I stopped myself. Some local man was approaching her, apparently intent on conversation. It was a stranger, not the man I'd just left, thank goodness. Still, I wasn't sure if Helen would want me to intrude at that moment. At the house, she'd told me to pretend I wasn't with her. Did that still apply? Since I wasn't sure, I held myself back.

He and Helen weren't really that far away, so I could hear every word they spoke. Their voices weren't loud, but the street was quiet and the brick walls carried the sound.

"Hola. ¿Como le llama?" the stranger asked.

"María," she replied. I recognized her Spanish name.

"No le hé conocer a usted."

"Porque no vivo aqui. Vivo en los Estados Unidos, estes dias." I didn't know exactly what they were saying, but it all sounded very light and chatty to me. Then the stranger switched to English.

"If you are of the United States, it is better we speak English, more—how do you say?—discreet." He had a heavy accent. The stranger paused, but Helen said nothing. "Why do you come here, if I am permitted to ask?"

Helen said something too quietly for me to hear.

"Welcome back." I looked up for a moment, and the stranger instantly locked eyes with me across the distance that separated us.

He strode quickly towards me. Helen was on his heels.

I assumed this was a vampire from his "for us" comment. Not sure what to do, I made the sign Helen had shown me. The vampire came right up to me with smile that didn't reach his eyes. "Whose property are you, boy?"

Helen had just said that I would be asked for a name. I'd ask her about that "property" bit later. "María Helena Morales," I told him.

He turned back to Helen. "Yours then."

"Yes." She said it emphatically, but I heard a note of desperation there that frightened me.

He turned back to me, "Anyone else have a claim?"

For a weird moment, I pictured Jane as I had last seen her, outside her house by her mailbox. I shook my head in denial, "No."

The stranger turned back to Helen, whose eyes looked tense and frightened even. "Are you willing to do what might be necessary, I wonder?" he said staring at her. Then, he swiftly walked away.

Helen swore softly. She took my arm and said, "We must quickly get to a place of safety. I wish you hadn't given him my name."

"You told me to!"

"I know. I know! I was just trying to keep you safe." We were walking quickly down the street, and she got out her cell phone. "Julio, I'm in deep trouble. I met an officious mind reader who is on his way now to the police station to report me for Alex. Will you and Nabila help me?" She gave a description of the vampire we had met and gave a street address. "No, I have to get Alex to safety. I'm taking him to a new place—the Iliumfuit Hotel. Meet us there." She snapped shut her phone.

"Will the police come after us?" I was starting to grasp how bad the situation was.

"I hope he won't get that far. We'll see what Julio can do. Don't worry yet. Just walk fast." She was brisk.

"That vampire called me your property. Is that how vampires think of me?" I was too cowardly to ask whether she felt that way about me. Maybe I'd finally learned not to ask questions when I didn't want to know the answer.

"Alex, when I say 'You're mine,' it just means I'm a jealous girlfriend." She sounded frustrated. "But most vampires *do* think of humans as property. For them, people are like animals. Some are wild and can be hunted if you follow the rules. Some belong to vampires who use their services or keep them for slaughter. Others are kept as special companions—I told you why before—and have special protections."

"Like pets. I guess I am kind of like a dog. I did the one trick you taught me for that vampire, and it turned out to be the wrong time." It was humiliating how apt her comparison was. I hoped I didn't sound as bitter as I felt.

"Alex, I wouldn't kiss a dog the way I kiss you."

I laughed at the exasperation in her voice and the image. It made me think of my brother letting the dog lick his face. "You haven't seen Simon with Inskeep. It gets pretty disgusting."

"Did your mother name both your little brother and your dog after National Public Radio morning hosts?" Helen sounded completely incredulous, and it distracted me.

"What? No!" Her suggestion was outrageous, but I really couldn't say it was impossible. "Well, maybe the dog, but Simon's full name is Simon Peter, like the saint, so she can't have meant Scott Simon." I said it confidently, but Helen had me wondering if anyone named Alexander worked at NPR. It didn't occur to me until we got to the hotel that Helen had probably just been trying to distract me from the danger. It worked.

She paid with what looked like a whole lot of cash and gave a false name. Apparently you can still get away with not having a credit card some places in Mexico, or maybe the cash was a bribe rather than a deposit. I don't know.

We were given a key and went to the room. Helen was pacing and didn't want to answer any of my questions. She said, "Be patient. We need to hear back from Julio." I sat on the bed and tried to listen to music on my phone, but I felt worried. Helen didn't seem to be taking her own advice. She was walking rapidly back and forth, doing something on her phone, and pausing every minute or two to look out the curtained window.

She got a call at last. She listened for a minute, and said, "Shit!" She added, "You and Nabila better come here. I'm texting you our location." It must be bad news from Julio then.

Twenty minutes later, there was a knock on the door. It was Julio and Nabila. Once inside, he explained, "I'm pretty sure I saw the guy you meant, Helen. The trouble is he was coming *out* of the police station."

"You guys have police stations?" I asked.

"Yeah, but they don't look like yours. Unmarked and hidden. You have to send a text to a special number to get the location."

Helen got really upset, "You didn't send your code to get the station's location, did you?" Helen's chest was heaving, like she was having a panic attack. "If there's an electronic trail, then central could follow it back to you later. Then there's nothing we can do."

Julio was cool. "Nah, I never use my own code on general principles. I used a stolen one I picked up a decade ago." Belatedly, he seemed to pick up on Helen's agitation. Nabila was silently staring at Helen, so that might have clued him in. An expression of comprehension came across his face. "*Hermanita*, damn! You mean to attack the station. You're planning on killing all the officers before they come after you."

"Please, Julio, I'm begging you." Helen's voice was agonized. "I'm desperate. Help me do this!" She went over to him and reached out like she wanted to grab him but held herself back. Nabila looked back and forth between the two.

"Helen, honey, you can't fight the police. They're gonna win in the end." He sounded resigned, like it was a bad thing.

"Please!" Helen practically shrieked and dropped to her knees. She grabbed Julio's kneecaps. Julio looked at Nabila, giving her a what-the-hell expression.

Nabila said quietly, "The police will demand she kill Alex."

Well, that was something I'd have been happier not knowing.

Julio let out a low whistle. There was a long pause while he considered. Finally, he said, "I'm in. Let's do this thing." Helen allowed him to pick her off the floor. Julio turned to Nabila. "What about you?"

She looked at him seriously. "I've got your back, as always." She looked at Helen. "Explain the situation."

Helen briefly summarized her encounter on the street. She and the strange vampire both had 'the eye.' When he asked if she would be 'willing to do what might be necessary,' he'd read in her mind that she would never kill me, no matter what the circumstances. In that same moment, Helen read his mind: he intended to go to the chief of police and inform on her.

"Damn him for a meddling snitch," Julio muttered. "Who the hell acts like that? Going to the police for something like this! It's not like Alex is trying to expose us. Vampires should mind their own business."

The tension was getting to me, so I tried a joke. "Effing vampires! You can't trust them."

Julio looked at me and burst out laughing. He clapped me on the back. "I like you, Alex."

Nabila said, "We need a plan." Everyone was quiet for a moment, thinking. "How many police are here?" Helen thought Zinapécuaro had a chief and two officers. Julio said the three of them could take that many if they had the element of surprise. He added that they needed weapons. Nabila said to Helen, "It's pointless to attack the station if they aren't all present. You need to make sure they are all there."

"No," said Helen. I didn't understand why. Nabila was making sense. Nabila looked at Helen like she thought so too. She stared her down. Helen said, "I don't want to bring Alex to the station. I don't want him in danger."

Nabila said flatly, "If they think you're coming to bring Alex to die, there'll be doubt in their minds. They may not believe this mind reader you met. They'll want all their officers there for safety, in case you lose your nerve. They'll probably wait to tell central authorities anything because you're cooperating."

Helen looked at Julio. He said, "Sis, you've already put Alex in danger. This ain't worse than what's coming if you go on the run. Your only other choice is to go underground."

Helen turned back to me. "Alex, are you ready to share the evil spirit in me? Become a vampire with me? Live underground much of the day for decades? It means you could never see your family again."

I hadn't ever progressed beyond the daydream stage in imagining the life Helen was suddenly proposing. My eyes teared up at the thought of never seeing my parents or brother again. "I'm not ready for that."

Helen nodded acceptance. She took a deep breath. "Then you're coming with us. As bait."

I wasn't ready for that either, but it seemed like my one choice had been made.

Julio said, "See if Mom and Dad will help." Helen took her phone into the bathroom to make the call.

Julio said to Nabila, "I'll go buy some weapons. Do you want anything special?"

Nabila flashed a white-toothed grin. "See if you can get me a big-ass knife."

"Wouldn't guns be more useful?" I said. "Surely the police have guns."

Julio shook his head. "Vampires heal instantly. You need to do massive damage to slow them down."

Nabila said, "Like cutting off the head." I was starting to feel queasy.

"Don't feel too bad for these guys, bro," said Julio. "Vampire police are some of the nastiest killers you don't ever want to meet. They enjoy having an excuse to drink humans dry, and nobody can do anything about it 'cause they're the police."

Helen came out of the bathroom and shook her head. Julio said, "Yeah, I figgered." He handed her his phone. "I got their number when I looked up where they are. Call 'em and tell 'em you'll be there in two hours, with Alex. That'll give me time to get weapons."

Julio was back in an hour with two hatchets and a foot-long camping knife with serrations down the spine. He gestured with one of the hatchets and said to me, "Massive damage." Nabila looked pleased with the knife.

Helen looked at me. I think she saw the fear in my eyes. "You can do this," she said. "Be brave."

I was.

"Let's roll," Julio said.

I called Mom's cell from the bathroom. I didn't want Alex to hear this. She answered on the third ring. "Your dad and I are on the beach. There are some people nearby, but since they don't speak English, it should be safe to talk." Mom sounded wonderfully relaxed. I was the opposite.

"Mom, I need help." I think the desperation came through in my voice because she called out to Dad to come over. I heard a rustling of blanket on sand as he settled himself.

I told Mom what had happened. It took some time, and she had lots of questions. Mom didn't put me on speaker, but I could hear her passing along what I said in tense whispers. Both my parents were horrified by the situation.

I told them what Julio and I had planned. *"Can you help us?"*

Mom said, *"Even if we wanted to do this thing, we couldn't get there in time."*

I could hear Dad in the background. *"She wants us to fight the police? Has she gone crazy?"*

"No, I think—" she started to say quietly. Then she said louder, *"One moment, sweetie, I'll be right back."* She silenced her phone's microphone but didn't end the call. I waited a tense moment, and then they were back.

Mom said, *"We can't be with you, now. I love you, dearest daughter."* Dad took the phone, *"I love you, too. It has been an honor for me to be your father for all these years."* He sounded like he didn't expect to see me again, and that broke my heart.

"I love you, too, Dad. We'll win this fight."

"If you do, we'll see you again in Minersville. But there may have to be some changes then." He hung up. My parents wouldn't be joining the fight, and they didn't seem to think we could win. It shook my confidence a bit. I wondered if they thought I was trying to die.

20. HUNT

We walked towards the police station in the late afternoon sunlight. I was surprised when we didn't turn towards the town's center, but instead Julio led us up a hillside. We entered a dusty road running along the slope, lined by poor houses with small yards and a few trees. Some of the houses had brick walls for security, and some just had sturdy doors. We stopped at a one-story house that looked to be made of painted cement. It was built into the slope, so that the inside must've been basically underground. There was no fence, but vampire police wouldn't really need security against human burglars, I guessed.

Julio said to Helen and me, "You and Alex go in first. They're expecting you, and they expect you to plead for Alex. Try to get close to the police chief. Once you're in place, Nabila and I will burst in and surprise the two officers from behind."

Helen nodded and checked the hatchet she had put in her waistband. She was wearing a tank top with a loose flowing shirt over it to cover up the hatchet. Julio handed each of us a pair of sunglasses.

"So we look cool?" I asked surprised. This seemed too Hollywood for me.

"That too, bro," Julio said smiling, "but these will help against mind readers."

"It'll show I'm hiding something," said Helen. Then she shrugged. "Which I am, so I guess it's a good idea."

Nabila said, "We only need a moment of uncertainty to get close."

Helen and I walked up to the door. It was made of steel and painted blood red, which seemed the appropriate color to me. Julio and Nabila stood on each side of the door. Helen tried the handle, and it was unlocked. We walked inside to a dark room, so it took a moment for my eyes to adjust, especially with the sunglasses and all.

That's when the whole plan completely fell apart.

We knew they were expecting us, and they were. However, they weren't going to listen to anything Helen had to say. They'd planned an ambush. As soon as Helen and I walked in the door, two vampires launched themselves at us from each side, and a third tried to push the door closed. Nabila and Julio struggled to keep him from closing the door and cutting them off, along with our retreat. Helen lost a valuable second tossing me to the side and out of the fight.

She tossed me hard, and I flew ten feet. I lost track of what was going on for a moment while I recovered from hitting the floor. When I looked up from where I'd fallen, I saw Helen struggling with a vampire who had a machete held above her head. Helen was holding the arm wielding the machete, up and away from her head with both her hands, while the two writhed and the guy tried to punch her with his free hand.

I looked to the door and saw Julio and Nabila fighting with the other two vampires. Nabila had her knife out and was holding off another one armed with a machete. His weapon was longer than her knife, but she moved faster. I saw Julio was fighting a vampire holding a strange gold dagger with a hilt that made the whole thing look a bit cross-shaped.

Julio punched his opponent in the face with his left hand, and then he brought down his hatchet on the guy's head, burying half the blade in the skull. There was that "massive damage" Julio had promised. His opponent fell to the ground. Julio plucked the gold dagger from his own stomach and let in drop on the floor. Apparently the other vampire had struck him at the same time just above the belt and buried his dagger hilt deep. I waited for Julio to fall, but then I remembered how quickly vampires were supposed to heal. Julio simply stood, clutching the place where he'd been struck.

Nabila's opponent brought his machete down on her knife, which broke her knife by pulling the blade from a broken grip. He brought his machete up for a killing blow. Nabila moved so quickly, I almost couldn't see what she did. She leapt in the air, executed a somersault over his head and landed in a crouch on the floor. She snatched the gold dagger from where it had fallen from Julio's hand. Then, incredibly, she reversed the move she'd just performed backwards. Her opponent had brought down his machete on the spot where Nabila had been and was now bent over it. Nabila plunged the gold dagger into his spine.

I heard a clatter from where Helen was struggling. Oh God, I thought, Helen! She had fallen to the floor with the other vampire on top of her. She still maintained her grip on his hand, but with his other hand he was raining down punishing blows on her face and torso. Nabila saw it too. She leapt into the air again and flew across the room. Literally flew. I realized that what I'd thought was gymnastics had actually been Nabila's tightly controlled flying. In less than two seconds, Nabila was on the other vampire's back. She pulled his head back by the hair and brought the dagger to his throat. I looked away.

When I looked back, Nabila was helping Helen up from next to the body of the vampire that'd been on top of her. The head was severed. To my great relief, Helen looked okay. She looked at me with a terrified expression on her face, but I couldn't see any injuries to her. I relaxed, not quite believing how lucky we'd been. We'd won. All of the police were down.

That's when Julio fell.

We all heard him fall. When I turned towards the sound, Nabila was already at his side. With her left hand, she cushioned his head. Her right hand casually buried the knife she'd still been holding in the eye socket of the vampire Julio had taken down with his hatchet. While I was glad Nabila was on our side, there was something about the easy efficiency with which she dealt death that made me sick to my stomach. Or maybe that was post fight jitters. I looked over at Helen, who was staring in horror at Nabila and Julio.

That's when Nabila screamed.

It was a cry of the deepest agony imaginable. The only thing in my experience I could compare it to was a sound I once heard on a nature documentary where a lioness had managed to frighten one of two elephant calves into bolting away from his mother's protection. The calf had made little noise as the lion killed it, but the mother elephant, stuck protecting her remaining calf, had cried out like that.

Helen went to Nabila's side. "Where is he injured?" she asked. Nabila indicated the wound in Julio's belly. "It's not healing," Helen said in disbelief. Nabila shook her head and retrieved the knife from the eye socket where she'd stowed it. We three all looked at the blade as it began to darken. It no longer looked like gold, more like tarnished, old brass. "Oh, no!" cried Helen. "You don't think this was for executions, do you?"

Nabila didn't answer. She just plunged the knife in the center of her own chest, angled upwards towards her heart, and let go. Helen screamed. She grabbed the knife handle, and Nabila didn't try to stop her as she withdrew the blade. We were all frozen in position for a time, waiting for something to happen. Since nothing did, I got up and joined Helen.

Nabila said, "No more magic left in that knife. I should've known it wasn't going to be quick and easy." She looked down at Julio's face tenderly. His lifeless eyes looked back at her from the floor.

"Don't give up, Nabila," said Helen. "Maybe he can recover."

Nabila looked at Helen wearily. "You know, same as I, that was a magic knife. You don't see any of the ones we just took down getting back up, do you?"

We all looked around, and it was true. I didn't see how the guy with the severed head could've healed anyway without help, but neither the hatchet-in-the-skull nor the severed spine showed any signs of healing either. They just looked—dead.

"You can't give up, Nabila. This isn't over." Helen was shaking her fists together in front of her own chin.

Nabila just stared at her.

"When my glasses came off, we read each other's minds." I noticed that Helen wasn't wearing her sunglasses any more. Neither was I for that matter. I think they must have fallen off my face when Helen threw me. "I was thinking that we needed to get them all, that they were all here together. He was thinking, ironically, that we wouldn't have had a chance except they were a man short. I got the hazy impression that one officer didn't think we would come and had already set out to track us home."

Nabila seemed puzzled. "Why would he do that? Some stranger reports you, and you offer to come in. They should have had every man present in case there was trouble."

Helen laughed without humor. "Headless over there agreed with you."

"No, I don't get it. The chief must've authorized the one tracking you home. Why would he do that?" Nabila sounded irritated, not angry. Like it bugged her that she didn't understand, but she didn't really care.

"The stranger we met must have told him I planned to run. I didn't change my mind until later," explained Helen.

"It still doesn't make sense. Why would they believe some stranger? When you called up offering to do the right thing? They split their forces on a stranger's hunch. Idiots."

Nabila was staring into space. I thought she was thinking about Julio, but then her head snapped back around to look at Helen. "Was there anything special about where he found you?"

Helen briefly told her the story of how we had gone to visit the house that morning, about the markings on the house and that she'd left me to deliver her note alone. That led to telling her about the markings on the fists of the father who'd assaulted her. Nabila wanted to know how the markings had gotten passed down if the baby had been adopted. Helen explained about the connection to the Order of St. Michael.

Nabila nodded as if all this made sense to her. "Magic is the only way humans can fight us. Even then they have to be careful to be as secret as we are because we're always looking out for them." Nabila looked down at Julio and sighed. She said a little bitterly, "I notice you didn't mention your trip to the house and the connection to St. Michael before we attacked the police."

Helen seemed confused. "Why would they matter?"

Nabila looked at her pityingly. "The police had the house staked out. They'd probably watched for years, getting ready to roll up this guy's network. Once they had all his contacts identified, they'd kill them all." She shook her head. "You showing up—of course the guy on stakeout followed you and checked you out."

Helen looked shocked. "So the mind-reader I met was a police officer?"

"They didn't split their forces on a stranger's hunch. They knew you weren't sincere. They probably pegged you as a traitor, working with the Order. They figured they could ambush you if you did come, but the chief let the other one track you home because he didn't really expect you here. It all makes sense."

She stammered, "Nabila, I didn't know. I would've told you."

Nabila didn't seem to care. "You were trying to save Alex." Nabila looked at me and then back at Helen. "I'd've done the same for Julio." She looked down at Julio's body again.

"Nabila, we can't stay here. We need to find the one tracking us before he reports my name to any other police. This isn't over." Helen was holding Nabila's shoulders and practically shaking her with urgency.

Nabila was unmoved. "It is for me. It's over. Go."

Helen looked at her stubbornly. "I can't leave you like this. Anyway, we need you with us."

Nabila took off her sunglasses—by some miracle still on her face despite all her flying. She looked at Helen with sad eyes. "Go," she said. "I'll clean up here. I promise I'll join you back in the states once I arrange to have Julio's body transported there." She looked down at Julio again, and closed his eyes with her fingers. "I don't think the spirit's still in him, but it makes sense to give it time to see if it is."

She looked up at Helen again. "You and your parents deserve some kind of funeral I suppose."

Helen was unsatisfied. "You need to come with us, to help me protect Alex."

"That's your job now. I'm staying with my Julio. Go." There was no compromise in her tone.

Helen waited a moment more. Nabila gave her a warning glare. Helen got up from her knees and helped me to my feet as well. She took my hand and gestured to the open door. It was getting dark outside.

"What are we going to do?" I asked Helen once we were outside.

"Do you have your passport?"

I felt my pocket. "Yes," I confirmed.

Helen looked relieved. "Then we're driving straight to Mexico City and taking the first plane we can get to Philadelphia."

It was a long walk to where we'd parked the car. I tried to put my hand around Helen's waist, and I was surprised to discover that she'd put her hatchet back in her waistband. "Why?" I said.

"In case we run into the other police officer. He's looking for us on the run, and since we're running now, maybe he'll find us." She almost sounded hopeful. I was terrified and nauseated with reaction to the violence I'd just seen. She might have noticed me shaking because she added, "Don't worry, Alex. I won't be caught off guard again. I'll keep you safe." Fine, I thought, but who will keep you safe? This time, we won't have Nabila.

What I said was, "You're not going to try to bring that hatchet through airport security, are you?"

Helen laughed, and that made me feel better.

The next moment my memory replayed the scene of Nabila casually sticking the gold dagger in her fallen enemy's eye. I threw up.

There wasn't much in my stomach to come up—we had skipped lunch in all the crisis of the day—but I fell to my knees and heaved. There was a little vomit in my mouth, on my face and on the street.

Helen dropped down beside me and held my sides. "Alex, are you okay?" She made a disgusted noise. "No, obviously not. Is it your head? I threw you pretty hard."

I was sore and bruised and miserable, but I also didn't want to burden her with all that. We needed to get to the car. "I'm fine."

Helen was busying herself feeling my scalp with her fingers through my hair. It felt sort of good until suddenly it hurt like hell. "Ow, Helen, stop that!"

"Pretty tender, eh?" Helen sounded sympathetic.

That's when my memory replayed the moment where Julio pulled the dagger out of his chest and simply stood there, holding the wound. I had thought he was going to be all right, but now I realized he must've been dying on his feet. I started heaving again, but nothing came up.

Helen held me until I stopped. She helped me up and wiped my face with a corner of the loose end of her shirt. Because I didn't want her to get my vomit on her shirt, I tried to pull away. She grabbed the back of my neck and held me tight and kept wiping. She spit on the end of her shirt and wiped once more. She finally announced, "Okay, you're clean."

She looked over my face carefully. "Tell me how you're feeling. I need to know whether you're concussed." She stared into my eyes.

"I'm fine," I said. I didn't want to slow her down. That's when my memory replayed all of Nabila's lethal moves with the gold dagger in order, followed by her stabbing herself.

Helen must've seen what I was thinking. She flinched. "That's enough to make anyone sick to his stomach."

I looked away from her kind, concerned face. It was nice of her to say, but I couldn't help but notice that she wasn't losing her breakfast on the street. "Sorry to be such a baby. Do you think you could use your 'eye' to make me braver? So I don't slow us down."

"In case you hadn't noticed, I already did. I pushed you far past your limits." She sounded upset. I thought she was upset with me.

"Oh," I said, disgusted with myself. I had given myself credit for walking bravely to the fight—where I had been useless—when actually that had been Helen. "Thanks for making me brave then. I'd thought it was me doing it."

That seemed to make Helen exasperated. "Of course it was you, stupid. That's why *you're* the one that's sick right now."

All I heard of that was that she called me stupid. I was clean out of bravery, and I started to cry.

Helen instantly looked upset again. "I'm so sorry. I didn't mean... You've been so brave this afternoon. You've done so much more than I possibly could've expected of you. I... Alex, look at me." I did. "Kiss me." I did, briefly but passionately. My chest unclenched.

Afterwards, I noticed a curiously frozen expression on her face. At the same moment I realized that my mouth still tasted like vomit. She must've forgotten and was trying not to hurt my feelings by looking revolted. We both started laughing.

As I wiped tears from my eyes, I said, "Julio told me that angry Nabila was scary. I guess I know now what he meant."

"I guess you do. Her knife work is truly intimidating."

"Do you think he's really gone? Or is there hope?" I didn't want her brother to be dead because of me.

"With vampires, there's always some hope, but if that dagger was magicked to kill the evil spirit, then he's really gone." Helen sounded a little defeated, like she didn't really expect a miracle.

I thought of Nabila trying to use the knife on herself, like Juliet trying to drink from Romeo's empty poison bottle. "Is Nabila safe to be alone with that knife?"

Helen nodded her head. "We all saw that it's harmless now. We might learn something useful from studying it. I hope she brings it back with her."

I cocked an eyebrow at her. "You don't think she'll try bring that big ass dagger past airport security, do you?" The dagger hadn't been that big, and my joke was still lame the second time around, but Helen and I both started laughing so hard we had to clutch each other to hold ourselves up.

Then we went to go get the car.

Alex slept a little while I drove to Mexico City's airport. He slept a little more waiting several hours in the middle of the night at the gate. Few people were as early, so he spread out along three seats with his head in my lap. His sleeping face looked painfully young. Oh my poor baby Alex! I was miserable thinking about the danger I had put him through.

I got out my phone to make the call I didn't want to make. "Mom?" I said.

"You're alive." Mom's voice was filled with relief. "Here, we're in the hotel. I'm waking Victor." I could hear her waking him up. "I've put you on speaker."

"Mom, I need to tell you, we won, but..." I closed my eyes. "Julio's gone." I heard my mom's sharp breath and moan. My dad said bitterly, "Life is cruel. It isn't fair."

I wondered why my dad would rub salt in my wound. He wasn't always kind, but he was usually considerate. "What are you saying? That if life were fair I'd be dead right now? And Alex? But not Julio? Is that what you are saying?"

Mom said, "Your dad didn't say anything like that. I'm sure he doesn't think that."

I sighed, defeated. "No, you're right. I said it. Because it's true. It's my fault."

Dad said, "We are all hurting right now. This is terrible news."

"Is it over, then? You won. You and Alex and Nabila are safe?" Mom wanted to know.

"We're safe for now, but it's not over. There is one more coming to look for us. I'm headed home." I was rubbing my forehead wondering what Mom and Dad must be thinking. I had really screwed up their lives.

"We're coming home too, then," said Mom.

"We'll do what we can to help, but we don't promise to take on all the police in the world," said Dad.

I could hear Mom say quietly to Dad that she's not asking us to do that. It's true. I wasn't. We wished each other love, and I ended the call.

I sat looking at my Alex's sleeping face. I wasn't asking them to fight all the police in the world because I knew they'd say no. I wasn't asking them because it was futile. If either one of those things hadn't been true, I would've asked. Pointless as it was, I would've asked.

21. PRICE

Helen and I got on the first available plane to Philadelphia. On the plane, I quietly asked Helen why she thought the remaining officer might come after us. It did not make any sense to me. The logical thing to do would be to alert the central authorities and send out an all-points bulletin, right? Helen explained that vampire police were less professional and more ruthless than human police and that could sometimes make them less efficient. She said that the local police had been defeated so badly, the central authorities might kill the remaining officer to send a message. Then the whole station in Zinapécuaro would be re-staffed. However, if the remaining officer managed to kill us and survive, he might be made the new chief.

When we got back to Minersville, Helen did not want me to go to either my house or hers, which were obvious targets. My parents wouldn't be expecting me yet, but I was worried about their safety.

"If the police come to my house, will they kill my parents?" I felt like panicking.

"I won't let that happen," Helen promised. "Since you'll only get in my way in a fight like that, I want to get you to safety." Even though I hated to leave her, I agreed with her logic. I knew from experience I couldn't help in a fight against vampires.

Helen gave me her mom's car keys. I don't know, maybe they were really her car keys. It was hard to tell in Helen's family what was real and what was subterfuge.

"I want you to take this car and drive to Jane's. The police won't have any reason to connect you to that place. I'll take on anyone who comes to your house. I think I can defeat one lone vampire. I'm hoping the remaining officer won't have reported to the central authorities what happened in Mexico yet. If he *has*, you and I may have to go on the run permanently."

I didn't want to leave my family. Since I knew I didn't have a choice, I drove to Jane's place.

"Hey, Alex," she said at her door. "What brings you here?"

I told her I needed a safe place to hang out, and I didn't want to go home.

"I thought you hung out at Helen's." She motioned me inside. "Isn't that safe?"

Because I'm not a good liar, I told a partial truth. "Some people Helen doesn't want me to meet are expected there."

"Fine by me. Dad's in town getting an engine fixed." Jane and I chatted a bit in the living room. I was surprised that she didn't ask anything about the people Helen didn't want me to meet.

Jane's doorbell rang, and I jumped nervously. Jane said, "Will you get that, Alex?" and headed down the hall toward the kitchen, which connected to the garage. Not sure why she left me like that, I answered the door.

I found myself eye-to-eye with the police officer from Mexico. Shit, I thought, he's here to kill me.

"Sit down with me at that table behind you," he commanded.

I found myself backing into the entryway and through the arch to the dining room. I was doing what he said before I could stop myself. Then I realized I literally couldn't stop myself.

He sat down across from me at the dining room table. "Before I kill you, I need you to tell me if you have told any other humans about vampires. Tell me now." I couldn't think. I had to answer.

"No, I haven't," I said. Technically, this was true. Jane had told *me* about vampires. I took advantage of the moment to ask him a question. "Have you told anyone about Helen or me?" I wanted to die knowing that Helen still had a chance to escape.

"No, but that won't save you—or her," he sneered. That "no" was what I wanted to hear before I died. Helen could still kill him, and no other police would know to look for her. At least she could live.

At that moment, there was a loud bang and a large, ragged red hole appeared in his forehead. My ears rang, and I smelled gunpowder. He slumped off his chair and onto the floor.

Free of the compulsion of his eyes, I turned around and saw Jane standing in the hall with a shotgun. "He was a vampire here to kill you, wasn't he?" she asked.

"Yes," I said. I was in shock. "How do you know about vampires?" Helen had made her forget. We'd argued about it. "Last time, you didn't remember what Mr. Martin said, and you never believed the story anyway."

Jane lowered the gun. "Helen visited me and unblocked my memories. She seemed to think it was important to you. The fact that she could mess with my mind in the first place kind of convinced me on the whole vampire bit." She grimaced, and I nodded. Jane added, "Thanks for making her fix my head."

"Thanks for saving my life." I meant it. Then I had a really bad thought. "Jane, we've got to get out of here and fast. Vampires heal quickly, and he'll be after us. In fact, I don't know why he's still down." I looked at him and felt rising panic.

"Silver shot." Jane looked pleased with herself.

"What?" What she'd said was so unexpected that it took me a moment to process it. Silver shot? Why would anyone load a shotgun with precious metal? You couldn't buy ammunition like that, could you?

"You shot him with silver shot?" It just didn't make sense.

"Yup." Jane sounded smug.

Silver shot would explain why the vampire was still on the floor. Helen said silver interfered with the spirit's ability to heal. "How in heaven's name did you happen to have a gun loaded with silver shot?" That was crazy.

"I wanted to make silver bullets, but after I watched a YouTube video, I realized I'd have to use something really hot, like a blowtorch, to melt silver. So, instead I used a bolt cutter to cut up some old silver forks Dad had from Gran. I hammered them a bit and used the pieces to replace the shot in some shells. Don't tell Dad about the forks, or he'll be pissed."

Jane's resourcefulness never ceased to amaze me. "When? Why?"

Jane looked away. "As soon as I got my memories back. I wanted to be safe from vampires."

"You couldn't have known this guy was coming."

Jane gave me a cold stare. "I needed to be ready in case your bitch girlfriend came back." Her posture was rigid, which was usually her way of hiding strong emotion. It occurred to me that the interference with her mind must have left her terrified.

Since I wasn't in a position to complain, I begged. "Please, please, please don't kill Helen."

"Yeah, I see how it is with you two," she said with a sigh. "What are we going to do with this one?" She pointed to the body.

"Silver only messes with their healing," I informed her. "It's not a guarantee. We need to burn him."

Jane thought about that for a moment. "All right then. Help me carry his body out back to where we got a barrel. Then I'll get some gasoline." We carried him between us, and I learned that people are heavier than they look. We had to half drag him. Jane went for the gasoline and returned with a can and a large boning knife.

I got squeamish. "Can you do that part, please?"

Jane deadpanned, "You bring the evil undead to my house; you do the honors." She handed me the knife. "We've got to get done before Dad gets back."

Fortunately we did. Jane was going to need a story to explain why we'd burned something, but I left that to her. My job would be to find Helen and tell her what had happened.

"Jane, thanks again for saving me." I didn't know what else to say.

"I watch out for my friends." That's what she'd told Helen in the nursery, I remembered.

"What you did for me—killing that vampire—goes way beyond anything I possibly could have expected or can ever repay. The fact that you did it and the way you've handled yourself is incredible. I don't deserve a friend as amazing as you."

"Damn straight, you don't." We both laughed briefly. "Take care," she said.

I got in Helen's car and drove to her house. I entered by the front door and found Victor and Marisol standing with Helen in the living room. I told them what had happened at Jane's house. Helen looked horrified.

"I had no idea he would find you there. I thought for sure he would come at us directly. Alex, I'm so sorry I put you in danger." She looked shocked.

"Well, now he's dead. Thanks to Jane." I hoped that meant the danger was over.

"Yes, I must thank her. And you say the police officer said he hadn't told anyone about us?" She put her hand on her chin, musing. "I guess the danger really is over," she concluded. She smiled.

Victor looked angrily at Helen. "The danger is not over! The same problem exists. You aren't willing to follow the rules with Alex. And what's this about silver shot? How does this girl still know about us? I thought you'd fixed her." Victor was incensed.

Helen squirmed a bit. "I did, but later I thought it'd be better to unfix her."

Marisol said, "What would possess you to do that?" Her tone suggested she was very disappointed in Helen.

Victor looked at me pointedly. "Alex, I welcomed you to this house, and you've cost me the life of my son, Julio."

I couldn't look him in the eye. "I'm sorry, sir. I only wanted to love Helen." I felt a weight of guilt I could never escape.

Victor raised his chin. "Keep doing that, and I may eventually forgive you—and her. That is if you two can manage to stay alive." He turned to Helen. "You are a danger to your family, to any vampire with whom you live."

"We are leaving," said Marisol. She was shaking her head at Helen.

Helen was distressed. "I can't live alone in Minersville where I'm seventeen. I can't go anywhere else to be older because I can't leave Alex."

"We know that," said Marisol. "We don't mean to make you desperate. Your father's contacted an old friend who's both willing and reckless enough to agree to live with you. We'll think of a story."

Victor added, "We'll come back for Julio's funeral. Once you graduate from high school, we will make the house over to you, and you can do as you like."

"Will I ever see you again?" asked Helen.

Marisol sounded sad. "*Querida,* I believe in my heart that you will."

"However, you must regularize your relationship with Alex first," said Victor.

"Kill him or turn him," Helen said bitterly. "That's my choice? You won't see me again until I do?"

"You just have to be *willing* to kill him and just if the secret is in danger," said Marisol. It sounded like she was pleading with Helen to be willing.

"If you care about him too much for that, then share your spirit with him," said Victor. "Trade it back and forth as your mother and I did." He acted like Helen was being irrational.

"I love you," said Marisol to Helen. "Take care until we see each other again."

"I, too, love you," said Victor, "Stay safe, *hija.*" He gave me a look as if to say they'd let me witness this parting scene so I'd know how much Helen was giving up for me. The truth is she'd already given up too much for me. I wondered if I'd be willing to give up as much for her.

"Helen, I need to get back to my house. I need to see that my parents are safe." I was worried how the police officer had known I was at Jane's. What if he'd interrogated my parents? Of course, they hadn't known I'd be there. They thought I'd be in Mexico still. Then I realized that he must've plucked the image of Jane from my mind.

She had been next to her mailbox. He could've used an Internet search engine and street view to find her house. I felt a little relieved.

"The danger should be over now, but I'll walk you there." She did, and then she came inside, too.

My dad came out of the kitchen looking agitated.

"Alex, why are you back early? Jane's father just called. He said you were back and over at their house this afternoon. Why didn't you come straight home? Bob wants to know why Jane's in bed shaking and crying. Did something happen over there? Did you two have a fight?"

I thought: yes and we won. I had no idea what to tell my dad. Fortunately Helen rescued me.

"I think I know what it is, Mr. Clarke. I'll go see her right now." Helen was acting the part of good-girl volunteer.

"Do you know what's going on then?" Dad sounded relieved.

Helen nodded, "Yeah, and I think I can help her."

"What's wrong with her?" Dad looked concerned.

Helen shook her head and smiled a little bit. "You really don't want to know."

"Should Alex go with you?" Dad asked.

Helen said confidentially, "I think it would be better if it were just the two of us *girls.*" Dad looked a little frightened at that.

"Okay, I get the picture." He turned to me. "Alex, after you say goodbye to Helen, I want to talk to you." Dad went back into the kitchen.

I walked outside with Helen. Once the front door was closed, I said to her in an urgent whisper. "Are you crazy? She made that silver shot for you!"

"I can help her. I understand what she's going through. I'm going to need you to call her and let her know I'm coming."

My whisper got a little louder. "So she can *reload?*" I was incredulous.

Helen was unmoved. "So she knows I'm there as a friend."

"*I'm* her friend," I insisted. "*You,* I'm not so sure about."

"You've no idea what she's feeling. Just convince her not to shoot until I can talk with her." I thought Helen's faith in my ability to control Jane was seriously misplaced.

"Don't mess with her mind, Helen," I warned her. "That's not acceptable to her or to me."

"I know that, and I wasn't planning to. It has not escaped my notice that she was only able to save your life because her memories were intact. After this afternoon, I'm feeling particularly well disposed towards her. I want to help." She got into her car and put the key in the ignition.

"All right. Don't forget to duck." I shut the car door, but not before she said, "Don't forget to call Jane before I get there."

I got out my phone and called. This was too urgent for a text.

She answered right away. "Alex, you okay?" She sounded worried.

I told her that Helen was on her way.

"I've got more silver shot, you know."

"She is not there to mess with you. She just wants to help."

"I don't trust her."

"Do you trust me?"

"I guess."

"Then, please don't shoot her, and let her help you."

Jane's father met me at the door. I introduced myself as Jane's friend, and he told me she was in her room and gestured for me to come inside. I

guessed her room would be up the flight of stairs. There was a short hall with four open doors, three bedrooms and a bathroom. Jane's room was crammed floor to ceiling with junk. Mismatched shelves had been added here and there to accommodate books, various 4H trophies and ribbons, travel mementos and a large framed picture of a woman who was presumably Jane's mother. Dirty clothes were discarded on the floor and a pile of them overflowed from the closet as well. Jane was lying on top of her covers on the bed.

"I didn't want you to come here." Jane sat up and looked at me.

"I'd just like to help."

"I don't need your help." Jane crossed her arms.

"I can see that. I can see how strong you are." The determination in her eyes was impressive. I tried a different approach. "Alex told me how you saved his life today. Nice job on the silver shot, by the way. Thank you. You have my literally eternal gratitude." She'd done what I should've. Now she was paying the price. "He told me you made him cut up the body. We both know you could've done it better. You let him help you, to let him feel useful. Why don't you let me help you, too?"

"It's over. There's nothing left for you to do." Jane shook her head.

"It's not over for you, though," I pointed out. "Your father says you were in bed shaking and crying."

"I wasn't crying." She was defensive against what she mistook for criticism.

"I believe you," I said truthfully. This child was strong. "I notice your right hand is shaking. Is that your dominant hand?"

Jane held up her shaking right hand in front of her face like it was a curious object. "What do you mean?" She sounded puzzled.

"Is that the hand you used to pull the trigger?"

Comprehension dawned on her face. "Yes," she admitted.

"May I?" I indicated a spot on the bed. When she didn't say anything, I sat down. "It won't be over for you until your brain replays the trauma again and again to try to understand it."

"What trauma?" She gave a contemptuous snort. "I killed that vampire bastard before he hurt Alex."

That attitude might be enough to protect her, but it might not. "Yes, but you just said it: 'before he killed Alex.' You were afraid because you imagined it. In your mind, you saw him do it. That's why you shot him."

"I'm not sorry I killed him."

"I'm not sorry either. You have no idea how glad I am he's dead. You're going to remember his face forever though."

"You could make me forget it."

I nodded. "I could, but I won't unless you ask. I'm not sure it would be a good idea either. You need to work through this on your own."

"Then why are you here?"

"To help in any way I can, to give whatever support you need." I thought about what I could do for her. "I can lend you strength if you need it. I can listen to you tell this story that you can't tell anyone else." I reinforced that by looking in her eyes. Her heroism would be pointless if she got us all killed with loose talk. "I can be your friend. I can hold your hand."

"Friend?" Jane sounded surprised. Then she looked down and noticed that I'd covered her right hand with mine for much of our conversation.

Her hand was still.

22. OFFER

The excuse I gave my dad for why we came back early was that Mr. García had something come up at work. Dad wanted to know why I hadn't called, so I told him I forgot. He shrugged and said "Yeah, that happens," which made me really glad I wasn't having this conversation with Mom. Dad was a lot more suspicious about why I went Jane's house, instead of coming home. He also wanted to know why Jane had gotten so hysterical afterwards—his word, not mine. I put him off with the somewhat lame "because I didn't think you'd be home" and "I don't have any idea what's up with Jane." He gave me grief about the former, but he shrugged and accepted the latter as a totally valid response to womankind. Sometimes I think my dad judges me solely by what he would've done in my place.

I don't think that Dad remembered to tell Mom that I'd gone over to Jane's—or maybe he just chose not to. Mom was happy to have me home and asked for every detail of the trip. Fortunately I was able to get away with describing Morelia and Zinapécuaro in great detail over dinner. No one else had any idea how much I was leaving out. Simon kept telling me how "lucky" I was, which basically meant we were both jealous of each other's Easter breaks. Inskeep kept jumping up on me and licking my hands, which I hate (because I then feel the need to wash my hands). That made me think of Helen's idea that he and Simon had been named after public radio personalities.

That evening, I did an Internet search for "Alexander" and "NPR." I didn't find any reporters, so maybe that wasn't the way my mom came up with names. I breathed a sigh of relief. I did find various famous authors with the last name Alexander who'd been interviewed on NPR. I found an author who wrote about how the police basically oppress young black men. I thought about how Helen lived in fear of the vampire police. Simon was right. I was lucky.

I didn't see much of Helen that week. She was helping Nabila make arrangements to return Julio's body to the United States and plan his funeral. It was going to be in Philadelphia, not Minersville. That's because the Garcías didn't plan to admit to anyone that he had died. "It's too memorable, a tragedy like that," Helen said one afternoon when she found some time to update me. "We don't want people noticing us too much, and this would make them notice." She pointed out that neighbors had never seen Julio much before because he was at college. The story would be that he was studying overseas, and eventually that he was living overseas.

Being without Helen was good for my homework situation, but bad for giving me far too much time to think about Mexico—and Julio. He really was dead, it seemed. I'd watched him die. If I was upset about it, how must Helen feel? He'd been part of her life for longer than my parents had been part of each other's. I felt guilty because I was the cause of it. If Helen hadn't decided to tell me her secrets, she wouldn't have been in trouble with the police, and Julio never would've fought them.

Helen had lost a brother for me. That was too high a price to pay. If I loved her, I shouldn't put her family in danger. I couldn't bear the idea of forgetting about her, which is the only way I could stop putting them at risk. It felt selfish to me. Of course, if I tried to forget her, I wasn't entirely sure she'd let me. Also, that would have made Julio's sacrifice pretty pointless.

I realized there were two ways I could stop endangering her family. I could ask her to make me forget and just be her clueless boyfriend (again). Or I could ask her to share her spirit and make me a vampire. She'd more-or-less offered that in Mexico. But she'd said that meant I wouldn't be able to see my family again.

I thought uncomfortably about my family. I didn't want to compromise their safety. Being with Helen was also putting them at constant risk. I'd attracted that vampire police officer to Jane's house, but I might've just as easily gone home. If I had, he probably would've killed anyone he'd found at home with me. Putting my own family in danger felt even more selfish to me than risking Helen's family. At least they'd known what was going on and had some ability to protect themselves.

All this thinking wasn't getting me anywhere. If I wasn't willing to ask Helen to make me forget or to share her spirit, all this self-examination was pointless. I was just being secretive and selfish. I was endangering my family because it felt good to be with Helen the way I wanted to be with her. I never felt more worthless.

Being alone wasn't helping either. Helen apologized for not inviting me to Julio's funeral in Philadelphia. It wasn't much more than a family affair in a funeral home, but she said I deserved to be there after Mexico. She explained that her parents refused to come if I'd be there, and I told her I didn't mind staying away. I hated cutting her off from her parents, and I didn't think I should push them out of their son's funeral.

The day after, Helen came over told me all about it. She cried a bit. I told her that I'd never cease to be grateful for his sacrifice. "I'll also never forget that you fought for me, instead taking the easy way out and killing me."

Helen shook her head. "That wouldn't have been easy at all."

She told me that her parents had said they wouldn't come back and she should cover for them until June. That was when Victor's friend would be able to come. The story would be that both their companies insisted they transfer to new territories or lose their jobs, but they wanted Helen to be able to finish school in the same place. Helen's "aunt" would live with her for her senior year.

Helen also told me that Nabila wanted to speak to me.

"Me?" I squeaked. I wondered why she'd want to speak to me. I was terrified she'd blame me for Julio.

"You," Helen confirmed.

"Why? Is she safe?"

The answers I got were "I don't know" and "I'll be there to protect you." Helen smiled as she said the last one, which was good. Having seen Nabila in action, I doubted Helen would've been much protection, but I also doubted Helen would be smiling if Nabila were likely to intend me harm.

I went over to Helen's house on Saturday afternoon to hear what Nabila had to say. Wearing a colorful African headscarf, she was sipping tea in the dining room. I sat down, and Helen brought me a Coke before sitting down next to me.

Nabila began by saying something to Helen in Spanish, who replied in Spanish. I realized that my lessons hadn't gotten to the point that I could understand them. Usually the Garcías spoke in English around me, but I'd begun to suspect Helen of sometimes using Spanish when she didn't want me to understand. I wondered what Nabila and Helen were saying, and why they hadn't said it before I came over.

Nabila said, *"Antes de empezamos, digasme algo. ¿María Helena, es este joven el uno para ti? ¿Es tu Julio, cariña?"*

"Espero que si. De verdad, lo espero mucho."

Then Nabila turned to me. "I have something to say to you, Alex, an offer for you to consider. With Julio gone, the time has come for me to leave this life."

"No!" interrupted Helen. "Don't say that."

Nabila fixed her with a glare. "I've made my choice, and I want you to respect it."

Helen looked worriedly at me and then at Nabila, comprehension dawning. "Oh, no," she said, "please, we're not ready."

"I am. I am *done*. He's going to hear this, or will you take from him the choice, as was done to you?"

Helen looked stricken. Nabila said to her, *"Bueno. Cállate. No me digas que lo hiciste y después decirme que él no puede escuchar esto."*

She turned back to me. "As I was saying, I'm ready to leave this unnatural life. I was ready in 1942, but Julio made me reconsider. With him gone, I'm ready to go. When I die, I'll take the evil spirit with me, destroying it forever."

"¿Como?" whispered Helen.

"Fuego," said Nabila to her. Then she continued to me, "Now, I wonder if that evil spirit should be spared to do some good for my sister. She's determined to try to be with you. If you stay human, what happened in Mexico may happen again. I'm offering to let you drink my blood—all of it—and take the spirit within me."

Helen looked distressed but said nothing and merely looked at me. Truly I wasn't ready to make this choice. It was like Mexico, all over again, when Helen had offered to take me underground. I'd be cut off from family, friends, everyone I knew—except Helen—and that exception had me pausing to consider. It was completely revolting to think about drinking Nabila's blood, and my revulsion made me wonder whether I was cut out to be a vampire. Still, it would let me stay with Helen. I didn't think this kind of offer came more than once to anyone.

Nabila said, "This way, you wouldn't have to spend years underground, weak, trading the spirit back and forth. You'd be strong, as strong as Helen."

"Would I be a killer?" I asked.

"That part's up to you," she said.

I thought about it. "I'd be killing you," I said. "That seems wrong to me, like murder. You're Helen's sister. She loves you." Helen beamed approval at me.

"Boy, you don't get it. I'm dying already. I'm old, sick and weary of life. Death isn't a tragedy for someone like me. It's a release." Nabila was starting to sound like Grandma Fulton, and silent tears started in my eyes.

Nabila unwrapped the lovely headscarf she had been wearing. I saw with shock that her hair was pure white. Helen looked shocked, too. I noticed wrinkles on the skin of her face that I hadn't noticed before. I'm not really that good at estimating the age of black people, but I realized that she didn't look like a woman in her early twenties any more. This might be fifty—or a well-preserved seventy even.

Helen drew a sharp breath. "Nabila, you must eat! You must drink!"

Nabila looked at her wearily. "I have neither eaten food nor drunk blood since Julio. I won't go below ground again. I am dying, and I'm taking the spirit with me—unless this boy says otherwise. He has a week to decide."

She turned to me. "If you want to try to be to Helen what Julio was to me, I'll give you my blood, Alex." Then she left.

It was only later that I realized that that was the first time Nabila had ever addressed me by name. I thought Helen and I should discuss Nabila's offer, but the only thing she'd say was, "This choice must be yours."

I didn't really understand what she meant. I wouldn't even have been considering it if it weren't for her. The only point of accepting would be to be with Helen.

Nabila came to my house the next day and asked to see me. My parents were out, and Simon just sent her up to my room. Apparently, he hadn't gotten the whole no-girls-in-Alex's-room lecture. Also, Nabila was beginning to look like an old lady, so I don't know that Simon would have considered her a girl.

I was sitting at my desk, working on my math homework for Monday. Helen had gotten me to the point where I didn't really need her constant tutoring in math though I never minded spending the time with her. I was really surprised when Nabila showed up at my door. "Hi," I said.

She gave me a little smile. "Hi," she replied. She sat down on the edge of my bed, a little stiffly. Then she said, "When I made my offer yesterday, I thought it was the obvious solution to your and Helen's problem. I thought you two might jump at it. Now I'm wondering what's making you hesitate."

I thought about that. "I was going to talk it over with Helen yesterday, but she says she won't tell me what to do."

Nabila smiled, a real genuine smile. "Good that," she said nodding approval. "So, what do you want? Do you want to be with Helen?"

"Yeah." Of that I was sure.

"Then why're you hesitating?" She didn't say it like she wanted to know. It was more like Nabila was helping me ask the questions I should ask myself.

"For one thing, I don't want to kill you. If I drink your blood and you pass the spirit to me, you'll die in short order. That's what Helen told me." Part of me worried that Helen would hold it against me if I killed Nabila, even if Nabila were determined to die.

"I've already told you that I'm ready to go. You'd just be helping me along. Hm, how can I explain this to you?" Nabila looked around and saw my bookshelf. She peered at it and picked out a book. It was a book of myths about shapeshifters, illustrated by one of the artists who'd worked on *The Lord of the Rings* movies. I loved his work.

Nabila opened the book and said to me, "Have you read these stories?"

"Yeah," I admitted, "They're easier to read than Ovid's originals, and I like the pictures."

She found a place in the book and showed it to me. "Do you remember this one here, 'Hospitality Repaid'?"

I looked at it. "Oh, yeah, this is the one where the poor old couple play host to Zeus and Hermes in disguise. I like the part where they chase after their two geese to try and have some food to offer. It seems sweet." I looked up at Nabila, and then I understood why she'd chosen this story. "Zeus offers them a wish in repayment, and they ask if they can die at the same time. They don't want to live without each other."

Nabila smiled. "You ever wondered why they were hospitable when everyone else turned the gods away?"

I hadn't. I'd just assumed they were good people.

Nabila said, "It's because they had love. Those two loved each other so much they didn't feel poor. They felt rich. They wanted to share what they had."

She sighed. "I used to be a selfish, soulless, death-dealing machine. Until Julio made me laugh so hard I could love. I loved him so much,

I felt full of his love. I realized I didn't need so much blood to fill me up. I didn't need to kill. The people I'd been killing had people that loved them. We loved each other so much we couldn't bear to take that feeling away from anyone—even strangers." Nabila looked at me with pride. "For the last fifty years, no human guest under our roof has come to harm."

I really liked the way Nabila saw the story, and I liked what she'd shared about herself, but I wasn't sure how it affected my decision. "What are you saying?"

"I'm saying that if you took my spirit, you'd be doing me a favor, granting my wish." Nabila was being very patient. I'd remembered that Julio said she only explained if she really liked you.

"I'm not sure if I want to be a vampire," I admitted. That's really why I was hesitating. That and the ick factor. If I said I was ready, was she going to open a vein right here in my room? God, I hoped not.

"That, I can't help you with," said Nabila. She started to get up, but I stopped her with a question.

"What's it feel like to be a vampire?" That's what I really needed to know.

"It feels great!" Nabila flashed a triumphant smile that was all white teeth.

"It feels great when you're killing people." She paused and reflected. "Until you realize that killing people is wrong. No matter what you tell yourself about how it's different for you, that you're different, that the rules don't apply—it's still murder, and it's still wrong. Then being a vampire doesn't feel so great anymore." Nabila shook her head. I started to speak, but she raised her hand to stop me. She smiled.

"It feels great when you love." She paused again and then looked pained. "Until the one you love is gone. Then it doesn't feel so great anymore." Her eyes were glassy.

I waited to be sure she was done. Then I said, "I don't mean this as a judgment on you, but I don't want to be a killer, and I don't need to be a vampire to love Helen."

Nabila nodded her approval before she left. "Well, I'll be. Maybe my little Helen ain't so crazy after all. I don't want to see you ever again."

She didn't.

Nabila asked me to come to the large funeral home where we'd had our tiny funeral for Julio. The clueless human funeral director had respected our wishes and left us in private. Everyone there had been in on the secret, and we told one Julio story after another until laughter and tears came and went.

I didn't know why Nabila wanted me to come here in the middle of the night. The building was in a working class section of Philadelphia, and I was having unhappy memories of searching for victims on the streets and back alleys. I was starting to feel faint cravings for blood again. Alex's rich blood hadn't cured me of hunger permanently, and I guessed I'd need to drink again before May was over.

I wondered why Nabila had wanted me to go to the back entrance, which was down an alley. When I got there, she was already inside and opened the door for me. She looked terribly old and weak.

"Come on in," she said.

"Nabila, why are we here?" I'd wanted to ask before, but she'd hung up quickly and never responded to my text. I couldn't really believe some miracle had happened with Julio. She would've trumpeted that news.

"I wanted your help. I could do this myself, but not as secretly."

Nabila seldom asked for help. "What can I do?" I asked.

"I chose this funeral home because it's also a crematorium." Suddenly I had a bad feeling about this. "I've signed papers for Julio to be cremated tomorrow. I plan on doing it tonight, with me included."

I had known she was planning on burning herself—so the evil spirit couldn't ever bring her back—but I hadn't expected her to ask me to do it.

"Why do you need me?" I tried to keep my distress out of my voice. I loved Nabila after all.

"I could hotwire the machine that runs the burners, and set a timer on it, but when they come in the morning they'd know someone did it." That would be bad. Neither of us wanted an investigation, especially one connected to Julio. "If you do what I show you, they'll just think someone did Julio overnight. Since they're supposed to cremate him anyway, I'll bet they either don't notice or hush it up. Why call the police if you screw up by doing something you were supposed to do anyway?"

I wished she'd left me out of this, maybe asked Dad. Then I realized that not asking Dad might have been her way of showing that she was still close to me. Maybe this meant I was forgiven. I looked in her eyes and saw that I was.

Through tears, I asked, "Isn't this a little too much like the ancient barbarity of a widow throwing herself on her husband's funeral pyre? You were always more than Julio's wife."

Nabila nodded approval. "You're right about that. No, I'm not doing this because I'm nothing without Julio. I'm still me. This is my choice. You know we don't die except by violence, either from others or from ourselves.

I've done everything I wanted to do in my life, and I'm not waiting for others to come after me. I want to end as I lived—as I choose, as I see fit. Will you help me?"

Of course I would. She let me kiss her. "Show me how?"

She took me to the room where they did the cremations. She opened the oven with Julio's body already inside. She showed me how the machine worked and she climbed in with him.

I almost couldn't bring myself to push the button. However, I was sure that Nabila had told me the truth. She didn't need me. She just didn't want the human police asking us questions. I guessed that meant she'd given them Julio's real name. I pushed the button. I hadn't insulted Nabila by asking why she chose what had to be a painful way to go or whether she was sure she could bear it. Those weren't factors with her.

If Julio and Nabila could leave me a legacy, I would want Julio's humor.

And Nabila's pride.

23. PROM

When Helen told me that Nabila was gone, I didn't know what to say to console her. She'd lost half her family because of me. I wondered if she was disappointed that I hadn't taken up Nabila on her offer of the spirit, but I didn't bring it up because it was too late to change my mind.

The end of May brought the Minersville Junior-Senior Spring Prom. We'd missed the winter one for juniors in December. At the time, I'd asked her in a vague way, "Is this the kind of thing you'd like to do?" She had begged off, saying that she had her class in Philadelphia. Of course I knew now that she'd needed to drink blood. At the time, I'd been a little relieved I wouldn't have to dance, but I'd also been disappointed I didn't get to see Helen dressed up.

We were definitely going to prom this time.

On the day of prom, Helen had come over in the early afternoon to make sure I had tickets, suit and flowers. She'd suggested I come to her house where we could talk privately. "Alex, I'm going to need to drink from you again. That is, if you're still willing after Mexico." She bit her lip nervously.

"Mexico didn't change the way I feel about you."

Helen cocked her head. "I thought maybe you'd turned down Nabila because you'd had enough of vampires."

"No," I said, "I want to do this for you." Although I wasn't sure drinking blood was right for *me*, I had no problem with Helen doing it. As long as it was *my* blood. I worried whether she felt the same.

"Can we go to the mine after the prom?" she asked.

We could, thanks to a curfew extension. "My parents said I could stay out until one. Apparently, prom is 'special,' so I can stay out late."

Helen's eyes narrowed. "You don't think prom is 'special'?" Her tone alerted me to consider my words carefully.

I tried, "It's special because I'm going with you." That was true enough, but I don't think it's why my parents relaxed the rules. She looked mollified anyway. I changed the subject. "How long has it been since you drank from me in February?"

"Fifteen weeks. I used to drink the same amount and would need to drink every week, but your blood was so much more satisfying than what I stole." She smiled.

Excellent, I thought. That sounded like Helen would be happy to let me be her exclusive supply, and I guessed that I could afford to donate a pint every three or four months. I was happy I could be enough for her. I said expansively, "Who knows? Maybe if I love you enough, we can recreate the legend you told me on Christmas."

Helen suddenly got really angry, like she had at Jimmy and Jon on the ledge. Like she had when I'd spitefully asked if she'd killed her husband. She was shaking with rage.

"Is that what you're thinking? Don't you dare think like that! I told you that I'm not trying to recreate that legend. It's just a story!"

"I'm sorry." I was taken aback. "I don't know what I said to make you so angry. I didn't mean to. I just..." Her reaction was so unexpected. "Wouldn't you want to be human again?"

Helen closed her eyes as if trying to summon patience. She calmed herself at little. "Alex, I'm never going to be human again. That part of my existence is over and dead. I've grieved for it, and I accept it. I need for you to accept it, too. I'm never going to be able to have your children." Her voice broke on the word "children," and I finally understood why she was upset. I hadn't thought that far ahead. I'd always assumed I'd marry and have children someday, but clearly I couldn't if I was going to be with Helen. She'd already understood all that.

Helen continued sadly, "I'm never going to be able to have a normal life with you because I'm not normal. I'm never going to be normal again, but you still can be. You'd be better off with someone else." There were tears in her eyes.

"Given the choice between a normal life and you, I'll take you." I took her hand.

She looked into my eyes. Hers were still shining. "If I selfishly let you make that choice, it needs to be a real choice. You have options. You can't pretend it doesn't matter." She paused for a moment. "I need you to promise me something. Any girl who asks you to dance tonight, you say 'yes.' Do you understand me?" I gave Helen my stubborn look. She repeated, "Any girl who asks, you say 'yes' to her and dance. You don't say you're there with me. I'll make myself scarce."

"I only want to dance with you." I honestly didn't know if I still had a choice because Helen had been looking me in the eyes when she gave the order, but apparently I could still argue. It was a relief to discover even that much freedom.

"Tough. I know it's bad form to back out of a date on the day of prom, but if you don't promise me this, I won't go at all."

"No! Helen!" Then I sighed. How'd I get to the point where she was threatening to back out of prom? "Okay, I give up. I promise to dance with any girl who asks—not that anyone is going to ask me. I'm not really in high demand by anyone but you." Helen squeezed my hand and smiled tightly.

Me and my big, fat mouth. "Look, I'm sorry I brought up the whole legend thing. It's just that I was feeling a little proud that my blood is working out so well for you and maybe that went to my head."

Helen looked sad again. "Even if the legend were true, you weren't paying attention. I'd have to drink you dead, and you'd have to want to die for me. That must never happen. Mexico was bad enough. I hate that you risked your life for me."

"If I made a list of people I'd consider dying for, you'd be at the top of it."

"I know you're trying to be sweet, but you are going to make me angry again if you keep talking like that. I don't want to hear you talking about dying for me." She added intensely, "Do you not understand my feelings for you *at all?*"

"I don't understand you right now."

"Let me try to make myself clear. When we were in Mexico, I put you in danger. Even when we came back, I put you in danger. I didn't mean to do it, of course; it was ignorance and miscalculation on my part. Still, I remember how it made me feel: desperate. The most important thing to me then was keeping you safe. Even if I died, I wanted to know that you were safe."

"Am I not allowed to feel the same way about you?"

The tears started to fall from Helen's eyes. She came towards me, and I thought she was going to kiss me, but instead she put her head on my shoulder and crushed me in a fierce hug. She held me tightly, furiously—until it began to be inconvenient I couldn't get a good breath. I put on my best Simon impersonation and said, "Enough hugging now."

Helen let go immediately and laughed at first a bit sheepishly, perhaps at herself, and then more deeply at me, until she was wiping the tears from her cheeks. She checked the time and said she needed a couple hours to get ready for prom. Her eyes twinkled a bit despite the fresh tears when she told me she had to have enough time to make herself beautiful. I told her since she'd obviously done that already, what'd she want to do until five? She rolled her eyes and said she'd pick me up then. Before she left, she asked me to remind my parents that she wasn't allowed to have her picture taken. I was sure they'd expect photos, but Helen said I could blame it on a stalker the family had left behind and her parents being protective.

Helen picked me up punctually at five. She basically had her own car now, and my parents weren't the kind of people who thought renting a limousine was worth the expense. Mom and Dad had already done the picture thing with me. Mom was sad that we wouldn't have any pictures with Helen in them but she said she "totally understood" how Helen's parents must feel. Dad didn't, especially since we were ready to promise not to post the photos. But he did agree that it would cause trouble and possibly ruin the evening, so what would be the point of photos to remember it by?

When I saw Helen, I didn't think I would need a photo to remember how she looked at that moment.

She was wearing the most amazing red dress. "It's not that dress," she whispered to me, "but I'm reclaiming the color for myself." She'd done up hair, wrapped around her head with pins, in such way as to give the impression it was longer than it was. I looked to be sure that it wasn't actually longer, but no, she must still be cutting it daily. I wondered how she could possibly be managing that with her mother gone.

Simon handed Helen a red rose he'd pulled from the flowers I'd bought her and told her to put it in her mouth so we could dance the tango. "Shut up," I told him. I was already nervous enough about dancing. Dad put his arm around Simon's neck and pulled him aside to give him some private advice.

At prom, Helen proved to be a graceful dancer. I'm not much of one myself, but dancing with Helen in my arms was different. She made me want to dance. There were slow dances and fast dances in alternation, and I did the best I could to use Helen's pre-prom dance lessons to good effect. She pretended to be impressed, but I don't see how she could've been. Fortunately no one else was looking at me.

We took a break, and Helen offered to get drinks, leaving me alone at one of the tables. I said hello to Jon, who'd come with a girl I think he met at Anime Club. Jimmy wasn't coming tonight. We'd tried to convince him to come by himself and pal around with us, but he said nah, he'd have a better time at home. I texted him to tell him we were thinking of him.

"May I have the next dance?" Jane asked. I looked up from my phone.

I glanced to see where Helen was and saw her waiting to get us some soda. "Yeah," I said.

"Checking to see if your girlfriend will let you dance with me?" asked Jane lightly. She'd seen me looking for Helen apparently.

"What she doesn't know won't hurt her," I joked. Jane looked really pleased with herself.

The music started again. Since it was a slow dance, I took Jane's waist and hand and began some pathetic version of a fox trot. The music was quiet, so I felt the need to start a conversation.

"Actually, she literally made me promise to dance with any girl who asked as a condition of coming to prom with me." I don't know why I feel compelled to be honest at times like these. It wasn't a good idea.

"I remember when you used to think for yourself," Jane said with a frown. "Perhaps you should take me back to the tables. I don't need anyone's pity dance." She didn't immediately pull out of my arms and that gave me a chance.

"Jane, I'm sorry," I said, stung by her words and my own insensitivity. "I would've said 'no' had it been anyone other than you. Please would you do me the honor of allowing me to dance with my oldest friend and one of the prettiest girls in the room."

I don't really know how to talk to a girl at a dance, especially when she's mad at me, so I think I just retreated into Jane Austen diction.

It was no lie either. Jane looked terrific in her dress. It was canary yellow, with an asymmetrical hem at the knees and bare shoulders. She had put on makeup and done her hair, which she almost never did, and it made her look girly. Jane never looked particularly girly. She could be beautiful when she was doing farm work, but it was never studied, always the natural beauty of competent strength in motion. However, there was no denying that she was one of the prettiest girls at the dance.

Jane relaxed. "Damn right dancing with me is an honor," she said. A moment later she added, "Anyway, I just saved your life, didn't I? Doesn't that mean you belong to me now?"

"Helen saved my life first, so she has a prior claim."

"When was this?"

"Jimmy, Jon, a high ledge over an escarpment—You get the picture."

Jane nodded. "Clarke, you do need a lot of watching." She calculated for a second. "It seems to me that since Helen put you in danger again, you two are even now. That leaves you belonging to me."

"Very clever, but I'd say the title was disputed at best. I'm going to take advantage of the uncertainty to assert my squatter's rights to prove my own title. As I've 'lived openly and notoriously' with myself since long before either of your claims, I figure I own myself now."

"Good for you. Also, owning another person is prohibited by the 13th Amendment."

"Maybe I should have had you tutor me in history, instead of Helen."

"We both know you didn't need tutoring in history. Also, I think your girlfriend would still be the hands down choice in that department." She snorted.

"Good point. We seem to have danced our way into a second dance," I said, noticing that the song had changed. Wasn't two quieter, slow dances in a row considered a no-no by deejays? "Won't your date object?"

"Oh, I came with a group of girls. We're going to Margaret's grandfather's hunting lodge afterwards for a sleepover. No boys allowed," she said, fixing me with so-don't-try-anything look. That's Jane's humor, totally dry. "Tomorrow, we're going hunting. I've got my rifle in my truck," said added matter-of-factly.

"I promise not to crash your sleepover. Will you hunt in your dresses?" I like dry humor, too. Then, the picture got to both of us. We started laughing. She put her head on my shoulder, and wiped away tears of laughter.

"I brought camouflage orange. Honestly, this yellow dress would probably do as good a job of keeping other hunters from shooting me."

"Probably warn off the does though. On the other hand, if you're after bucks, that dress might draw them for miles." She shook her head but smiled a bit.

The music stopped. "Thanks for the dance, Alex," Jane said and went back to her friends.

I found Helen. She was sitting at a table. "Good job," she said. "I wasn't sure you'd dance with anyone else. That's exactly what you should be doing." She didn't sound completely happy, and she wasn't looking at me when she said it.

"Shouldn't I have?" I was worried I'd done the wrong thing.

"No, you absolutely should do exactly what I tell you," she said with conviction. "It's always for the best."

I sat down and we drank our Cokes in silence through the next dance. "Come," Helen announced. "Let's go outside. I need some air. It's so loud in here I have to shout at you, and I can't hear myself think." The school had a no re-entry policy to discourage teen drinking, but I didn't mind leaving. I'd danced a number of times with Helen and seen all my good friends, so what was the point of waiting any longer?

We left.

Once outside, I felt how overheated I was. It had been hot at the dance because of all the warm bodies, even though the air conditioning had helped. Outside, the heat of the day had cooled a bit and there were no bodies pressing around us, but it was still hot. Of course, I'd been dancing, and my suit had a jacket.

Since it was already ten o'clock, I suggested we go to the mine. It would be cooler in the mine, and I wanted to leave enough time that

I could make it back by my special extended-for-prom, one-time-only one o'clock curfew.

Helen drove us partway there in her car to cut down on the long walk. "Good idea," I said when Helen proposed it. "I notice you're not wearing the most practical shoes for either hiking or spelunking." We got in the car, and Helen started driving.

"We're not exactly caving. It's a mine, and you've been there twice, so you know that the floor is hard and packed. I'll manage."

"True, but those heels you have—well, I object to them on general principles."

"Were you afraid I'd give you the same treatment I gave Manny at my last dance?"

"No, until you mentioned it, that thought did not occur. If it had, I would have kept it in perspective. Unlike Manny, I'm well aware that your spiked heels are probably one of the least formidable weapons in your combat arsenal."

"True. By the way, I'm now giving you blanket permission to put your hands where Manny did without fear of repercussion—if we're suitably private. If you're in any way unsure about how private we are, then you'd still better check with me first. Also, if I seem in any way angry with you, check first. Otherwise you're good to go."

Helen was smiling and almost gleeful as she said this. I don't know if that's because she thought she'd enjoy it if I took up the invitation or whether it was because she knew she was blowing my mind. Anyway, her statement totally stopped the conversation while my imagination went completely out of control. I shut my eyes, just in case Helen turned to look at me.

A little while later, she asked, "So, what have you got against my heels? I thought they made my legs look good."

"Your legs look good all the time, no matter what you are wearing. My objection to high heels is that they seem to serve as a torture device imposed by cruel fashionistas on women as a means of oppression. Additionally, they lead to crushed toes and twisted ankles."

"That may be true for normal girls, but I've had far more time to practice—and my toes and ankles heal instantly."

"You are the exception to every rule."

"I've made you the exception to my rule, so don't take exception to my rule."

Apparently this was to be one of those times when Helen revealed how much smarter she was. I knew she could talk circles around me, wind me up in verbal acrobatics until I was completely tied up by her logic—just like one of the court jesters in a Shakespeare play. I sighed as I worked out what she'd said. "You're saying that you've chosen to make me your one permitted exception to the vampire rule of secrecy, meaning that I now belong to you, so I should agree to accept your 'rule' because you are the queen of me. You're the boss." I sighed again. "Okay, I agree." Helen just smiled.

So much for the 13th Amendment, I thought, recalling Jane's reminder. But I wasn't really Helen's slave, was I? She had said I had options, implying that she would let me walk away with a human girl and not exercise her rights to me as her property under vampire law. I mostly believed that was true. I wondered whether Jane would also expect to be the boss if we were more than friends. Probably, I concluded. That wasn't slavery though, not if it was my choice.

When we parked, Helen said, "If anyone sees the car or if we get caught walking to the mine, people will just assume we're two teenagers up to some typical post-prom action. It's the perfect alibi."

"Fine for you. I'll be grounded for the rest of my life."

"I promise to break you out if the grounding extends past our high school graduation."

"That's over a year!"

"Blink of an eye."

I shook my head. She got out the backpack, and we started walking the path to the mine entrance. I experienced some relief when we passed the concrete seal without being seen. Also, the mine was the same temperature it always was, but instead of cold it felt nice. When we got to the spot where Helen had drunk from me before, I was glad to take off my jacket and shirt. I put my flashlight on the ground pointed up to serve as a lantern while I pulled my undershirt over my head.

"Alex, about how we're going to do this?" Helen was holding her open backpack and the first aid kit. "You seemed a little grossed out last time, you know, by the messiness of me drinking from your arm. I brought a needle and tubing, so I could drink from you that way if you'd prefer. It's cleaner."

That seemed very clinical to me, less personal. Like she was drinking me through a straw because she didn't want to put her lips on me. I was really embarrassed to say that out loud though.

"Alex?"

"No, I liked the way you did it before. I'm over my issues with messy. Why didn't you offer this last time?"

In the light of the flashlight, I could see Helen blush. "I wanted to drink directly from you. I didn't want it to do it like I do with strangers." I felt myself grinning uncontrollably, possibly looking like an idiot.

Helen turned around and asked, "Can you help me with this zipper?" I had forgotten she was wearing a dress. I suddenly realized she couldn't just take off her top; it was all or nothing. I drew a sharp breath and helped her with the zipper. She stood there in nothing but her underwear, turned around and removed her bra. I stopped breathing entirely. She was glorious.

"The underpants stay on," she said.

I nodded, speechless. I sat down and she cuddled up to me. I raised my arm, so she could drink.

"Helen, I love you," I declared. I trembled waiting for her response. She was silent and then opened her mouth and gently bit.

I'd hoped that she would tell me that she loved me, too. Here, in the darkness of this place where she'd first shown me what she was, I'd hoped that she would say the words. Maybe drinking from me was her answer. Maybe it was her way of telling me that she could be herself with me, that she needed me, as I needed her. Maybe this meant she wouldn't leave me.

It was enough for now.

When I drank from Alex for the second time, I finally admitted to myself that I was irreversibly in love with him.

He was not a child to me any more. He was Alex, my Alex, and I needed him.

I didn't tell him so because I wanted time to consider the implications for us: what my committing to him absolutely meant for me and for him. I didn't make love to him either though I could tell how much he wanted it.

That part seemed increasingly ridiculous to me. My body wanted his as much as his wanted mine, and I could no longer pretend I was an adult protecting his innocence. I'd already taken his innocence in so many ways that were more important: I'd asked for his blood, shared my scary magical world, placed him in danger, made him a witness to violence and made him commit butchery. Honestly, what good did it do his innocence to withhold sexual experience at this point? Still, part of me hoped that by going slowly, I was keeping one part of our relationship normal.

Now that I'd drunk from him twice, I wondered how was I ever going to stop. If he let me keep doing that, could I really say no to him when he asked for anything? Would I be able to refuse him when he inevitably asked to drink from me? That would start to seem like a solution before he aged past the point where we could appear with decency as a couple in public. Would he be too essential to me by then to refuse? We could trade the spirit back and forth as my parents had until we were both damned. In agony, I contemplated some dark day the future might bring. Would Alex come to me some day covered in the blood of an innocent? Would he ask me for help as I'd asked my parents once? Would he need me to bring him a shovel? I fervently hoped that my nightmare would never be his.

Still, I knew in that moment that I was ready to give him everything he asked. The nightmare alone wasn't enough to stop me. Alex felt like the answer to the prayer I'd made at Trinity Church. I no longer wanted God to strike me down. I no longer hated myself. I'd forgiven myself for the innocents I'd killed. I'd try to be good.

I wasn't ready to give Alex up for anyone, even if it was for his own good. I felt too selfish: I loved him, and I'd stay with him, as long as I could. I'd stay with him his entire human life and pretend to be his daughter and granddaughter, or I'd make him a vampire like myself, whatever he chose. There would be dangers. We risked more encounters with vampires like the one we had in Mexico if Alex made the former choice; we risked the nightmare if Alex made the later. However, in that moment, I was determined.

We would go on the journey together wherever it led.

24. CYPRIA

After she was done drinking, Helen cleaned us up as she'd done before, and we both got dressed again. It was starting to feel chilly in the tunnel. Helen had me zip her up.

"That didn't take very long," I observed.

"I only drank a few ounces this time. I learned last time that I can't handle any more. I didn't want to fall asleep and leave you alone again."

"Oh, that's sweet."

She smiled. "I may need to drink again from you sooner though."

I said, "No problem," thinking about how much I'd enjoyed seeing and touching her body tonight.

She snickered. Oops, I'd been looking her in the eyes. Well, she surely knew how eager I was by now.

"So, is there more to this mine? Than just our place here?" I wanted to change the subject.

"Oh, yeah, I've explored it. There's quite a complex of tunnels and shafts. We came down a tunnel that was used by mine personnel. We're very close to a shaft where an elevator used to be. Do you want to see the landing?"

"Yeah." She led me down to a place where the tunnel got much wider. It continued ahead. Helen pointed it out with her flashlight. "This was a seam of coal they mined." She moved the beam to show me a room carved from the right wall of the tunnel. There were broken planks and pieces of discarded equipment lying all over the ground. In the back of the room were two rusted iron frames with bars, like a prison. You couldn't see through the bars because someone had bolted plywood to them. I wondered if that was because the bars had rusted. "This is the landing for the elevator. There's a shaft behind those doors that goes down to where they mined a deeper seam."

"Oh," I said. I hadn't realized they were doors. I guessed the iron bars kept the miners from falling into the shaft when the elevator car wasn't at the landing. They must swing open so the miners could get in the car.

"Be careful while I open the door," Helen warned. "You can look down the shaft, but they've removed the equipment."

"Ah, I'm not sure about this. I'm afraid of heights, remember?" The thought of those doors opened onto an empty shaft made me nervous.

"I do. You remember that I can easily save you, right?" Helen sounded amused.

I did remember (give or take a dislocated arm). "Okay, just a peek." I was a bit curious to see the shaft, and I couldn't see anything because of the plywood.

Helen grabbed ahold of the edge of one of the doors and pulled. There was screech of rusted metal as the door swung open from its frame. I stepped up to within four feet of the threshold and craned my neck to peer down the shaft. Helen held her flashlight to illuminate it, but the light didn't penetrate to the bottom. It was creepy.

"Seen enough?" asked Helen. I nodded.

There was a sharp bang over our heads. I looked up and saw that the metal doorframe above us had buckled. There were two cracks in the stone above our heads coming from each side of the doorframe. I realized the door had been propping up the frame, which had been holding up the ceiling. I probably couldn't have budged the door in the first place.

Frozen in thought, I didn't notice that Helen had sprung into action, moving blindingly fast to grab me and push me out of danger. She saved my life.

A giant slab of rock, about the size of a small car, fell where I'd stood. I saw Helen just behind me get struck in the back of the head by the edge of the falling rock. Then I couldn't see anything because her flashlight went out and the air filled with choking dust.

Frantically, I used my suit jacket lapel to cover my nose and mouth while feeling around for my flashlight, which I'd stowed in my jacket pocket. When I turned it on, at first all I could see was dust. I looked for Helen.

Once the dust started to settle, I could see the giant slab of rock on the floor, and my flashlight showed me a slab-shaped hole in the ceiling. I hoped that meant it wasn't going to be a total cave-in, and it was safe to keep looking for Helen. Of course, I was going to look, safe or not.

I found her dust-shrouded form lying on her side next to the giant slab of rock. I noticed blood coming from her mouth. Mine? Had she thrown up? Then I saw the back of her head and panicked. I started repeating, "Oh my God, oh my God, oh my God." The back of her head had been completely crushed inward on itself. It was a catastrophic injury. For a moment, I thought Helen was dead. I tried to imagine myself walking out of here and going to tell her parents. They'll kill me, I thought. They're vampires. Then I remembered that they weren't at home.

Then I remembered Helen was a vampire, too. I calmed slightly remembering how Helen described how vampires could survive a wooden stake through the heart. What had she said? Something to the effect that a vampire could recover if the object were removed. I looked to see if her head was clear of the rock and if her wound was healing. That got me upset again. Her head was clear of the rock, but I didn't see any magical healing happening. What else had she said? Oh, that a staked vampire might require blood to recover.

I looked around for a sharp object to cut myself. Maybe I could use Helen's teeth—though I was reluctant to touch her wounded head. Then I spotted the backpack she brought. I remembered the needle and tube she had offered.

I opened the pack and searched for them. Once I'd found them, I took off my jacket and rolled up my sleeve. Since the needle was already attached to the tube, all I had to do was insert it in my arm. I had no idea what I was doing. I vaguely remembered how the nurse had done it when I'd had blood tests previously. I took my tie out of my pocket where I'd stashed it and used it to tie around my upper arm. I flexed my hands until my veins became prominent. I stabbed myself with the needle on the inside of my elbow. God, it hurt. I must've done it wrong because no blood came out.

What had Helen told me when my grandmother died? That love can be painful, that it can require sacrifice? I wasn't giving up. This is where those idiots Pyramus or Romeo would've thrown themselves down the elevator shaft. Because they thought their lovers were dead and it was their fault. Well, it was my fault, too. I was sure she could've moved out of the way if she hadn't stopped to save me. However, one thing I'd learned from Pyramus and Romeo is that *the girl is not dead, so don't give up.* I rolled Helen onto her back. Looking at her this way, it really seemed as though she could be alive. I leaned down and kissed her. Her lips tasted of blood, and they were cold.

I stabbed myself in the arm again. This time a black bruise started to form, spreading quickly. Great, I thought sarcastically. I'm bleeding internally. That's no use. I was seriously considering trying the needle in my neck or thigh, but I held back because my first aid training taught me that uncontrolled bleeding from those arteries could be fatal within minutes. If the needle puncture didn't seal around the edges, I might not be able to contain the flow. I might bleed out. Desperate, I considered risking it anyway.

My arm looked a mess after I'd tried many times. I gave it one last stab, careful to angle the needle and choose what looked like a vein. It was hard to tell at that point, what with the purple bruise and all. Luckily, it finally worked. The tube started to fill with my blood. I quickly got the other end of it into Helen's mouth. I made sure it went partway down her throat.

I waited, standing there for what seemed like forever, pumping my arm, looking at the red tube and wondering if any blood was going through it. I started to feel light headed even though most of the dust had settled—or maybe it was the ventilation Helen had told me about. I sat down next to Helen. I watched her face in the light of my flashlight, which I'd put on the ground, hoping to see any sign of change.

I waited and waited, feeling a bit sleepy. Then I saw something: her lips moved and tightened around the tube. It looked like she was sucking. I looked at the back of her head. It was hard to see because

I'd flipped her over, but it did seem like it was repairing itself. I went to shift myself to see better and discovered something terrifying.

I didn't have enough strength to get up. I must have lost too much blood. How much was too much? I didn't know. I went to see if I could move my arms at all, and I could. I had enough strength left to take out the needle from my arm.

I left it in.

I knew I would die, and Helen would wake up and hate the choice I'd made. Too bad. She didn't have to like it because it was my decision. Sure I wanted to live, but I wanted her to wake up more than I wanted anything else.

"Please, God," I prayed. "Forgive her. Let her live."

I didn't pray for myself. I wasn't worried God would be angry I'd allowed myself to die. This wasn't suicide; it was sacrifice. I wasn't killing myself in despair, like Pyramus or Romeo. Pyramus falling on his sword and Romeo taking poison didn't help anyone, certainly not Thisbe or Juliet. Helen needed my blood to recover. I didn't worry about her future. She would grieve my death, but she wouldn't throw away my gift.

I'd been lucky to win her; I wasn't going to lose her. This was for me, my final act: winner, not loser.

I closed my eyes with hope, ready to meet the God who taught me to love like this.

I became conscious of a tube in my mouth choking me. I spat it out and sat up, finding a thick layer of dust on my dress. I was in the tunnel next to the large slab of rock that had fallen from the roof. I'd felt it strike me in the head, and that was the last thing I remembered. A flashlight on the floor illuminated the scene.

Alex sat next to me propped against the slab with his head down. I saw that the other end of the tube I'd spat out was in his arm. "Oh, no, Alex!" I said. He didn't move. I lifted his head and saw that his eyes were glassy and there was blood on his lips. I kissed them, partly in the hope that would rouse him and partly to check: they were still warm and the blood on his lips was vampire blood, my blood.

I took his pulse at the neck. There was none.

That was the worst moment of my long life. Worse than drinking the monster's blood. Worse than Zinapécuaro. Alex's death was completely unacceptable to me. If this was reality, I rejected it.

My medical training kicked in. If his lips were as warm as that, his heart must've just stopped beating—perhaps at the moment I regained consciousness. Maybe I could save him yet. I laid him on the floor and began chest compressions.

I thought about what I could do. I needed to get him to a hospital, obviously. He was going need intravenous fluids to replace lost blood volume. He should be ventilated. If I got him outside where I could get cell service to call for an ambulance, would help get here in time? I could continue chest compressions outside if I brought him with me. I stopped the chest compressions to pick him up.

I couldn't. I tried with all my strength, and it wasn't enough. I scraped the back of my hand on the floor trying, and I stared at it stupidly. It wasn't healing magically. I thought the spirit in me must still be too weak. I wondered why that would be. Sure, my injury had been horrific, but I was underground and full of Alex's blood.

This wasn't helping Alex. Unfortunately, if I couldn't move him, I wasn't sure what could. I could give him my vampire blood, but I wasn't sure how to do that if he weren't able to drink it. I saw the tube in Alex's arm. I wondered, my vampire blood tested as A negative. Alex was A positive. Could I give it to him intravenously? Theoretically, I could directly transfuse A negative blood into him and improve his blood volume. As a doctor, I knew this idea wasn't good medicine. It was crazy. However, with the patient already dead, there was nothing left to lose.

I had no idea what vampire blood would do to a human if introduced to the bloodstream. Likely it would make Alex a vampire, and I'd need to share my spirit with him so he didn't become one of those short-lived revenants. Of course, I would. I'd meant to give him a choice, but fate had intervened and taken away all his choices.

I went into action. I had more than one needle in my first aid kit—habit from when I used to visit Philadelphia. I wouldn't reuse a needle, of course. I clipped the end of the tube that had been down my throat and fixed it with a new needle.

Then, I checked the one in Alex's arm. The evidence of the terrible job he'd done was plain to see. He'd really poked himself good. "Poor boy," I said, "you must really love me." I'd have preferred to put it in correctly myself, but I realized that with Alex's heart stopped, I probably couldn't set the needle again. This would have to do. It had worked before, and I hoped it would work the other way.

I put the new needle in my arm. There was no way to tell if blood was flowing because the tube had already been red with blood. I resumed chest compressions. Tears ran down my face. Then I started to pray. "Please, God, let me save this innocent boy. Forgive me. I am trying. At least, don't punish him. Don't let him die."

I realized I was bargaining with God. This wasn't good. I'd gone from shock, to sadness, to bargaining—all stages of grief. Would I have to proceed to acceptance? I refused. Anyway, I'd try to be good no matter what God did. I'd determined that's who I wanted to be.

The second time I checked, I found a pulse. Maybe there's justice in the universe after all. *Gracias a Dios.*

Eventually his eyes fluttered open, and he looked into mine. "Helen," he said, "my angel."

Alex can be a real cheeseball sometimes. I smiled and sighed in relief. "I'm not an angel, and I'm very much alive, thanks to you," I said. I felt myself getting angry. I very much wanted to scream at him right then for killing himself. Since he hadn't, I bit my lip and shut up.

"Then why am I in heaven?" he said. "Oh, ouch! Not in heaven. I hurt everywhere."

If he was complaining, that was a good sign. I gave him some water from the bottle in my backpack. He put down the bottle and said, "I love you."

I was shocked to discover that I had no idea whether he meant it or not. I was staring right into his eyes, and I had no idea what he was thinking. "Alex, I can't tell what you're thinking."

"That I love you. I just said so." He looked puzzled.

Something was wrong with me. I urgently needed him to understand this. "No, I mean I can't read your mind."

"Welcome to the club. Even I don't know what I'm thinking half the time." Damn it, he wasn't taking me seriously.

I looked down at the unhealed scrape on my hand, and I couldn't feel the evil spirit anywhere inside me. I had thought that meant it was weak, but what if... "Alex, how do you feel?" I asked. Had my spirit passed to him? But that made no sense. That wouldn't make me human; that would make me a dying vampire—unless he gave it back.

"Like crap. I just told you that, too. Are you all right, Helen?" Alex was beginning to sound worried. Something of my urgency had gotten through to him.

"Here, let me look." I grabbed his face and put my finger in his mouth. His teeth were normal, but they should have been changing by now with all the vampire blood in him. He was reacting as if I had transfused him with normal, human blood. That was my first inkling of the truth.

The legend.

Despite being unable to read his mind, I had absolutely no doubt that Alex loved me. He'd just given so much of his blood to me to drink that he'd been clinically dead for several minutes. Was it possible that I was human again? The legend said that the vampire's evil spirit was so perfectly satisfied that he never needed to drink blood again. Vampires assumed that he was still a vampire, still immortal, but what if he wasn't? If he'd become human, he'd never have had to drink blood again.

What if the evil spirit had been conquered by love?

I was afraid to tell Alex what I thought had happened. Maybe it wasn't true, and my vampire traits would all return soon. I unhooked the transfusion line, and cleaned us both up as best I could. Alex needed my help to get up and walk. I was glad I'd left the concrete seal open for air because I was sure I couldn't move it anymore. Managing Alex was challenge enough. Also, I'd left my high heels behind, and my stocking feet hurt as we walked on the tunnel floor. I was glad I'd brought the car.

I called my parents, and I pleaded with them to come home. I told them I'd lost my powers, and Alex had been hurt. I could hear Mom arguing with Dad. I had to promise no police were involved. It turned out they were staying in Philadelphia and could be with me in a little over an hour.

I got Alex back to my house. He was in no condition to be seen by his parents. There would be far too many questions to answer. While he was taking a shower, I worked in the laundry room on his shirt and suit, trying to clean off the mine dust. Once I was satisfied that they were as clean as I could get them, I went to find Alex. He was drying off from the shower. He seemed a little shy of my seeing his body, which made me smile, thinking of how much of mine he seen tonight. I gave him a robe of my fathers' and suggested he try to sleep on my bed.

My parents arrived some time past midnight. My father said he needed time underground and went to the basement. Mom asked me to explain what was going on.

She listened with wonder to my story. She said, *"Dame tu mano,"* so I gave her my hand. She bit my finger lightly and licked the drop of blood. *"Sangre humano,"* she said with reverence. Human blood. I was human again. "Victor!" she shouted. *"¡Ven acá! ¡Escucha esto!"* My father came, and once she'd shown him my bleeding finger, he just stared at me in amazement.

I excused myself to go tell Alex. I had to wake him up.

I told him everything that had happened in the mine once I was conscious again. I told him what I thought had happened and what my mom had confirmed: "I'm human now." I was so excited I was crying as I said it.

"What does this mean?" asked Alex. "Does this mean you'll grow old and die?" I was glad he didn't ask if I wouldn't want him now that I didn't need his blood. I hoped that meant he was past that insecurity.

"It means I can have a human life with you—if we want." He nodded agreement. I felt happy even though it wouldn't count until he was fully recovered—and a lot older. I was breathless as I considered the possibilities. "It means..." I didn't want to say it. I was afraid to hope.

Alex had seen it too, and he was less afraid to speak of it. "Do you think you could have children some day?" I noticed he didn't say "we," but maybe that's what he was thinking. I just didn't know any more.

I still couldn't say it. I nodded my head. "I hope," I clarified. I didn't add I wanted them to be his. I hoped he understood that.

Alex nodded his head, accepting my provision. "You know I won't be ready to be a father for years and years, right?"

I pointed to myself, "Long-term thinker, remember? As long as you're willing to try someday, I can wait." Eager as I was, I wanted some years with just Alex anyway.

He nodded and looked thoughtful. Then he asked, "Does this mean we're in trouble with the vampire police again? You were allowed one human who was in on the secret like me. Now that you're human, too—and in on the secret—does that mean they'd kill us both?"

Shit! That's exactly what it meant. But what if...? I had an idea which I didn't say aloud. I didn't want to make him promises I couldn't keep.

"Let's talk about that tomorrow. You need to get home now to meet your curfew." I took his vital signs before he left. His blood pressure was low, no big surprise, so I gave him some juice to drink. I made him promise to text me frequently to let me know he was okay, or I'd be coming over to check.

Once Alex had left, I sought out my parents with a proposal. Alex and I were human, and we knew the secret. Each of them was a vampire and entitled to one human servant. Would they consent to continue to live with me as my parents? I could belong to one of them, and Alex could belong to the other.

My dad approved. "That's lawful. Good thinking, Helen. But we would have to be willing to kill you to enforce the secret if necessary." He looked at me, and I got the message. Otherwise, none of us was better off than before.

Mom looked horrified. "I could never kill Helen, no matter what!"

Dad asked, "Could you kill Alex? If he were determined to expose us?" He said it seriously, like what would you do if this really happened? It made me upset just hearing him talk about killing Alex.

Mom looked thoughtful. "Yes, I think I would have to." I didn't want to hear her say that. I was human now. Could I even protect Alex from Mom? Probably not, I admitted.

Dad had the opposite reaction. He said, "Good. Alex can be yours. He can live next door with his parents. That's close enough supervision to satisfy the authorities."

He turned to me. He said, "Helen, I love you just as much as your mother does. I know you don't have 'the eye' anymore, so you can't tell if I am telling you the truth. You can be my human." I was really starting to hate the vampire attitude towards humans.

"What are you saying?" I said sarcastically. "You could kill me? If you had to?" I didn't want him to mean that. It made it possible to continue to live with Alex, but it made me doubt my father's love.

"I'm saying I have faith you won't expose us." He added firmly, "Please don't."

I frowned at him. He explained, "If I had to kill you, it would only be because you'd forced me to chose between your life and Marisol's.

I'd hate myself afterwards, and Marisol would leave me forever. But, yes, I'd do it to save her from the police." He looked at me fiercely. "Make sure it isn't necessary."

Oh, I thought, to save Marisol. I suddenly understood him. This wasn't the vampire attitude towards humans. This was his love for Mom, and there was nothing to forgive. He did love me, and I loved him, and of course I'd never make him choose between Mom and me. I felt closer to Dad than I ever had before.

I still had questions. "What about when we go to college? What if we get married? What if we have children?" I had no idea what direction my life was going to take.

Mom said, "You might want to go to the same college. Maybe Penn State. We could move, and you could live with us." I considered it.

"I don't think Alex's parents would be cool with that." The Clarkes would not approve of Alex living with his girlfriend in college, I was sure.

Mom smiled, "Perhaps he gets a dorm room, then. He might not sleep there very often though. It wouldn't be the biggest secret we're keeping from them." That was true enough. I smiled back.

Dad said, "If you have children, they couldn't be in on the secret. If that becomes a problem, we could always call my friend with 'the eye' and ask her to make you forget. Then you would be as safe as any human."

I couldn't bear to lose so much of my life. "I'd forget you."

"Everyone loses both parents at some point. But maybe that won't be necessary. You kept the secret from your first husband. Perhaps you could keep it from your children." Maybe I could. I'd have to give that some thought.

Mom said, *"Hija,* is this really what you want? This human life? The spirit I shared with Victor is strong again in both of us. Perhaps we could share it with you." Sometimes my mother didn't understand me. Or maybe she did, and she just wanted me to say it.

"No, Mom, I want to be human. I want this life. I never wanted to be a vampire." I had a choice this time.

"Then it gives me joy that you have been given this." She smiled, and my father looked approving.

That night, I prayed my thanks to God. The next day, I got dressed early, planning to go over to Alex's house to tell him what my parents had agreed to. The doorbell rang. Since I was already almost at the door, I answered. There were two men in dark suits, and one was holding a copy of *Watchtower.* Ugh, I thought, Jehovah's Witnesses. But after all the miracles of last night, I was in too good a mood to be ungracious to anyone.

"Hello, may we have a moment to talk about your relationship with God?" the man on the left asked politely.

I smiled. "It's better now than it has been in a long time. I'm planning on going to my boyfriend's church in Pottsville." The idea filled me with joy.

The man said, "Are you Helen Gracía?"

I nodded automatically, still smiling, until I realized he'd gone off the usual Jehovah's Witnesses script. How did he know my name?

The man looked at his companion, who shook his head subtly. I looked at the companion and noticed his hands for the first time. The knuckles had the same pattern of scars as the man from Zinapécuaro. My heart started to race as I realized this wasn't what it seemed. These were assassins from the Order of St. Michael's, here to kill me. They had tracked me down at last and caught me completely by surprise.

The man on the left said, "That's great. Do you mind if we leave you with some of our literature?"

I wrenched my attention back to him. "No," I said automatically, and took the proffered copy of *Watchtower*.

"Thank you, miss," he said. The two of them turned around and left.

Stunned, I watched them walk away. Why hadn't they attacked? I wondered.

Then I realized the obvious. Because I was human. They had come looking for a vampire, and they found a human. Just as the man in Zinapécuaro had immediately known I was a vampire, they somehow knew I wasn't. They would cross me off their list. They had investigated Brubacher's tip, just as we'd feared they would, but now they'd conclude he was mistaken. I closed the door and leaned back against it, breathing heavily.

"Who is at the door?" said Mom from the kitchen.

"It's the Order of St. Michael," I said. I was giddy at our close escape. Thank God one of my parents hadn't answered the door.

I was taken aback when Dad came charging down the stairs with an assault rifle. Mom had rushed from the kitchen with a sledgehammer grabbed from the garage. They were fearsome, and I realized belatedly what they must've thought.

"Where are they?" asked Mom.

"They left," I told her. My parents looked puzzled.

"Why didn't they attack?" asked Dad.

"They found a human." Mom and Dad stared at me. It took them a moment to realize what had happened. Then we all started laughing hysterically.

Mom wiped tears from her eyes. "Well, that's a relief," she said. She put down the hammer.

Dad said, "Do you think they'll come back?"

"I don't see why they would." If Brubacher had told them about me, they now wouldn't have any reason to believe it what he'd said. I nodded towards Dad's assault rifle. "Did I know you had that?"

He smiled. "It's legal in Pennsylvania. I keep it in my bedroom closet. For emergencies."

Since there wasn't an emergency, I asked if I could go see how Alex was doing.

Alex was doing fine. I explained to him how my parents had agreed to be responsible for us. I told him how the Order of St. Michael had come and gone. We could now be together without fear from either vampires or humans.

"What does this mean?" he asked.

"I means I'll never have to kill again."

Alex looked skeptical. "We don't have to keep the secret?"

I shook my head. "Of course we have to keep the secret. Now more than ever. If we don't, my parents will kill us."

"Then why are you so happy?"

I didn't say anything to give him a chance to work it out. He looked at me, chewed his lip and then nodded. He understood. The awful burden of responsibility was gone from my shoulders. It had shifted to my parents. As a human, I had to keep the secret, but I'd never be expected to enforce it. That was a job for vampires.

Now that I was human, I could be the person I wanted to be. I had a right to tell Alex how I really felt. I didn't think he was going to be a virgin much longer. "I love you," I said.

Alex just started laughing at me. I was hurt and a little angry. Maybe he'd get to keep his virginity for a while.

Eventually, he seemed to notice me fuming because he threw up his hands in apology and said, "No offense, but I kind of figured.

After all you've done for me." He smiled broadly, "And you know I feel the same—because I told you before and I gave you my blood."

That's my Alex. He doesn't always say the right thing, but he'd proven his love past any doubt by his impulsive act in the mine. I softened.

He added, "I love you, too."

So I kissed him. Not for the last time.

ABOUT THE AUTHOR

James H. Edgar teaches ninth graders English at Niskayuna High School in upstate New York. He also teaches fantasy and journalism and advises the Anime Club and school newspaper.

ACKNOWLEDGEMENTS

The inspiration for this story was Stephanie Meyer's gender reversed *Twilight* reimagined *Life and Death*. She's one of my favorite authors, and I felt that she could have gone much, much farther in reimagining. That led me to obsessively writing this book.

Not enough gratitude in the world exists to repay the consistent love and support of my family, all of whom read various drafts. Sarah ensured that Helen's character had color. My father, in his seventies, became the book's biggest fan and provided me with endless suggestions and encouragement.

I'd also like to thank my first audience, students and former students, especially those in the creative writing club and especially Joy and Niko. Their critiques improved my work and their enthusiastic reception gave me impetus to make the book a reality.

Made in the USA
Lexington, KY
10 September 2018